Nathan Haddish Mogos was born in 1982 to Eritrean parents in the city of Addis Ababa, Ethiopia. He completed his higher education at the University of Asmara, Eritrea. Nathan has held several professions along the years in half a dozen countries before realizing his dream as a published author in Norway. His first work of fiction, *Mottak: An African Tale of Immigration and Asylum*, was released in 2015. His debut novel was translated into Norwegian by Tor Edvin Dahl. His second self-published work, *Amid the Chaos*, appeared in 2016.

Dedicated to all the souls that perished in the Sahara Desert and the Mediterranean Sea in pursuit of a better life.

Nathan Haddish Mogos

Ripe Dreams

Austin Macauley Publishers™

LONDON • CAMBRIDGE • NEW YORK • SHARJAH

A CIP catalogue record for this title is available from the British Library.

ISBN 9781528907804 (Paperback)
ISBN 9781528958714 (ePub e-book)

www.austinmacauley.com

First Published (2019)
Austin Macauley Publishers Ltd
25 Canada Square
Canary Wharf
London
E14 5LQ

Chapter 1

"Before we start, is there a need for a translator to make sure everything said is perfectly understood?"

He shook his head.

"I mean it will be over the phone, and they have a confidential agreement, you know everything said remains between us."

"I understand." He was firm in his response.

"So, we can communicate in Norwegian with no problem?"

"Yeah, I don't need an interpreter to make myself understood."

"Impressive, I'm so proud of you." She meant the compliment. "You know many immigrants come to this country and it takes them years to have a rudimentary knowledge of the language. But I see you have a good command of it."

He nodded without a smile. Compliment not taken well, she noted.

"How long have you been in Norway?"

"Three years, going on four."

"So, you feel at home then?"

He shrugged.

She leafed through his file that she had received from the child welfare office. A thick one at that.

"So, how are you doing?" she posed with a smile.

"I'm fine." Curt reply.

"How is school going?"

"School is fine."

"Your classmates, ahhh; are you making friends, Teme?" asked the child psychologist from the much-maligned Child Welfare Services Department with a professional smile.

"Yeahh," he replied hesitantly. "I have no problem with my social life."

After a moment of a stare contest and some observation, the psychologist proceeded with yet another smile. This was her second session. The first being with a teacher and his state assigned guardian present. It was a mere introduction then almost like a transfer of supervision and guidance from an underage unaccompanied migrant child in custody to an adult teenager. He never showed up at the previous meetings. Nor answered the phone calls. But since then had moved from the shared underage supervised boarding compound to a private shared flat. Adulthood and freedom came at a full swing, she gathered. This state funded program, though voluntary, was essential during this transitional phase for these troubled teenagers.

"It has been a while since we last talked. Everything going well at your apartment?"

"Yeah, all is well." Teme avoided eye contact.

"Are you getting along with your flatmate?"

"Yeah, no problem." His feet were fidgeting, dying to hit the cold pavement outside.

"It's just two of you, right?" She tried to engage his attention without provoking him.

"Yeah," he sighed, already agitated with the inquisition.

"You cancelled our appointment two weeks ago. Was everything okay then?"

"Yeah, I had some school stuff to do, that was why."

Watching him attentively, she contemplated ways of penetrating the defensive wall without bursting it open.

"You know I have a son, almost your age. He is quite a handful, very restless but not as matured as you are. He has some anxiety issues. Unless he finds something to busy himself, he becomes so restless. So, my husband and I found him some sporting activities to try out."

Teme watched her passively, his mind already wandering to the wonderlands of nothing and nowhere.

"So, hobbies are very important to have, both for the body and mind, don't you think?" the psychologist continued.

"Yeah, I guess," he mumbled, avoiding the bespectacled eyes studying him. *Why the fuck did she have to do that, sit there and just stare like she was leafing through my soul? She just will never understand me. None of them will ever will*, he raged inside.

"Okay. So, have you been going to the gym, body building like you teenagers like to do, or you prefer more outdoor activities?"

"I play football at the indoor hall once a week, but I used to work out at the gym, but not anymore."

"Okay good, at least you're active in some sport. But why not the gym?" She finally found something he was interested in.

"Just too crowded. The machines are always occupied."

10

He wanted to add he was tired of sticking out like a sore thumb with all the blondies in there, but he held back, as it was not the real reason.

"Okay, okay. I understand. But it is also a nice place to get to meet new people, you know."

Silence.

"Has anybody said anything mean to you at the gym?" Her inquiry persisted.

"NO."

"But at the school do you have any Norwegian friends?"

"Yeah!"

"Like close friends or do you prefer to be with people from your country?"

"No, I don't care where anybody comes from…" he left it trailing, shifting his feet, crossing and uncrossing while his eyes aimlessly wandered around her gray-walled undecorated office. She observed his every move and scribbled on her notepad. That got his attention. Alert his eyes zoomed on her pen. She smiled back. A faint smile was the response.

"It is good to have somebody to talk to, Teme. Are any of your friends your confidants, with whom you share your feelings and thoughts?"

"Hmmm, got no best friends. But I have good friends."

Precise and defined were personal boundaries, she noted.

"How about your family, do you keep in touch with them?"

"Yeah, sometimes."

She took a peek at his file and continued with a measured smile.

"You are still very close to your cousin who lives in Switzerland, right?"

"Yeah."

"How often do you talk to him?"

"Not often, just once a month or so," he lied. A sign of his irritation growing, she noted.

"How about your parents or relatives; do you call them often?"

"I was raised by my grandmother. And no, it is expensive to call from here."

"Okay." She grimaced, failing to notice in time that his mother died when he was a child and his father was a decorated martyr.

"How is your grandmother doing? Is she okay?"

"She is dead."

She was taken aback with shock. That particular information was missing from his file. She drew a thick question mark to inquire about it later on her notepad. She sensed him drawing inward. She scribbled a note and waited until he got her attention.

"So, what did you want to talk to me about today then?" he impatiently questioned, dying to escape her office.

"No, I just want to see if you were okay. Just to talk to you, that's all. Are you in a hurry?"

"No, just asking." Both his hands were now jammed into his pant pockets.

"You sleep well of late?" She adjusted her thin glasses and peered at him with concern.

"Yeah, better than before but the same." His eyes accidentally landed on her breasts. He quickly looked down, '*but damn she's got nice breasts*,' he thought.

"Are you having any nightmares?"

Silence and a blank inward stare.

"How about the flashbacks in the daytime; have you had any of them lately?" She had read his file of recurrent flashbacks he was suffering from.

Eyes now glued to the floor, Teme shut off.

"You know that does not make you a weak person. Nor any different from any other person out there. You just do not have control over it. It is psychological." She drew her chair closer to add, "Our mind is a tricky thing. It is complex system like a closet you have at home, as it retains everything we go through in different compartments. Like a closet unless you sort its contents it will always be chaos . Very hard to find anything whenever you need it in a messy closet, right? You know like you teenagers throw everything inside, folded, unfolded, dirty, clean, every clothing you have inside. I know because my son does that all the time."

For once he was paying attention. The closet analogy must have triggered his attention, she noted. Treading carefully by not overcomplicating it, she wanted to break down the role the shady state of the subconscious mind had over traumatic episodes in life. Choosing her words, she continued, "So when something beyond our control happens in our life, the mind will be like that closet, total chaos. But it can be sorted back to order and back to normal, but it takes time. It is normal for the mind to react that way for people who have experienced very troubling or very traumatic incidents in their lives, especially at a young age, like you. Even for adults like me it is normal. The mind is like your phone registering all the contacts; it registers every image, scent, taste, even texture of a certain incident, but it could be shoved deep in the rubble of other things stored in your mind. Like stinking dirty underpants or a pair of socks in your closet. Since it is a shock, not ordinary experience, you do not want to remember it but it is still deep down buried in your mind. Like the stink of that dirty little sock the entire closet starts to smell. But it does not mean everything inside the closet is dirty and smelly. But unless you take your time to sort out where exactly that dirty sock is buried inside your closet, you will always be reminded of it every time you open the closet to get let's say a jacket, a sweater, or your jeans. You must take the dirty socks out of the closet once and for all, take it to the laundry and have peace of mind. So, you should address what is bothering you, what you do not want to talk about, and try to forget in order to move on with your life. Understand what I am trying to say, Teme?"

"Yeah," he nodded with a glimmer in his eyes for the first time since he walked into her office.

"So, what do you say we try to get the dirty socks out of your mind?"

Silence and a blank stare.

"You know even strong men, big men, courageous, and brave, who serve in the army suffer the same way." She once again moderated her words in not breaking the stride she had made with his wandering train of thought. "After serving in the army or participating in a war, even though they are serving their country, defending their country, they do things they normally would not do. Like you know kill people. War is terrible as people die, women and children included. People get injured, cities and villages are burned and destroyed. But while they are at war, their mind registers everything, but they do not feel it then. It is like they are there but not there, understand me?" She waited for a second to see he was hanging along. "They do not reflect on what they are doing and witnessing, their mind is busy absorbing everything. Too much of what is going on. All the crazy things nonstop; it becomes normalized. It still is not okay but since it happens every day, they get used to it; it will not be of any surprise. Most of them feel quite normal or not feel at all while they are there in the army. Their feelings are shut off. But after witnessing all the ugly, disturbing, not normal experiences and watching friends and enemies die, they come back home. At home with the normal, peaceful life around them, suddenly they start to reflect, and it becomes too much for the mind. The transition back to normal life is a process. The mind starts to replay like, you know, a movie of all the horrible incidents. They try to forget it but the mind, like I said, is very complex. Unless you

13

help it to help itself, it could lead to a serious problem where one cannot function in everyday life. It is called PTSD – Post Traumatic Stress Disorder – where the mind when you are not alert might replay an incident in your life you are trying to forget, like a movie, but you have no remote control to stop it. The more you try to avoid it, the more it gets worse. It might come in your dreams when you have no control in your sleep. Or worse as a flashback in daytime, like any smell, image, sound, taste, or feel can instantly trigger that incident you are trying to forget. So, it is not your fault and you are not alone."

Teme was attentively processing every word she was saying but not replying. After taking down a note, she continued,

"So, Teme, do you want talk about those nightmares?"

He mumbled something incomprehensible.

"Is it something specific? Very clear image you see, or is it like a loop, the same event that is running over and over again."

Silence.

"Or is it like totally unrelated scenes? Like full of symbols and people you have never met?"

He looked down, avoiding her eyes, yet she sensed him tensing with his clenched hands jammed in his pockets tightening.

"How about the flashbacks in the daytime? When do they occur, like unexpectedly or when you are bored and start thinking about them?" She was relentless.

Silence.

"Teme, you should open up, talk to me, so I can help you."

He looked up, studying her intention. He did not look convinced.

She took another flip of her notepad and skimmed through the previous report passed on to her on him.

"Is what happened in Libya that bothers you the most, or is there any other traumatic experience you have experienced in life?"

"Mostly it is Libya," he mumbled.

"Can you tell me what really happened? Talking about it helps, Teme. You know you can trust me; I am here to help you and as part of my profession all you say stays between us."

Silence. Jaws sealed as if words might spill out, eyes now staring with that inward look of a much older man. The defensive wall was up in full swing. The insecure boy was unavailable; the reserved, determined man was staring back at her.

"Shall we continue, or you want to talk about it some other time?" She gave in.

"Maybe some other time." He could not wait to get out of her office.

"Okay, shall we meet in two weeks? Three weeks? Or you will make an appointment yourself?"

"I will make an appointment myself," he said defiantly.

"Okay, if I do not hear from you for three weeks, is it all right if I book an appointment? You know it is voluntary, none is pressuring you into seeing me!"

"Yeah sure," he shrugged.

"You have my number, right?"

"Yep," he was already halfway towards the door.

"Have a wonderful day then, Teme, and take a good care of yourself."

He nodded, avoiding her eyes and stormed out of the office.

****

Smoking his cigarettes, Teme was raging. *What the fuck does that skinny white bitch know about what I am going through anyway? Talking about closet, dirty socks, and the post trauma blabla bullshit psychology. What does she know?* he sizzled inside. He imagined the cool, composed pyscho-fucking-logist witnessing someone she had just talked to being decapitated in front of her. *How would she react then?* he questioned as he made his way to the bus stop. The cold breeze slapped his face numb as he hurried his steps. *What does she know about going through days and nights in the scorching sun with no food or a drop of water? Telling me about duty to kill for your country and normalization bullshit, what does she know about being into the position of kill or be killed for just another day? I survived all that bullshit hellhole, and now all she wants to do is talk about it. I am trying to forget it. Everything. Delete everything, even all the good and the bad, everything and start from scratch like with a new name even, new, fresh, clean memory. Bitch talking to me like I am a baby, why don't they leave me alone? Why did I choose to come to her anyway? Why can't she just tell me how to yank the fucking dirty socks of the closet of my mind? No, she just wanted some good sad story to tell someday at a gathering. Why was she taking notes anyway? Report or record it for whom? I will have to ask her next time,* he debated with himself while rushing past the traffic, nearly getting hit by speeding cars, he made it to the other side of Kirkeveien. Nerve-cringing moment for bystanders and drivers alike he paid no heed to. There was some kick to it, beating the red light. Adrenalin kick for a wild, adventurous self amid boredom or suicidal tendencies, who knew? The bus he jumped in headed towards Tøyen. He looked left and right to get a sense of the ticket control, sneaky trolls. He usually could sense their presence from afar. No way he was getting busted this time, he would break their jaws and make a quick escape instead of making a scene like the other day. His crew would probably be hanging out in their corner right across Sørli children's park. He was hoping to run into Toure, Smokie. The only mate he could trust. He flipped his phone to send him a message of his whereabouts.

****

Indeed Toure and the crew, LocoCrew, were stationed on their spot, goofing around like usual. A warm sense of belonging calmed Teme's nerves upon seeing them.

Later, when Toure and Teme were on their own, just walking around the Tøyen Square like they often did as if they were police patrol, Teme hesitantly began, "Do you ever think about, ahh you know, all the Libya stuff?"

Toure looked around and grunted, "Sometimes."

"Yeah, me too."

"But we survived, you know," Toure snapped back trying to switch the subject.

"Yeah, we did."

After a moment of silence they both admired the graceful beauty of a girl much older than them walking out the pharmacy. She knew all eyes were upon her. Every movement accentuated and elaborated as she slithered past them. "Shit lucky whoever is hitting that one," Teme continued.

"Word is she is with this Norwegian dude, high flying with a Porsche, who picks her up every afternoon," recounted Toure, his eyes still following the bouncing muscular behind of a girl everyone salivated after in their block.

"How do you know all that?" Teme was astonished.

"Shit, you live in this hood, better keep up with hood news, my man."

"Hahaha. I hear you."

As they made their way past the square with the bustling cafés, library, grocery store and bars, another bout of silence engulfed them. Right when they reached a bench facing yet another playing ground, a familiar junkie approached them inquisitively. They directed him in a subtle way towards the end of the park, where he could score crack. The junkie began to get too friendly. "Fuck off now," Teme interrupted to dismiss him at once. The junkie scurried away to score his hourly dose. Sitting next to overweight mothers trading hot gossip on the bench, their eyes fell on the kids playing in the designated area.

"Junkies and kids are only separated by a fence, both in a different world of high; sugar high and crack high," remarked one of the older lady to the other.

"Horrible! Such a horrible place to raise a child. It used to be a nice place. We used to know everyone around the block, now it is a junkie playground and people from all over, God knows where," replied the other but soon hushed, realizing the presence of the two African migrants on the adjacent bench.

Teme was still reeling from the conversation with the psychologist as he wanted to get it off his chest. In a hushed voice, he inquired, "Do you feel guilty… you know what we did?"

"We had no choice." Sniffles agitated by a flash of a violent episode, "We had no other choice. It was survival," was the reply from Toure.

"Yeah, it was." He nodded, reassured. "Fuck it, we had to do it. No other choice." He strapped the glove tighter as if to stop the cold from seeping in.

"Yeah." Blinking wildly Toure felt his temperature rise and stood up, stretched himself, reached for his jacket pocket for the Marlboro lights. Lit one cig after several attempts with his fingers trembling for an unknown reason. He then offered the pack to his buddy in crime without turning to face him. Teme took one to stick it on his ear for later. Toure finally said, "Man, you got to forget what happened. Let the past be the past. Now let us get wasted somewhere."

"Hahaha, I feel you. You call the gang for any hotspot tonight."

"Cops raided the Polish connect. No booze, everybody is freaked out."

"Let's just score some weed and mellow down then."

"Yeah, I need some chillaxing."

"Me too."

With that they slowly made their way to the bus stop. Bus number 60 pulled up right on time as they hopped in. Two stops, eyes vigilant for the ticket patrol, they stood by the door ready to fly.

They got off at the meet-up place to score some weed at a discount in Grønland from one of their men. Hood affiliation privileges.

****

Back in Tøyen, the entire crew huddled around the bench on Sommer fly garden. At around this time ordinary citizens abandoned the site, circumventing it instead. Retired grumpy old men and women sipping beer in their corners. Junkies doing their evening Tai Chi and Zen, after crack or meth, moves on their own corner undisturbed. In the middle of the garden though it was their crew that reigned. If need be the other occupants could be dismissed without protest. With neat apartment brick walls and office glass buildings surrounding it, the place calmed down after six. Ironically, the Oslo prison was a block away, with its watch tower visible from their spot.

****

They had just smoked their third joint when a patrol vehicle rolled up on the sidewalk behind them, unannounced. But it came to nobody's surprise as the cops ignored the junkies and the old folks to zoom in on them. Hearts dancing in their mouth, all tried to keep calm, especially those holding. Some possession, others with intent to sell. Most were strapped with knives; one Teme suspected was carrying a replica gun.

"Well, well, well, how are we doing this evening, boys?" Two cops approached them from both sides. The clique waited, glued to their spot.

"So, have we done anything wrong, Officers?" Teme was quick off the block.

"No, this is just a routine check. You boys out of trouble?"

"Yeah." Muffled one or two voices,

"We chilling," confidently Teme retorted.

"There have been complaints by some neighbors of drug dealings going around here. You boys know anything about it?" asked the older police while the female cop studied the faces of the five young men one by one.

"No. Since when is it illegal to get together and catch up in your own neighborhood?" asked Teme. The rest fidgeted in their places, nervously following the exchange.

"No, it is not illegal. Disturbing the peace in a residential area is illegal. Loitering around a business area is prohibited and, of course, selling drugs is also illegal," lectured the male police.

"Yeah, we know the law. We have not disturbed anyone and none of us is doing drug deals either."

"Yeah, but we saw you earlier as well, you were standing close to the kiosk entrance, thus obstructing customers from going in and out undisturbed." The police pointed to the kiosk 200 meters across the park.

They all giggled and sighed at that. The police were just making a round to make their presence felt. All was safe.

"Maybe we are customers too. Have you considered that?" snapped back Teme. The other boys, giggled suddenly relieved Teme had turned the tables on the cops.

The unimpressed female officer zoomed her eyes on Teme while the older cop smiled and scanned to register all the faces. This new kid indeed got balls. Through experience he knew the older two at the back, more reputed and repeat offenders, had something to hide as well. He could smell their fear on their faces. He could sure nab them on patrol later but to frisk them now would cause a scene in this quiet residential alley with a cocky kid leading the way.

"Besides, is it not against the law to harass law-abiding citizens without probable cause? Are we suspects of any crime committed, sir?" His confidence grew as Teme stared down and faced the cops, demanding an answer.

"No, you are not suspects. We are here on patrol to maintain peace and order and to keep even you guys safe as well."

"We understand it is your job to protect and serve." The clique was now definitely enjoying the exchange. Whatever reservations anyone had about Teme were won over. He quickly added fuel to the flame, "Or is it because we are black and brown and such natural-born suspects that you had to keep an eye on us? Just keeping us in check, reminding us that we don't belong here? Is that part of your job as well?"

Even the cops smiled at the last remark. Not out of joy but the kid profiling his introduction into the game and the law itself was indeed a great self-inflicted tip-off.

These stupid kids never learn. From the get go all is about showing off, feeling all invincible, contemplated the older, tired male cop, analyzing Teme. The older cop signaled his partner towards their patrol car. Right before they bid the boys farewell, he gave Teme a grin and a wink. Teme replied to the wink with a cocky grin and a final dig, "Drive safely, Officers." The entire crew burst into laughter. The cops got into the car exchanging glances and whispering to one another to keep an eye on the cocky little black boy.

He sure earned a couple of points with the pushers as they gave him and Smokie a fair discount. They rolled a joint on the spot and took a stroll down the playground open park in Tøyen, more obscure from any intrusion, for an undisturbed smoke session, their meditation. The locals knew what was up, the stench of marijuana meant almost a no-trespassing sign as they either turned around or quickened their steps to get away without stealing a look towards them. That was their territory.

****

Chapter 2

High as a kite, when the cold breeze begun to be unbearable, Teme and Smokie split up to go their own ways. Teme was spending the night at his girl's. She lived on the west side, the deadly quiet area he dreaded heading to every now and then. Around the Tøyen metro station there was a new clique making their presence felt; he was quite unnerved by the way they were looking towards him the last time he got off that stop. Now they were stranded, *fucking fronting like big shots, pussies just because they were in numbers doesn't mean they earn respect,* he mumbled to himself. He would take them all at once, he challenged himself, strutting his lean athletic stature towards them. He would not start trouble but if they did, *I would go all berserk on them, make a statement,* he promised himself as he neared the sliding door to the underground station on the south side. They were all clowning when he approached them, specially this little boy with pimples all over his face or was it acne or whatever, he looked like a painting half completed, profiled Teme, his target firmly planting his eyes on him. The kid flinched first to look away towards his crew for a sort of backup. Teme smiled in triumph, slowed down his pace and eye-balled every one of them. Not one of them spoke. He entered the station totally alert for any movement. None came but he heard one of them being held back, told off by the others to cool off. He was not worried by any of them any given day as he checked the monitor; line number 2 to Østros was to depart in 1 minute.

His girl lived by a residential area near Røa. Not many of his people lived around there, it used to make him a bit conscious whenever he took the bus or the metro to her place, but not anymore. They were just like that, mostly white and mostly quiet, which was good, none of that eyeballing and clowning he often met on the east side. Their effort to make him feel unwelcome on the west side astounded him at times though. Grabbing their purses when he sat next to them, electing to stand rather than sit next to him, made him laugh at times, watching them change their mind when noting it was a dark face occupying the seat. At times, they looked away quickly after strenuously studying him. That collective fear of the stranger, that tense atmosphere they create around someone like him was unnerving at times. It was unsettling in the beginning but now he was getting used to it. Teme was grateful he was not subjected to that kind of treatment on a regular basis though. The last thing he needed was to be conscious of another person's insecurity. *Got plenty of shit to deal with right now!*

He got off at his stop along with other commuters and raced ahead; he was starving, the munchies had him good. The one thing he loved about his girl was there always plenty of stuff to eat. All that sweets and chocolates in abundance, fruits and all in display waiting for him to gorge on them. He licked his lips in anticipation as he made his way across Sørkedalveien all the way to Røa Kirke. Besides her sweetness what he missed most was the warm body, her moan, the way she looked at him. Damn, he was hungry for everything in her house, including her.

****

After steamy sex, she lay on top of him. His high had long faded but being inside her was almost like a reboot to his system. He was at peace feeling her warm body on top of him.

"So when are you going to tell me about these scars, babe?" She broke that beautiful trance he was hovering in for a little while.

Silence.

Caressing the edges of the bulging circular rough-edged white scars dotting his back. "I meant your tattoos," she added. "I like this one. It is smooth, like some abstract art."

He smiled faintly at the analogy, "This is better than tattoo, you know. Like a tattoo is on the outside of your skin. But a scar is from deep within. The flesh and all."

"Yeah."

"Did it hurt, this one?" She ran a circle with the tip of her ring finger on the most pointed white scar tissue protruding just below his shoulder blade.

His mood instantly changed, taken back to the moment when those fuckers were burning plastic on his back. The explosion of a searing pain when the dripping plastic landed on his bare back, the scream and then one felt numb. Still hurt but it became bearable, almost accepting one's fate. It went on and on for days as part of the indoctrination.

"Yeah, my tattoos, had them done by a professional." He loved it when she gently caressed his wounds. So soothing and reassuring, he wished she never asked questions. *Just rub them gently, baby,* he sang to himself.

"Does it hurt?"

After a long pause, "No."

Oh but they did every time he accidently glanced at his reflection, a spasm of pain electrified his body. Like buttons he felt them tighten at times when he was edgy. Especially there was this one spot on the small of his back that took too long to heal. Infected, the sore had spread its perimeter by the weeks, pus that was barely cleaned. His own urine as a disinfectant, unattended, languishing in that container, how could he forget? The scream, the sizzling tremor that blinded him in pain the moment the melting plastic drop landed on his back. The nauseating smell of his own burning skin and flesh. The lingering fire on his back until one became numb was a recurrent scene upon his abduction upon arrival in Libya. His hands tied over his back, dangling from a rope upside down, his captors toyed with him. Intoxicated with the bango the man child militants were hoping to terrify a loved one into sending a ransom for his life. The agony often forced relatives living abroad into coughing thousands of dollars wired at once the longer the tormenting songs of torture played over the phone from the circus arena. Indeed, it was a circus or a theatre that Teme woke up to everyday, waiting for their turn, while listening to the cries of agony followed by a cacophony of boyish giggles, every fucking day. The routines dragged until the full ransom was paid. If relatives fail to deliver, the torture ended in a peaceful death, execution style. Even death was a relief under those circumstances. Even the beatings one got used to those dark times.

They had given up on him; he had no use for them in keeping as a ransom after a few burns, cuts and cries. None had claimed him nor had he requested for a lifeline. None had negotiated at least for his skin, it was all on him. But he heard it all for those who had people in diaspora. Some phone calls were unanswered, screams on the phone to make their points had become unbearable. To wash their conscience, the relatives had given up. How many times had he heard screams on one end reciprocated by a helpless sobbing, *May God be with you* on the other end. *Where was God? Which God, in fact?* He survived through it though.

"Did you bleed when it happened?" asked Elise pleadingly again.

Another pronounced pause while his face dug deep into her warm breasts. Oh, he felt like crying but he fought it back. He felt so safe lying on her chest. The only source of warmth in his cold existence. God, if he could tell her how much she meant to him! Was it loving or not ever being loved, maybe it had been a long while since someone loved him like that; he cherished her, but the words never came out right. But he hoped she sensed it.

"Okay, baby, I won't bother you. But you are safe here with me." She kissed him on his forehead. "I love you, babe."

He opened his mouth to reciprocate with his feelings but stuttered. He finally mumbled, "Love you too," and fell asleep.

It had been a while since she last heard him utter those three magical words. Elise felt a warm sensation envelope her. She held him tight in euphoria as she listened to his breathing on her chest. Wishing this beautiful moment lasted forever, caressing his kinky dreads, she begun imagining what their life would be together in a few years. Sure, by then she would definitely break that impenetrable defensive wall Teme had built to protect himself from himself and others. Underneath that hard shell she knows is a boy, an innocent, love-hungry, she shall allow him to grow into a man. She would let him heal in time, she will, Elise promised herself to not push him.

****

Chapter 3

He was back at the psychologist's office, fidgeting in his seat as usual, wondering what he was doing there in the first place.

"So how have you been, Teme?"

"Good."

"It has been a month since we last talked. Anything new or interesting in your life?"

"Not much."

"It is not like I am snooping around but I hear you quit school."

Silence. Blank stare.

"You want to talk about it or…?"

"Talk about what?"

"Why you quit school?"

"Nothing to talk about, I just could not concentrate."

"Concentrate in class during lectures? During study at home or homework?"

"Overall, I just can't." He sighed, agitated, pressing his left temple with the white of his right thumb incessantly, she noticed, when anxiety kicked in.

"Okay, okay, I understand!" The child psychologist nodded.

No bitch, you do not understand, the voice within him was raging. *Why am I here anyway?* he questioned his motives.

"Maybe it is not for me. School stuff," he mumbled.

"So how do you expect to survive, Teme? No school, no grants means no income."

"Yeah I know, I started working once in a kebab joint a while back."

"You get enough money to cover your costs?"

"Yeaaah."

"You know you could apply at the local social welfare office NAV to seek any financial assistance if you are struggling, right? You know you have the right to?"

"Yeah, I know."

"So you have become your own man then, Teme?"

25

"Yeah, I guess." His eyes lit up at once.

"Proud of your progress, Teme, not every teenager steps up like you do on their own. It is not easy to be independent. Take a time out, but you are still young to get back to school. It is always good to take a breather but one must not be idle. You have to have something to keep you busy. Something constructive."

Nod of recognition.

"So what else is new? You sleep well at night?"

"Not bad." He looked down again.

"How about the nightmares?" she asked in a motherly tone.

Silence and head fell down.

"Are you able to go back to sleep after you wake from a nightmare?" She suppressed her emotion to kick back with the professional objective mode back on.

"Sometimes."

"What do you do the moment you wake up?"

"I say a quick prayer. Sit up or drink some water."

"Good, good. If it helps try to think of something positive then to calm your nerves. A prayer helps as well to calm your spirits."

Nod. Fidgeting in his seat.

A quick glimpse of her journal before she continued with a smile, "Is it some episode from the time you spent in that underground prison in Libya that keeps flashing in your dreams?"

Silence.

"Or is it the boat trip across the Mediterranean?"

"It is all of it."

"Is it people, faces that show up in your dreams, or is it images?"

"Mostly images, not clear or exactly like it happened, just I don't know how to say it in Norwegian, but the image instantly takes me back to a certain episode I would like to forget." He was in a sort of trance.

"Vague symbols that represent the traumatic event. I understand." She doodled something on her note, which his eyes followed all the way. She almost asked him if he wanted her to hire a phone interpreter next time, but she checked it, recalling his reaction last time. She smiled back at him and continued her inquisition, "Is it one image or several ones?"

"Ahhh, it depends, sometimes it comes in flashes, happening so fast that I do not remember what exactly it was when I wake up. Then at times it is in slow motion."

"In slow motion, can you remember any of the images or scenes? Something that stands out?"

"Yeah, sometimes it is the ocean. In the middle of a calm sea with no land on sight. But you can feel something is on the way."

"And that is when you wake up?"

"Yeah!"

She once again jotted something down in her journal.

"Was there anyone in the sea, any people along?" she asked in a soft tone, trying to keep him in that trance.

"No, I am not even on the scene; it is just the open sea. But I sense the breath of people around."

"Right, right, very symbolic." She jotted it down again. His eyes followed her fingers but this time their tone had changed.

"What do you think the open sea symbolizes, or represents? Does it instantly trigger or refresh something from your experience?" she quipped.

"I, hmmm, it's like, I don't know exactly. I just never observed the ocean to be that calm. You know like they say something like the silence before the storm or something."

"Surreal experience. Hmmmm, then from a dream state your mind becomes active and you are awake and aware. Alarmed like seeing some stranger's hand reach into your back pocket?"

"Yeah, like this force in my dream is sneaking into my memory without my permission."

"Exactly, that is how the mind works. It's crazy but I am truly impressed, Teme, how well and articulately you have tried to figure out the wonders of the mind."

He smiled at the compliment.

"You know you are sharp and brilliant for your age."

His smile froze as he stared directly into her eyes. Reading her mind. A long moment passed before his eyes eventually trailed away. It gave her the break to note down her observation.

"Can I ask you something?" Teme asked in a grave tone.

"Yeah, sure. What's on your mind?"

"What are you jotting down there?" He pointed with his right index towards her journal.

"This is a journal I keep so I can follow up your progress. Every session is a step, and I keep some record to keep track of them." She noticed that suspicious look in his eyes, he was not convinced. "But have no worries, no one is allowed to see my journals. Everything you say or we say to each other remains between us. All of it is

27

confidential. If I reveal anything you say to anybody else, I could lose my license, you know my job and perhaps go to jail as well."

"Okay. What happens to the journals after I, ahh, let's say I move to another city or decide to quit our sessions? Do you keep a journal of every session of your clients forever?"

"It is only for our reference in our sessions that I keep the journals, not as an official record or anything. Confidential laws are very strict in this country; you have nothing to worry about."

"Let me ask you this, if someone confesses a crime to you in their session would you report it to the police?" His eyes were firmly set on hers.

"The confidentiality agreement between a patient and doctor is unconditional. That means the doctor has the moral duty to report a grave crime to save a life. You know some things are more than just a promise. But still it means one has broken the confidentiality agreement one has with a patient, so it is a gray area. You know it depends from doctor to doctor and from place to place." She instantly saw his suspicion of her grow, the wall she dreaded begun to close in between them. "But if you ask me it is a rare case that a psychologist or psychiatrist reports their clients to the police. But I would not do it, my duty is first and foremost to my client, that means you."

The analyzing stare was not satisfied but the suspicion dissipated.

"Have you witnessed a crime, Teme, you want to talk about it?"

"No!" quick no, she noted. "I was just wondering."

"Do you want me to stop jotting things down during our session? If so, no problem."

Silence followed by a shrug.

"Shall we continue then or you have had enough of me for today?"

Another silence followed by a smirk she never noticed on his face before. A kind of cocky manly smirk with an attitude. He had caught her off guard with his question and was now gloating over it. She would let him have it, but that is the beauty of the profession; one never stops learning, it was always on job training, every session…

"You know sometimes the ocean is not that calm. I see a red ocean lapping back and forth. Blood red…" he trailed off. Her heart was skipping its ordinary pace. She even monitored her breathing to escape soundless for him to open up by himself. Just waiting.

"The bloody ocean though I see it sometimes in the day time too. Wine spilled on a table cloth or even my eyes play tricks on me the longer I stare at the ocean by the coast, I see it turn red... Hmmm," he sniffled a bit, eyes gone inward yet fixated on the window behind her head.

"Does the blood-red ocean remind you of something in your past?"

Shrug followed by silence.

"The moment you see the sea or ocean turn red, what image comes to your mind automatically?"

He studied her for long minutes, the cocky attitude was back again, smacking his lips several times he continued, "Let me ask you this, have you ever witnessed somebody getting killed?"

After a long hesitation, she shook her head to reply. "No, I have not. Have you?"

"You know the first time it is shocking. You feel like you do not believe it is happening. Then like you said last time about the mind and normalization." She nodded attentively. "Yeah, the more you see it happen on a day to day basis, it becomes normal. You feel nothing. It is crazy, you know. Because I am not an evil person."

Her face turned red. She was shocked how composed he was, this little boy of 18 talking about death like his best friend. Quickly regaining her composure, objectivity is the cause, no room for emotional attachment, she reminded herself to switch back on the pro face.

"That is now progress, Teme, to understanding the making of our minds. They call it the subconscious state of mind; you have no idea, even to this day it remains a mystery." His mind was somewhere else though...

"Yeah," he interrupted her, "Sometimes I hear the screams. Like an echo inside my ears. You know screams of agony that send shivers up and down my body. But it happens seldomly."

"Is it the scream of someone you know or just the scream of a stranger?"

"We all screamed everyday back then. Pain, scream and then you laugh it off, knowing tomorrow will be the same."

Her knees were shaking, but she held back from betraying her role and breaking the lucid trance he was in. Very articulate he got like he was almost there, back to then as it happened. Envisioning every grotesque scene his young mind had to comprehend. As much as she felt sorry for him, as much as she wanted to reach out a hand and caress his soft face and heal his tortured soul, she held back. It was a mission he must fulfill on his own. Her job was to usher him without distracting or biasing his recovery.

Uncomfortable silence ensued as his eyes blinked almost in a slow motion yet they were somewhere very far. His face had a serene odd look though. Almost disturbing and paradoxical to the events he was unraveling.

"Were you tortured daily?" She finally broke the ice.

"Torture, yeah. But after a while you feel nothing."

Another silence ensued. She waited pensively, not moving a finger. Waiting for him to open up, under his own terms.

"Have you ever heard your own scream? In your dreams or in the daytime."

Dumbfounded he stared at her.

"Or do you see the faces of those that are responsible for the torture?"

"I see them every day. They are everywhere."

"Where, you mean here in Oslo?"

"Everywhere, they are everywhere. They look like them, talk like them."

"Do you think about them sometimes?"

Silence.

"Let me ask you this." He shifted in his seat eyes firmly set upon hers. "Do you think I will ever going to be normal again?"

"Yeah, absolutely. If you try to hide from them, they will haunt you down when you least expect in your sleep or in the daytime, triggered by something you have no control over. But if you understand the mind, give it time, it is a process but you will get there."

He smiled at her answer. A wide boyish smile of satisfaction.

"But it is a process. You are making some progress. Now you are talking about it that means you are no longer in the denial stage."

He looked confused.

"What I mean is that you are now tracing back your memory on purpose to look back and reflect upon the traumatic events in your life. Then you will learn to accept them. Come to peace with them, and in time they will be just a part of your past. A harmless memory."

"So there is a chance that I will be free again?"

"Yes, no doubt. But it takes time to heal the mind."

"Do most of your patients heal at the end?"

"Yeah, most do eventually." She lied and he knew it. She quickly added, "But only those who accept the challenge. And you are on the right path."

He rose to his feet. "So I guess it is next month same time or?"

"Yeah sure, but do you want me to set the appointment or you want to do that yourself?"

"No, I will take care of it."

He was on the way to his door, once again not looking back. He waved his hands at her as a goodbye and quietly slipped out the door. She breathed a sigh of relief. Tears flooded but she fought them back. What if he raced back to her office? '*Hold your front woman,*' she reminded herself.

On his way out, already dialing his buddy for a meet up, he kind of felt guilty for telling her all. It felt good though. *But how can I trust her? Besides something about her does not add up, I have to keep my guards up. Never trust anyone!* he admonished himself. Skipping past the red light with no regard, he waited for his friend to pick up the phone. Apparently, Smokie had tuned out. He decided to go home, eat something and read something before he headed back to the kebab joint for the late shift. What was it she said, about the confidentiality law as well, he reminded himself.

****

Getting off the back towards the council towers, he called home. Teme made a detour stop at the library on Tøyen square. Though still restless inside, watching the world map somehow entertained him. Tracing the path he had taken over the map. He sure had come a long way; he would reminisce and be kind of proud of what he had braved. Then his imagination would take over, fantasizing the places he would visit, memorizing the names of the cities and towns in weird countries sure killed time. But reading the encyclopedia was even more interesting. He would flip through the pages to randomly read the profiles of countries, the language, ethnicity, population, currency, and people. From Andorra to Venezuela. That day it was Czech Republic. Scanning through the brief historical accounts of Bohemian history and culture engaged him a little. Reading about the well-known fact of beer-drinking culture even perked his interest. Occasionally glancing through the window at the activity around the square, aided by the pictures on the encyclopedia, he imagined himself drinking beer and walking through the narrow cobbled streets of the old town Prague. Soon he got bored and walked out without even bothering to place the book back on the shelf. Outside a strange face caught his attention. He followed him with his eyes, the boy smelled trouble. One should always be looking for invaders, unwelcome visitors and suspicious fuckers encroaching in their territory. If it's a civilian acting up, better know whose territory it was. If it's a wrong soldier in the wrong neighborhood, well better learn your lesson was the unwritten law of the streets as Teme causally shadowed the stranger, making his way past the square. It was a duty he gladly performed in his neighborhood as well. The stranger recognized the threat and quickly made a retreat towards the highway past their demarcated border. Job done, Teme trotted back to his place with a chip on his shoulder.

****

Chapter 4

Teme went home. Entering his bedroom, he was welcomed by a whiff of pungent trapped air. Blaming his gassy guts of late for the unfortunate smell, he chided himself with a naughty loud grin. He could crack the window open and let some much-needed fresh air in, yet the blend of northern cold sea wave gliding past the hardened ice for further freezing effect was whistling violently outside. Grateful that it was his own gas that circulated inside the room, he brushed aside the overwhelming stench and stepped towards his unmade bed. Nonchalantly, he readjusted the trampled blue and white colored winter duvet over his flattened pair of pillows. His pillows had to be changed. A combination of sweat and drooling saliva had abstractly formed a figure on both pillows. He bent lower to pay closer attention to the stain. This was artistic, maybe he was subconsciously painting it in his dreams through his own fluid, who knew? It looked like a global map drawn by an amateur over his creamy pillow cases that retained none of their original whiteness when he had been supplied back in his underage camp days. Knowing he expected no company, he ignored the stain and tucked them inside the bed cover with a delicate tap. He must change his bed set one of these days, he noted and looked around his tiny bedroom. His bulging bedroom chest, stuffed to the teeth with unfolded clothes of all sorts stood in front of him. Unfazed by the shambolic site, he looked away towards the overflowing cloth bin standing awkwardly between the bed and the window. He strode with intent towards the packed bin and inserted his left hand with disgust as if he was dipping his fingers into an open sewer and trashed his way deeper in search of a pair of socks. Flailing his wrist left and right, he finally fished a pair of neatly folded ball of socks and yanked it out, a pile of pressed litter of dirty underwear, t-shirts, sweaters and shorts spilled all over the floor like a coffee filled to the rim spills its contents on the plate when a spoon is dipped.

Unfolding the ball of socks, he studied it closely. The thick white socks with a black Nike swoosh on its side had unnaturally soiled toe marks to his annoyance. It baffled him how his feet produced their own soil ingredients to mark their prints when the very shoes he trashed along in the streets were covered with nothing but white snow and ice. White was never his lucky color anyway as he tossed them back into the bin and dipped his hands once again with sheer force that he rocked the plastic bin from side to side, spilling its filthy contents once again. He dug out two pairs of balls. One of them was a silk thin silver, which he tossed back at once and retained the other thicker black blend of wool and cotton pair. That would do it, insulate his weary sensitive toes from the cold tiles for a while as he begun to put them on with haste.

He hurried his way back into the shared kitchen/living room as if racing past a hotel lobby late for an appointment. The other occupants were often either at work or at school. The couple were not in talking terms with him after some incidents and late parties he had held despite their repeated protest. He was walking on thin ice with his landowner. Leaning onto a wooden semi divider that stood between the sofa and the ever-droning fridge with two wide arms arching with intent on his hips like a landlord, he pondered. Something he could not pinpoint bothered him dearly. Then he realized the apartment was awfully cold that day. Even though it was never warm in that basement apartment, today was a tad unbearable. He retraced his steps back and picked up the water boiler and filled it with water from the sink faucet that gushed adjacent to the electric oven lodged between it and the fridge. Switching on the boiler, he raced back to his living room threshold, walked past the tight spot between the leather sofa and the oval-shaped glass coffee table and reached for the curtains. He swung them across the rod with some gust like drapes in theaters were opened for premieres. A frosted windowpane welcomed him. He inspected the window from corner to corner, yet no cracks appeared. So where was all the cold coming from? He was puzzled. Pacing restlessly, clinging to the window frame, Teme looked down towards the flat heater fused to the walls underneath the window. He cautiously sent his tame fingers towards the electrical heating board. Anticipating a warm sizzling heat wave, his tactile sensors were disappointed. This was getting weird! His open hand approached the flat heater closer this time. Yet he picked up no source of heat from the appliance. Teme tapped the flat metal a couple of times. Yet it was ice cold! Relieved it was the heater being off and not he being overly sensitive of the cold like a grumpy grandmother, he bent down to switch it back on!

Still the heater was not emitting heat. He once again tapped the flat end, maybe it took time to heat up the cells or whatever, he wondered. Impatient he switched it off and back on. To his frustration the red round indicator beside the switch button was still not glowing. You too! He shook his head in disappointment and off he went ranting once again about why things always start to fall apart when lady luck turned her back on him. It beats him why the tests in life go harder when he was short of luck and money, provisions run low, appliances stop working and on and on the run goes to run him down. What was he to do then? He never asked for it! Ever since he quit school, transition to adulthood has come as a shock. Opportunities were limited, just as he was to run the list of all the things gone wrong in his life, he recalled it was him actually who had unplugged the heater's chord in place of his phone charger late last night! Laughing at his forgetfulness, he instantly reached out at the divider and yanked out the charger. He definitely had to stop smoking too much ganja, maybe they were right, it killed the brain cells. Plugging the heater chord into the divider, he reminded himself to buy a bigger divider next time he went to the store!

****

Smokie finally arrived, accompanied by the Kurd twins Aras and Sina, a laid-back Palestinian and a Somali friend, Nasib and a blond giggling kid they called Cold Martin; they had all gone to school together. Most had dropped out, with the exception of one of the twins, Teme was not sure which. Now all were in the hustle game. They had a couple of beers and a cocktail of hard liquor – a blend of red bull, vodka, mineral water, ram in a coke plastic bottle and some grounded oxycontin and other relaxant pills as extra spices. Smokie was right away on what he does best, rolling joints for the entire squad. The party was on the way. Music blasting. One of his flatmates gave them a scorning glare before he stormed back to his room and banged the door, to which all burst into giggles. X box hooked to the TV, they alternated in playing Grand theft auto.

"Man, wish life in Oslo was like GTA. All guns blazing, you get what you want," one of the twins remarked.

"I hear you, man, too many rules; the pigs and their potato blond families and the cameras everywhere. You can't do shit in this town," Smokie replied, shaking his head.

"It's like GTA in Iraq right before we left. Bombs and shit was just normal. Boom all the time. Dead bodies in the streets was part of the day, bro. It is normal. These Norwegians are lucky, bro, all shit they see is on TV. But us, we seen it all, you know."

A disturbing silence ensued. A sort of collective recognition to all the violence they had overcome. It was obviously an uncomfortable moment for Martin, who opted to remain invisible when nonwestern realities were related in his few encounters with the crew.

"Shit man, in this world though," one of the twins finally broke the ice, "unless you make some noise, don't nobody respect you."

They agreed unanimously.

"All the great men in history were hard men. Killers and gangsters. They become heroes when they are dead and gone. But when they were alive, they were feared," Smokie added.

"It's fucked up. Everything don't make sense, I tell you," Teme finally said with a flashback of all the violent episodes coming back at once to trigger a splitting headache centered around his right temple.

"You ever heard of Salah ad Din?" asked one of the twins, arranging his sleek long hair around his ear. None replied. "You remember the movie about the Christians and Muslim war they showed us at school? You know the Muslim king he is talking about?"

"Oh ya," Teme beamed, recognizing the movie, perhaps something in common to engage with the twins he had been uneasy about for long, "yeah, he is some Arab hero right?"

"No, no, my friend, he was a Kurd. Like me," the animated Aras continued, "He once ruled over every Muslim land, imagine. He conquered Christian armies time after time. But now you see, we Kurds don't even have a country. It's fucked up."

All begun to recount heroes. Mythical figures from their homelands. Teme was amazed at how every one of them, now stateless and almost heartless, could all retrace the selves to ancient glory days for solace during testing times. In every one of them there was either a civil unrest or an international crisis that had uprooted them off their motherland. Perhaps never to get back again. Thus, he questioned in a haze of intoxication, will Norway ever feel like a home? Will these guys be his new family, broken traumatized pieces from all corners of the world completing each other? With different yet similar experiences at such a young age, they never questioned each other. There was a distance maintained, no inquires on their past deeds nor judgment for their ill-conceived decisions they had to make to survive. Only those who had been through it all

36

understood you sadly, the rest with their high moral values were only there to either belittle, dehumanize, distance, or pity them. None of them understood them, though pretend like they did.

Two Thai chicks and a Norwegian blonde soon joined the party and whisked away the twins and Martin. The reticent Nasib disappeared without a trace, leaving Smokie and Teme by themselves.

****

They ran out together to buy a pack of smokes at the neighboring kiosk. Scanning and patrolling their territory, subconsciously an unfamiliar movement grabbed their attention. They have seen him before, either one of the Grorud guys or from Storo, either way he was in the wrong place in the wrong time. And he knew it too, looking over his shoulder time and time again. Game recognizes game at once, and the duo applied the pedal to their feet in tandem, shadowing this boy their age fidgeting past the maze of the council towers. Boy was lost, they knew it; they followed him, split in two directions, like lions set on a prey to lead him and corner him at a dead end. Right before Teme was about to jump him, a police patrol pulled up the corner, as if smelling some trouble. They backed off, signaling their intent. The fear in the boy's eyes was evident, the relief at the sight of the police car. But regardless, they smiled and high-fived, having delivered their message.

****

Back in the apartment they were on a chill back mode, killing time.

"Why you chill with these guys I don't know, man," posed Teme the question he had been contemplating while puffing the thick joint stuck between his fingers. Greasy one too, he noted.

"The question is why you don't with them, Killa," retorted Smokie

"Don't call me that!" exclaimed Teme, glaring at Toure with that deadly killer look.

"Okay, okay, anyway the problem with you is, you spend way too much time thinking about your own life, man. Try to listen to other people too, bro. We all got problems. Maybe we are all the same."

"We are the same, fuck you! You were there, were we the same people then? Treated the same. Felt like I was in a slave ship. Christian and black, we were just disposable commodities, man. Fuck you talking about? We are the same shit."

"I know, I feel you." Toure took back the joint. He was filling the buzz. He got up to spike the volume of his favorite rapper Rich Homie Quan's song *some type of way* and took his seat back. Rather collapsed on the leather sofa. "As a Muslim yet with the wrong color, I felt the same man. I remember, man, thinking how the captured slaves 500 years ago used to feel, waiting for the boat to ship them to the plantation, right. Shit we had to pay for that and everything for this life, right? But you seen what they do to one another, man! Shit too fucked up out there!"

"Yeah, this shitty life." Teme got up to pour himself the guava juice they had bought earlier from the Grønland Arab store. Fucking magic after some ganja session. He poured two glasses and sat back. "The problem is they remind me of them, you know who am talking about. They look like them. Sometimes I feel like killing them all, you know."

"Hahaha, Killa, they sense it too. But never forgot we survived, man. And mostly if it was not for you, we would not be here talking and chilling in Norway."

They both cracked up at that for what was like minutes until silence took over. Dub reggae mix *Konshens* was playing *We no worry about them*. They both enjoyed the drum and bass fucking good. Everything in fact felt better with ganja.

"You know the two Kurds, the Palestine, the Somali and us too, are all outcasts to our own blood. We chose to or were forced to. That is personal. But we all been through shit in life. We all been forced to do things at a young age, and we all survived. Even that kid Martin has been through tough times despite growing up here, man. We are no victims nor are we heroes or psychos. We are no longer boys either. We grew as men too fast. The rest of society don't understand us. We do not need fucking sympathy. We just want to chill, not remember any of that shit that happened and be left alone. And I tell you being around them and even you, makes me feel normal. Feel me?"

Totally faded, red-blood eyes buried in their sockets, two forearms lazily resting on his knees, Teme hung on to every word streaming out of his best friend. He agreed with him. Indeed, he was lucky to have someone who had gone through the same trauma; fuck trauma it's the fucking doctors trying to victimize him, he was a survivor, it was just a tough life experience he passed. He made it. Not many did. It was remarkable how he had missed that element that made him uneasy about the other guys was the same strangeness he felt about himself. They were alike. Lost souls. No! Not lost, wounded but hardened. Maybe he should ease up on them fellows. "I hear you, Smokie. I hear you. But never compare our life with white people problem Martin has gone through, my man." Teme leaned back on the sofa and dozed off, listening to the soft reggae tune of Toure's playlist.

****

Chapter 5

A couple of days later, back at the shrink office, the psychologist began the session about anti-social behavior, isolation, and me against the world mentality. Teme was in no mood for a lecture nor an argument as he kept interrupting her. She was trying her best to relate the psychological phases everyone had to go through in one's life time. Erikson's eight stages of psychological development she studied and applied many times in her work was totally inapplicable in this particular case. Some stages had overlapped and entwined inconveniently. Adolescence and its trials had been sadly skipped to give in to the crisis and existential dilemmas of early adulthood at an alarming pace. Thus, she was left to improvise in a vague manner. As of Freud's bourgeoisie white kids who afforded therapy were his pool. A narrow scope to see the world through. The libido theories seen through affluent white men's perspective, objectification of women and nullifying other races, the Freudian range was beyond the young African men in child's body who frequented her office these days.

"Wow, wow, who said I was anti-social or lonely? I have nothing against others," Teme protested at once, confused with all the technical jargon.

"I understand, I am just speaking in general, Teme," she pleaded, trying to wrap up a point. Her attempt to open with a scientific approach misfired again, she noted. She instead rephrased her question to directly appeal to his case, "You do not want to live with your own people?"

"It is not like that. I just…I have no problem with my people." Teme was all defensive but he was in a no confrontation mode.

"I read from your file that you were having hard time with living with people from your country when you first arrived." She was at it again.

"I have no problem with my people."

"Yeah, I understand. Maybe you preferred not to be roomed with some particular person or persons?"

40

"Something like that." He gave in.

"They moved you to several rooms with other nationalities, but still you insisted on being moved. Your request was to live alone; did you want to be left alone?"

Silence.

Okay.

"Do you hate your people, Teme?"

A pause. A long staring contest, then he shook his head almost in disinterest. It showed his indecision, she noted.

"Do they remind you of something you want to forget?"

"Maybe." He quickly added, "But like I said, I have no problem with them."

"Do you have friends from your own country?"

"Not at the moment."

"Have you asked yourself why?"

He took a long moment. Scratching his head, he pondered if he should tell the psychologist why. He sure came across people from his country all the time, but he often kept his distance. And for a damn good reason. Word travels fast, and the past follows you, as they say.

"Are there many people from your country?"

"Listen, what is this an investigation? I don't want to talk about my countrymen. If you want to, you can go out and meet them yourself," he snapped at her.

She waited until he calmed down. Cleared her throat and added, "Sure, sorry to badger you about it."

"Yeah, no problem." He ruffled his jacket to compose himself.

An uncomfortable yet necessary silence ensued for both to compose themselves. Maybe she was going too hard, she figured.

"So, what was it you wanted to become?" The shrink diverted the inquisition to a less intrusive subject. "You know your dream career or job when you were a little boy?"

He was lost in his thoughts again, trying hard to refresh his memory on what it was like when he was a boy. That part of his life, which was just few years ago, has been totally obliterated. Almost no recollection of it. It was almost like another boy's life.

Realizing his struggle to connect with his earlier dream, she tried to rephrase the question, "What were you good at, Teme, when you were a kid? Does something stand out about you that people used to talk about? Something? Anything that you were praised for?"

His eyes lit up all of a sudden, "Football. I used to be good. The best goal scorer in town. I always wanted to be like Ronaldo, you know." His mood shifted into a sorrowful look at once, realizing the death of his childhood dream.

Focus, no time to sympathize, she reminded herself, though her throat was strobing, fighting a sob. This was the hardest part of the job; the moment kids realize the loss of their innocence. No kid should ever experience it. A child must grow as a child.

"There is still time for it. Do you still play football?"

"No, not anymore."

"But they have plenty of clubs that would take you in around where you live. If you are interested, I could ask around for you. Who knows maybe you still can become Ronaldo. You are still young."

"No, I don't want to," he snapped. "I just lost all desire to kick a ball."

"But do you still watch football?"

"Not anymore. Not like I used to."

"What do you like to do then in your free time these days? Besides getting into trouble," she smiled jokingly, trying to brighten his mood.

His cocky look came back. He almost replied smoking weed and get faded. But he bit his tongue and just stared at her.

After another bout of silence.

"Do you remember the very reason why you left your country, Teme? Sometimes looking back to the very beginning can help you sort out the future. It can help you find a goal to pursue in life, something you can believe in. Understand me?"

He nodded.

"Let's make this as your assignment for out next session. Think about why you left your country. It has to be your own reason. Then think about what you are capable of doing. What skills do you have that you can apply here for a better future?"

Teme agreed and said his due goodbye. On his way out, he started thinking about why he had left his country. So much has happened along the way that he has forgotten why he had left his country in the first place. Shit was just too confusing.

****

Life was not supposed to turn out that way though when he left his country as a runaway kid with a dozen others to the greener pastures his fate had for him. He was just a 12-year-old hyper-active kid when he left his country. There was no concrete dream then. Everybody left. Future was dim, his only close kin his grandmother was ailing and on the edge of senility. It was never planned; it was just his time to try out his luck, like everybody else, in the West. Luck was on his side from day one. He was always the lucky one, who always got away with any stupid delinquency he conspired of since he was a kid. He had always felt he could get away with anything. He did not suffer like many of the undocumented refugees residing in the capital of Sudan, Khartoum. He had picked up the language very fast, despite no remittance nor any sponsor from abroad to apply for family reunification, he had survived well. The immigration police that were rampant in the city never bothered him.

Teme, along with other unaccompanied underage kids his age, had lived in a compound in Dem district, where they hustled and saved money for the Libya trip that would change their life. That sole goal in life had kept them together, focused, and most importantly, fearless. Unsupervised and unrestrained, they built up a close-knit nucleus of boys and girls with similar experiences and age group they called a family. They were protective of each other. Bailed each other out when apprehended. Shared meals and stories. It was there Teme had begun to grow with confidence and found his own voice. He realized people listened to him, they respected him. He was their undisputed leader. They survived on hard labor amid the intense Sudanese heat, they scrapped floors, they even stole when they could but always split equally among the family. Through ups and down amid the unpredictability of Khartoum life, they accumulated enough for the much-anticipated trip. Through hierarchy Teme was among the selected first batch to embark on the treacherous desert journey.

He remembered it like it had happened yesterday, the trip had begun flawless like he had imagined, the last phase of the Euro dream was underway. Deposits paid, the dusty pickup along with over-packed 24 souls took off from the outskirt of Khartoum in the pitch-black darkness sometime after three in the morning. Five women, one heavily pregnant, were allowed space to sit in between the guys cramped and protectively surrounded them. Some with half their bodies dangling from the pickup held on. Once the money was in their hands, the traffickers' tone gravely transformed; slapping and punching soon followed. Pushing and shoving was brutal, not even sparing the pregnant woman. Fucking savages were treating them like cattle driven to the slaughter house. But with dreams of skyscrapers on the horizon all bit their tongue. All from different backgrounds, all shades of black Africa marching towards the Arabs voluntarily to ship them to the white world, exactly like it happened centuries ago. *Slavery was still alive!*

The first few hours flew by like a blur. The gravel path was a bit rocky, the driver well used to the road, and hands clasped to one another, all the live commodity was intact for the smugglers in haste. The dust was brutally lashing on to their faces though despite the faces covered like a desert ninja on a pickup, holding hands to avoid falling off. Sleep, they had been warned, was almost death penalty in a speeding open truck.

Then came the first hurdle, a checkpoint in the desert. There was a hint of a settlement or a small town in the distance behind a hill they were skirting, the panorama of the light, but they were still in Sudanese territory. They were told to stay put. Three policemen, one dressed in military outfit, circled their pickup, constantly exchanging hushed words with the driver and the animated smuggler. After head counts and calculations, a heated argument took place while the live cattle kept silent. Abruptly, the two policemen in blue khaki outfits approached the back of the car from both sides and gave orders in Arabic. All raised their hands in the air. One by one the occupants were pulled down to the ground by one of the police and searched for a hidden stash, all the way to the underpants. When it came to the ladies, perhaps the man accompanying the pregnant girl and one passionate lover to one of the girls got a heavy stub with the back of the Kalashnikov for their protest. The women, whining and whimpering, were searched even in their crotches. After confiscating what little money they had hidden on their person, the car was underway with two heavily bleeding men on board.

The next day was torture by nature. The longer the pickup trashed through the Sahara Desert sand at a mind-numbing 150 kph at times, the drier the air, the scorching the sun and humid it got. Water bottles were emptied by then. The smugglers seldom looked over the shoulder, indifferently making headcounts but never answering any questions and complaints. That was quite some tactic to shut off the humane aspect of their arduous task of human trafficking. It was only a job, following orders, Teme would later learn about the cold nature of the job. The pregnant lady was surprisingly tough, barely complaining. While a skinny girl was sick. The gash on one of the victims of the night before would not stop bleeding. But they moved on. It was better to move on as well. Whenever they made the rare stops along the way, the sun and the still air of the desert would become unbearable. The dust and the wind generated by their own pickup was much preferred.

Incident-free they cruised past the second day as well, surrounded by nothing but sand dunes, the occasional swooshing desert wind and the disturbing constant state of stillness but not tranquility; the sand always seemed to as a swirling veil for some evil lurking underneath. Teme was vigilant though he was helpless and unarmed.

The third day deep in the heart of Sahara disaster struck. Their pickup overturned a couple of times, landing on and trashing the occupants across the sand. The first time they were lucky they had slowed down climbing a sand dune that crumbled in a heap when they reached its top, barely toppling its content onto the sand. The second time, though, happened while they were speeding and caught them by surprise as it tossed them violently before it toppled over a sand dune. One unlucky soul broke his neck. Many were injured, even Teme fell hard on his shoulder. Yet all tried to keep the unfortunate soul alive, some crying, some praying, some giving up and with a stoic look of sympathy bidding their farewell. The smuggler and the driver were pissed off though over the damage to their car. The windshield was cracked, the side mirror broken and to add insult to injury, one livestock fatally wounded. It took a while to repair the pickup, no shades under the unbearable desert sun. Water rationed by the unruly trafficker had long been depleted. Warning shots missing one of their heads stopped the angry mob from further protesting. The man died of his injuries, buried in an unmarked sand grave, with teardrops and long faces the pickup was on the way at last. A short ride later the sick girl succumbed to the heat, the angry smuggler dumped the dead body on the sand and threatened everyone to remain on the pickup. The girl Teme's age was hastily buried and the trip continued. Silence ensued among the exhausted, thirsty passengers. The humming of the diesel truck pluming through the sand dune must have disturbed the peace of the desert, hampering their pace.

The third night, right before they reached the Libyan border, one asleep passenger fell off the pickup. The driver never bothered to stop, regardless of the howling of insults, neither did the slapping of hands deter him. One shot fired of the passenger seat and all fell quiet. By then they had accepted their fate as being in the hands of the two passengers in the front. Submissive, they all succumbed to the sorrow in silence. What struck Teme most was all the passengers were as young as him. Most teenagers, apart from two adult companions, who were surprisingly docile and complicit. Three casualties paid so far for the three days on the road. Finally, the pickup stopped. They all received a curt order to step out of the car and file in one line. They complied. The truck turned around, and the driver took off back to the same route they had come from. The armed smuggler keeping his distance with the muzzle of the gun pointed at them, informed them in Arabic that they had a six-hour walk to the border town to sneak in undetected. None protested. They walked for seven hours, still no town in sight. The smuggler looked agitated but answered none of their inquiries. The sun arrived and started baking them for breakfast and then lunch. The line broke off several times, some dropping behind, seeking shelter on a sand dune that appeared and disappeared on their path. Stunning consistency all yellowish, no sign of life but the stench of death was evident. They ran into several dead carcasses of failed past attempts rotting in the open desert, some with their clothes intact over their white skeletons resting peacefully on the sand as if relaxing on the beach. Another casualty was paid, another girl left behind. But no room for grief, they kept going. 20 left!

After 12 hours, they arrived around dusk at the border town near Al Awaynat. They were intercepted by a heavily armed gang. They looked like militias and spoke different dialect of Arabic. They looked different from their Sudanese counterparts both in their facial appearance, demeanor and complexion, a tad darker, meaner and always in a hurry. They would later find out they were renegade militia from the neighboring Chad, renowned for human trafficking, kidnap, torture, and contract murders who knew the Sahara like the back of their hands. After haggling over price, two pickups split them in two groups of 10 and departed in separate directions. The one heading to the north with two females was the one Teme was on. After a short ride they reached what looked like the outskirts of the town, Kufra. Everyone seemed to be armed and communication was hushed. The beatings started right off as punches and kicks were the welcoming. They were thrown inside a container, the women separated and herded into the house. There were three containers side by side. Locked inside their container were three men from previous trips, looking all haggard and emaciated. Panic set in. That night was torture, hearing the constant screams of the two girls followed by loud outbursts of laughter.

Twelve days passed, none leaving the container, new faces trickled in. They were slipped a bowl-full of over-boiled macaroni sprinkled with oil and salt and a jug full of murky warm water every afternoon. The repulsive smell of the bowl and the tasteless macaroni one would forget after a day or two and long for it soon. After a week, one salivated at the sight of the bowl, and they would fight over it like hungry hyenas, licking the bowl clean.

The war in Libya was ongoing, Gaddafi had been deposed and killed like a dog. They knew all along as well there was a new dark force lurking in the desert that persecuted Christians. Cut off their heads for their faiths, enslaved women, and forced young boys to convert and join their militancy. They had been warned off plenty of times. Especially that YouTube video of his countrymen slaughtered like sheep on the Mediterranean beach was hair-raising. But he had done his homework for the trip, hid all the Christian signs including his name under the alias Nasir, rehearsed some prayers in Arabic, which he had some good command of. He was well prepared and had this gut feeling it was his time. He just felt it was the time to make his move, it was either then or never.

After Gaddafi, the military had been distracted, fighting off the different factions and militants and local militias for control of the land; thus, he had heard reliable rumors if one evaded the militias and those deadly radical militant group, the boat trip across the Mediterranean would be within grasp and for much cheaper price, conducted by locals. Rumors were spreading even Gaddafi had ordered his coast guard to ship thousands of Africans into loaded boats as a retaliation to the invasion of the Western world. Some friends had made the trip scot-free. He was halfway. And the sight of the open sea was what kept his spirits alive and alight languishing in the darkness of the container.

And now that he has crossed the sea what then? It was happening too fast to question and plan. Nothing he had ever done in life was properly thought through anyway. He contemplated checking out his crew in Tøyen but thought otherwise. Maybe head to his girl and chill, he figured.

Chapter 6

Reclining comfortably on Elise's sofa facing her flat plasma TV, he gently placed his feet on top of the other on to the glass coffee table. Stretching and sighing in fatigue, he picked up the remote control from the table and switched on the TV. What were the odds as a slalom championship was live on NRK 2. Hissing something incompressible under his breath, he switched channels in a dire attempt to escape from the pile of snow. It was just everywhere! After a futile attempt to find anything interesting, he finally resigned to BBC news channel. There was reportage on some Middle East conflicts that had erupted once again, with the images of young kids cursing in fury before they threw chunks of rocks on the police. He mused and joked to himself on how come they never run out of rocks to throw. Soon they would need to import in tons from neighboring countries. He cracked up at his own sick joke. TV was just for distraction, for the eyes to play along with something in motion while his mind raced as usual somewhere far, far away. He could not remember the last time he had given an undivided attention to something on TV; well, maybe a chunk of the divided part undividedly focusing on different worlds simultaneously, *multitasking, baby*! His mind once again tracked back to the icy winter. There was some instances in his life where ice was considered more as jewel, prized assets looked after and cherished to its last drop! And now he was trampling and trashing his way across everywhere he turned. Nature sure was a mystery!

Eyes fixated on the news, the mind wandered on and on his current state. Being independent for the first time he thought it would help but the problems grew. In fact, exploded. New responsibilities, new nightmares. Even the police mean business now ever since he turned 18. No more slaps on the hand, he was now considered a responsible adult in the eyes of the law; missteps that were looked over had now severe consequences. Even his girl had become a nag, acting all like she was his mother or something. Job situation was a worry though.

He had done it all, all sorts of odd jobs to get by. He had played with toddlers at kindergarten playgrounds as an unqualified assistant. With the ever-skeptical parents watching him with unease, over leaving their loved ones at the hands of an African, who probably had been a child soldier, made him conscious and reserved. The innocent offensive remarks uttered by the children, echoing their parents' jabs behind closed doors, probably over news coverage of another African genocide or hunger, would take him aback. Yet what was he to reply to a child; remind him of futile innocence lost? His childhood memory almost deleted from his memory disturbed him when spending way too much time on all fours bo bo bo boing at strange yet innocent blond kids for a living! After two weeks he stopped showing up at work without notice.

Then there was the elderly home stint that Elise hooked him up that remind him of death. A qualified assistant nurse's unqualified assistant, the ass washing business, as they referred to it bluntly. Teme, for the first time, was confronted on a constant basis with the decadence of human life. It was the top of the list most sought-after job as well, among the new comers, specially the women. Their job was to change the diapers and wash their asses that leak faster than the toddlers he kept watch on in kindergartens. There was a one weird week where he had actually changed a diaper of a two year old in his last morning shift at a neighborhood kindergarten and happened to end up at the elderly house the same afternoon. While changing the soiled diapers and running the faucet over the limp elderly man, he realized he had just witnessed the complete cycle of life while on duty on the same day. Apart from the wrinkled lanky legs of the elderly, it was a déjà vu moment that haunted his days for weeks to come. What was the point of it all, the toiling, the worrying, and the hustle if the ultimate preservation and goal was to end up back to where one started off? The helplessness and the hollow emptiness he observed time and time and again disturbed him dearly. At least the toddlers had that spark, the fresh innocence that tamed even the callous of hearts.

Subconsciously, his young mind was being exposed to the ordinary passage of life, from the cradle to the grave, in the most gradual natural path. It kind of confused his interpretation of life. A cheap commodity snatched violently at any given minute. He thought he was primed for the task. He had so much respect for those, specially the women, who worked long hours looking after the men and women who yearn nothing but a peaceful death. Slumped awkwardly on their side facing the door, the wrinkled bony faces expressionless, eyes locked on an empty wall as if watching a breaking news, greeted him many a times during a short stunt. Unless the overwhelming stench of their excrements stirred his nostrils, there was no way of knowing from that blank expression of theirs on his evening patrols. Would be hours before some have their diapers changed; fighting off his own vomit, Teme had found it hard to get accustomed to the occupational hazards, drawing a deep breath he would often reach out with tentative gloved hands to peel off the plastered jelly liquid of all colors off their private parts. Dragging their limp figures on an electric wheeled chair to the bathroom for a clean-up, never had he noticed any sign of shame, discomfort, or embarrassment on some of the old residents. Willingly abiding their limbs to be swayed left and right, they would always stare somewhere low on the wall, while he washed them up. To make matters worse, he overheard some were renowned, respected citizens who had lived their lives worshiped by many for their commanding achievements and charisma, finally let down by nature and suddenly could not even command the liquids flowing inside their own bodies. It was there he had contemplated, feeling like a teaser of death standing agile in front of them, if he really wanted to get old at all. The very idea of shriveling like a crumpled paper, helpless, half dead and never alive, just waiting and feeling like death had stood one up, but still not giving up was a painful thought. There was no trace of fear written on some of the senile ones; numb to all emotions except for sudden incompressible outbursts none understood, they just wallowed their days unconscious of neither time nor space. The memory fading, he was shocked at times how some meticulously run the details of their funeral arrangements. It was just the most depressing working environment he had ever been. Death was in the air, but never on the ground. Just hovering, teasing, and cajoling his next victim from a distance like a nurse. Not like the one he was well acquainted. Besides him and death knew each other on a very personal level.

Death was sentimental yet a cruel lover in that part of the world. A century of life was a common affair. Having long reclaimed their flesh of their emaciated bones, their spirit dissipated into a mere resilient acceptance of their fate, the artist death, squatting by the low end of the wall, looked admiringly at his latest work from afar, bones and a hint of memory through the soulless empty eyes flashing once in a while in front of him. But he never had that kind of patience back in the desert, just a quick massive sweep every time it swung by! A domino game he played back in the Dark Continent, just in a hurry to get out with maximum gain. Cold and distant, yet ever present, figured the young, confused Teme, rolling his dreadlocks on his index finger, all the grotesque images he had endured on a regular basis flashed by agonizingly. A disaster in a Western world was a kidnapping of a photogenic blond, a shocking earth-shattering incident dominating the headlines for weeks, while an ethnic cleansing wiping out an entire village was just the order of the day back from where the likes of Teme came from. At times making his night patrols on those death-quiet elderly halls, he would stick his head into the occupied rooms of the residents to see some barely hanging on to their last breath for far too long. Terrified Teme would bid silent farewell to the strangers who barely recognized him, and walk away briskly, wondering if he would ever get to see their haunting faces on his next visit. Yet again he was surprised to see them once again hanging by the same thin thread, indifferently staring down into the abyss from the ledge of life. That was when he realized he was not as tough and cold-blooded as he had assumed he was. He had so much respect for the women who run about their business from one deathbed to the next, totally detached from their emotions. It was too much for him as he went on to seek manly occupations, where he was not reminded of that dreadful eminent end. Repetitive routines stifle emotions once one mastered them to engage mechanically as he opted for a more physical job that required no communication with humans.

Thus, the much coveted sanitation business. The backbone of the immigrants that ends up breaking their backs. Once again in the background, making sure the glistening marble floors stay sparkling like the stars in the sky, moping away any smudge left behind the long airport corridors, public buildings, hotels and sport as a full-time occupation was a pinnacle for many immigrants.

Teme had not even been able to secure a full time-shift as a temp floor sweeper. He recalled quite well though the spell he had at a junior high school across town. His shift was from 6:00 to 10:00. Since he had to take two busses, he set off around 5:00 to catch the early morning bus, wait for 15 minutes for the connecting bus in the town center to get there often on time. The task was not tiresome yet the consuming silence in the empty school halls terrified him at times. The squealing doors, the sound of his own feet and mop shuffling across the marble tiles, resonating synchronized magnified echoes across the entire corridors, would conjure scenes from his dark past, where silence was only associated with terror. Conscious of even his own shadow, the wind whistling past the windowpanes, the motion sensor corridor lights that play tricks on his periphery vision, the gliding doors that send a gust of wind to slam a chain of classroom doors, he had forgotten to close behind him, would startle him over and over again until the school employees begun to drip in numbers. All the dark alleys he used to navigate in all the places he had been, all the evil people he fought and fled from, the prison drills he had persevered through, all the torment he had faced in his young life had probably left him shook off for a mere echoing gust of wind was all it took to startle him, he had reckoned in dismay. The giggle and the running foots, the curses and the cries of the students was a welcome sound, before Teme handed over the equipment and snuck out invisible in a crowd of youngsters. Though he dreaded the early morning torment, he always showed up until the person he had filled in for came back from his annual leave and like many others they soon will stop calling and he would be out of a job.

Teme sighed in frustration. Adulthood was just too fucked up. He tweaked the remote and put on his favorite documentary on. Cristiano Ronaldo, his hero. The documentary was so touching that it resonated with him, his determination at least, and, of course, his loneliness. The success, the envy, and the jealousy of the haters was what Teme aspired to have, to start from the bottom and conquer the world. Imagining himself in Ronaldo's shoes was not just his favorite pastime in those dark days but more like the sanest thought amid all the chaos. It was life right from the start.

While on the back of a pick up, huddled together with other migrants like livestock on their way to Libya, his imagination was a solace. He had imagined himself as football star just like Ronaldo. He had mirrored his imaginary rise to stardom like his idol Cristiano Ronaldo. All the beatings, the hunger, the dust, and the thirst clogging his throat that dream kept him alive. He was good at football back in the days, though he knew the dream was farfetched, the longer it dwelled in his fantasy, the more he believed it. The journey in the desert was part of his destiny of global superstardom. He had constructed and reconstructed the progress in his fantasy that at times he was having conversation with other superstars who looked up to him. Even Ronaldo had begun to notice his talent and envy him. That fantasy made those dark days roll by without a fuss.

In the meantime Elise had snuck in to her living room, unnoticed to his wandering mind.

"You going to work today, babe?" she asked.

"No, no work this week. It was just covering up for some dude. I hate that fucking job anyway."

"What do you plan to do then, babe? Come on we're not kids anymore. Talk to me," she pleaded, noting his agitation.

"Hmmmph, I don't know, I will get some job."

"And then you will soon get tired of it and look for another job. And another job, before you know it you will be 58. An old man with no education and skill to speak of."

"Uff, I will figure it out."

His irritation was giving in to anger. But she did paint the picture of his future as bleakly as it can ever get, he mused. It was funny as he never envisioned his life that far ahead in time, never. He figured he will probably be dead by then.

"That is not an answer, baby. Got to think about it. You have to have some long-term goals. Don't look away now, I am only saying this because I care about you." She reached out to caress his cheeks. He hesitated for a second and pulled away before he conceded to her warm touch. Eyes locked down though and lips sealed.

"Look, it is not the same for us new comers that it is for you guys," he protested, "Born and bred here. You get prioritized as well as have people always on the inside to hook you up."

"Wow, how many times do we need to talk about this, honey? I know but that should not be an excuse for you to give up. That should even fire you up. You know, to challenge you but…"

"You never understand, girl," he interrupted, frustrated, "Listen, I feel like we are unwanted here, you know? Like uninvited guests, so they make sure to remind us of our intrusion through checkpoints in the system every day. And that knocks your ambition. Besides, I know many who studied heavy-duty stuff and have yet to find a job."

"Oh, you think it is easy for me." She snickered, "You think I am the gorgeous Norwegian blond with stunning model figure with rich, powerful daddy and mommy connections."

"No, I know it is not easy. But I am saying it easier for you than someone like me. Besides, they trust you more than me since you came through their system."

He had a point there for once, not using the race card excuse. She nodded in agreement to give him a credit. "But the whole point is not to give up. Have a long-term goal to wake up to and pursue every day. Otherwise, those fools you hang with hustling and pushing are going nowhere."

"Humph, okay but…" he let it trail, knowing she would not stop badgering him.

"Anyway, let me know if you want any help with the job thing as well. You know, if you want help writing job applications or making some inquiries or someone to recommend, you don't hesitate, okay babe?"

"Yeah, sure," he finally looked up, relieved the subject was shelved for a while at least. She leaned over his shoulder to give him a wet kiss.

She hated it when he fell silent and stoic. It was disturbing. She had to keep him engaged, at times it even meant provoking him.

"You want me to introduce you to some Norwegian friends?" she added desperately.

"No, I am good."

"Wow, that was a quick 'No'."

Silence.

"I mean me and my girls and their boyfriends are going bowling tonight if you want to, join or on the weekend if you want to come on a hiking tour in the mountains. A friend got a cottage out there, we could have a bonfire and chillax."

Still he was not interested. Shaking his head, "No, maybe some other time. But I don't do mountain stuff as well. That is for white people."

"Here we go again with the white people stuff."

"Hmmf, listen you want to go, go! I don't want to fight about this shit right now. I'm fucking tired."

"Okkkkay." She sighed. "I'm just saying you need to make new friends."

After a long silence, Teme watched Elise applying her make-up meticulously. Deft and dedicated. Beauty is a sacrifice, she had said to him last time he had inquired, "Why all the fuss?" But she is beautiful, he exhaled, admiring his girl, with or without make-up. She was conscious of his eyes but remained focused to the task. One thing he had noticed about women regardless of the occasion, they never lost focus when a make-up kit was in their hands. They sure could put their make-up in a war zone or amidst an earthquake. He smiled.

She looked up and asked, "What?"

"What you mean what?"

"What you smiling about?"

After a long pause just watching her, he said, "Nothing."

"Okay," she was satisfied with the job in front of the mirror; she gave the reflection an air kiss.

"So you just don't like hanging out with white boys, is that it?" she reignited the conversation to his frustration.

"Puff, I never said that!" He was defensive at once.

"Then why do you avoid being around them? You think I never notice? Every time I invite someone, you never show any interest to what they say nor try to get to know them."

"Humph," he looked away, grabbing his joystick mechanically and switch on his Xbox, the ever-reliable escapade from monologues or dialogues.

"Do they bore you, or do you think they look down on you?"

"They look down on me I fuck them up on spot. I am no slave TV nigger who says, 'Yes, master,' and walks away, you know that."

"Ahhaah, my lil gangster." Hands on her hips she enjoyed the moment. It terrified her and thrilled her at the same time when he said stuff like that off the cuff.

"Yeah, girl. But it's not that, you know racism and stuff don't bother me. We are just too different, feel me? Some are cool, but I don't know we just don't click."

"Okay." Appraising him with hands still on her hips, she snickered at his response.

"Girl, once you finish school, they go their way and we go ours. They got their future all lined up while we make our own."

"That is a lame excuse. First off, you quit school." Her right hand index finger was pointing at his accusatively. "And second thing, everybody works for their future. My family got connections, but that don't mean I sit on my lazy ass and wait for my future to land at my doorstep. I work hard for it. I earn it!"

"Puff. There you go. I don't want to argue now," he sounded deflated.

"I mean what about Magne, you guys were tight in school, right? You don't call him anymore?"

"No, like I said they change on you too. Some even don't holla at you when they run into you."

"Yeah hanging with your crew, little sorry ass gangsters who the hell would want to be associated with you, huh?"

"Little ass gangsters?"

"Yes, little ass nobodies." She matched his outburst.

"You need to chill." He stood up with his right index finger threateningly pointed at her.

She did not flinch, holding her nerve and stare, "Face it, you are not going anywhere hanging out with them losers!"

An awkward silence resumed. It hurt her seeing him wallow in his own bitterness.

She finally sat next to him. He was irresponsive and did not even pay attention to her. His eyes were glued to the TV, but she was sure his mind was somewhere else. She had to break the ice. She finally said, "You want to go on a boat trip? You know cruise ship, a couple of days on a giant floating hotel?"

He tensed at the very mention of a boat.

She continued oblivious to his angst, masked anguish. "It is beautiful. I used to go with family and friends. My girlfriends that is," she clarified while pulling her hair back, "sharing a cabin, drinking like crazy, party, party, sleepless for two nights. Of course, we had to get fake ID, got to be 20 years to be on board by yourself. Or get someone older to accompany you as a guardian, you know. Anyway, it was three years ago, a friend nearly went overboard."

Elise went on to tell him about the drunken episode that had got her and her friends into a lot of problem afterwards while Teme nodded, half listening, half drifting on a dinghy boat of his own courtesy of his colorful past. Then abruptly, she fell silent to face Teme and was petrified at the sight of his blank look. She knew what that blank look meant, retreat! Then she realized, '*Oh my God, the cruise ship, the ocean, how can I be so stupid*?' She admonished herself in silence over her own insensitiveness. Blushing in embarrassment, she smiled at him. He was irresponsive, stoic. She got closer, gave him a peek on the lips. He looked at her. She peppered him with kisses that finally broke the icy look of his face. Taking his shirt off, which he obliged with pleasure, she pushed him back on the sofa. He smiled, he enjoyed it when she came on strong. Not aggressive but passionate. It just took his mind off everything. '*But that floating hotel thing sounds very appealing*,' he thought one last time before her naked perky breasts pointing at him froze all thoughts.

****

Chapter 7

"I am beautiful," Elise said to herself, looking at her reflection in front of her bedroom mirror. Her waistline was expanding of late; lucky her face never lost nor gained a pound. Pinching playfully the flap of extra fat on both sides of her waist, she sighed and winked at herself. Confidence was the only treasure she had left, besides it was not that bad, she cheered herself up. She was not yet fat, though far from the slim bony figure she had been a long time ago. She contemplated, admonishing herself that she was never good at anything anyway! She used to be good at school but something went wrong at some point, and she completely lost her focus. She had suspected it had begun in her late junior high school years when she had begun to be very conscious of how different she looked from the rest of her schoolmates. She had always known that she had a black father yet she never felt herself as black. Nor did it ever bother her when her all white friends and neighbors made those racist comments towards the distinctly colored people that crossed their path once in a while. But it eventually crept upon her, the complexities of being a mixed-race individual. She had never known her father, albeit from the pictures and snip snap stories her mother had reluctantly slipped every once in a while. She was brought up knowing and being assured she was better off without her father and that her mother loved her dearly. But gratefully, despite his several flaws, Teme has had a calming effect in her life. *He does not even know it*, she smiled, looking over her shoulder to glance at his splayed form in her bed. His mouth was open, snoring lightly. He had that weird appearance of alertness even when he was asleep. His eyelids were not completely sealed when asleep, there was a slight glint open, and maybe she was imagining it. But most often he would jump off the bed from a deep sleep at the slightest strange sound or movement. *Her guardian angel.*

Looking at herself with less bravado this time, the flaws glared back at her. At a tender age of 20, her big grayish green eyes had become an epitome of hollow sadness. More like the Nordic melancholy perhaps. The same look she saw in her mother and all the old decaying lonely soles at the elderly house she was currently doing her internship as an assistant nurse. She loved the job that she had already decided to further her studies as a qualified nurse and who knows all the way to a certified doctor. Her eyes fell back to the reflection of her eyes. Just unbearable emptiness only love could fill. The grayness did not help hide that either, it magnified it. She wished she had dark brown or black pupils that concealed all the turmoil that was displayed unto her translucent gray eyes. She bemoaned her nature. She was one of those people that defined one's existence through the eyes of the ones that love them. She had this crazy shoe theory about love she had formulated in her teenage years that desperately made sense the longer the years dragged on.

According to her theory, we were all born in pairs, spiritual and physical pairs. Like shoes straight from production, we were deliberately lost during distribution, so we could toil our days in search of the other. Innately, we were all aware of the other's existence. And no pair would ever take that place successfully; they were just made to wear out together, custom-made by nature, a riddle, sort of a challenge posed by our maker! Even when time wounds and wears one heel, the other would definitely cease to exist; it's just logic like no human in his/her right mind would ever go out and buy just a shoe, no matter how fine the shoe was, maybe that was the mystery behind the obsession of women piling up pairs and pairs of dozens of shoes they never wear, she had figured. In fact, lost in the jungle hustle of men, she had always known the question! What the purpose of it all they call living? It did not take one to be so existentialist to process; it was just to find the other pair. The rest was just an illusion created by those who had long given up on the search to distract the rest from pursuing the quest; no need to label it nor sophisticate it. You just got to fit in like the right key slid and glided inside the keyhole. You sure could pick the key and break in but you would never feel at home! You miss that moment, that magical moment, when the key clicked, locked in, a natural embrace, and released it to slide one without a fight each and every time one came home. How many keys had she lodged into her heart, only she knew the disappointment after disappointment she had lived through with one potential key being rejected after the other! She sure had forced some in, yet like they say, things always seem strange for a stranger. And they all had been strangers; none had felt at home! Still drifting haplessly in the open seas of the man's world, it sure had been rough and tough to get to him, yet she had long accepted her sole quest in life, it was just love.

The likes of her were constantly on the lookout for that one and only who would make them happy for the rest of their lives. With that fairy tale deeply ingrained, they were vulnerable to easily falling madly in love over and over again. At times on first sight! Her mother had explained to her that they had a very soft heart that saw the good in almost everyone. Making them an easy pick for the wicked, twisted, manipulative men who exalted at the sight of submissive, obsessive women who adored them. Her mother trying to sound upbeat had said it was a rare gift for the world yet full of suffering that is only rewarded blissfully in the end. She hated her mother at times for jinxing her love life with a soft ever-loving gene pool. She hated her for mixing her up confused between a distinct white and black world. She looked at herself once again with resentment and contempt in tearful gray eyes. Her thick wide nose was a total contrast to her milky white face. She had always been conscious of her nose her entire life, more than any part of her anatomy. She loved her nose when she was around Africans, who had the exact broad fleshy nose that broadens from the bridge to expose the nostrils when they smiled like her. The stiff straight bony noses she encountered at school and the tiny celestial nostril of her mother made her feel so foreign or even a freak on her low days. She was just on no man's land! Apart from that flat African nose and bushy curled brown hair, nothing stood out from the rest of her white friends. Her thin lips, pointed chin and high cheekbones were very Nordic. The muscular limbs infuriated her growing up, just like her blonde and brunette friends who blamed their genes for not magazine-like feminine features. But turned out it was an asset among the black side of life, who adored her curves.

It all changed when Teme came into her life, and boy he owned her! He just felt at home. She knew it was him but still needed some work. Mostly on his part. Too many missing parts; she had to reassemble him back into the perfect match she always dreamed of. She just needed some patience, he would definitely come around. She looked back to look at him again. He was sound asleep, still she had that weird feeling he was watching her. Not stalking her but protecting her. Never had she felt so safe around anyone than with him.

There were also some days where she failed to notice any resemblance with an African and notice that she fit right in and out of a white crowd without raising a second glance that her beloved

Africans wearily faced every day. Growing up her mother had tried to discourage her from connecting with her 'darker' side of life. Both mental and epidermal! Having been heartbroken beyond repair for many lonely years, her mother hoped to spare her from the allure of that forbidden love. More Eurocentric and Nordic values were bombarded upon her since her toddler days. Her childish curiosity regarding race were quickly brushed aside by her mother's family. They had showered her with all the love reserved for their only surviving grandchild. They had tried so much to instill a mentally strong and confident Norwegian woman. Yet it had backfired and now she resented them, all of them, for confusing her. Her mother's suspicious stories on the reasons why she should keep away from Africans had always made her curious and tempted. Mother's words, "They seduce white women with their endless misery until the misery is reversed," did however ring back over and over when her heart eventually got broken.

It was both a relief and shame at the same time to witness that her people were the subject of abject unfair treatment by the general public. From the feeling of being ignored to being ridiculed and stared at for no apparent reason than a superiority complex was a daily occurrence on all levels. Witnessing her African friends shrink at the intensity of communal stares to quickly recover with a weary smile was the most excruciatingly gruesome experience she had ever felt. She had cried all night the first time she had witnessed it helplessly as an African mother of five succumbed to the power of contempt in a supermarket during a busy rush hour. As a result of being unfairly hurried and hassled impatiently by white customers behind her, the trembling short lady had forgotten the very pin code of her Visa card. Grunting and mocking from behind, Elise had heard someone commenting, referring to why they should not let monkeys get hold of a visa card: they lose the card or the pin code. He had cracked in Norwegian, to which most impatiently shuffling in the queue joined the banter.

The lady had fled the store, abandoning her children and groceries behind to a corner to cry her eyes out. Stiff in horror she had felt the pain and felt like a black African for the first time. Yet she could not stop an innocent mother from breaking down in front of her children, in public, watching the queue relieved to proceed with their purchases as if nothing happened in horror. After her own breakdown in the safe comfort of her mother's house, over her indecision of not reacting to that incident, she had recovered from the sob a different woman. A black woman who would defend her dignity and people, and she promised herself to never stand back and watch people abuse her or her people. Recalling all the harmless jokes she used to make about Africans, she resented her white friends or her mother for allowing that to happen. From that day on, she looked at them differently. Veiled, reserved resentment.

But it was never smooth and all-embracing on the other side either as she was to learn through bitter experiences. The open but camouflaged division, the diversity and adversity among her black people astounded her. The superstition, the religion, the norms that were foreign to her were exciting and adventurous in the beginning but soon confused her. The vibrancy enthralled her, the diversity engaged her as she gorged herself with the all-black experience, to the dismay of her mother. At some point, she had completely distanced herself from her white half, her rebellious early teenage years as her mother would recall, in immersing herself into what she missed out. Her ultimate aim was indeed to reconnect with her father and his ancestors. However, her naïvety had shielded her from the envy and malice that was out there. She was blind to the mistrust other Africans had in her presence nor was she aware of that reserved distance. But it would all come crushing down to teach her a brutal lesson in life. The lesson was to love herself for who she was and not where she had come from. Embracing her identity took time, perhaps will take her entire life for a full circle, but she was at peace. But she felt at home and fully belonged as any Norwegian would feel. She considered herself as the mix of two worlds, the best of two hemispheres meshed into one; *fuck purity and fuck other people's opinion anyway* had become her new motto.

As for Teme, his humble African self seduced her at times. Those dignified gestures he gesticulated so naturally. Ironically, he had those African traditional traits he clung on to so stubbornly that infuriated her, slip of the tongue or rather obsessed with his own struggle, he would offend her and the centuries old stride made by women across the globe. Maybe he was too macho of a man to feel challenged when women expressed themselves freely in every way, Elise had thought in the beginning as she was drawn to the bad boy stereotypes. Yet he was sweeter and more honest than many of the men/boys she knew. Unlike some of the bastards in town, those pathological lying players who sweet-talked their way into her pants. Teme was different; he was just too African, who will always remain one as well. Funny, she smiled remembering many a times he had said, "I am city boy, girl," how compromising and understandingly flexible he was to any culture; little did he know how maybe he was too proud of his identity. His calm, authoritative demeanor and how others respond to it was the mystery that intrigued her, that mysterious pride of a stateless misfit, she had figured. She was sure he would never be able to integrate and accept Norwegian way of life as his own as well. He was just drifting in a no man's land. Was it the black and white thing he was so obsessed about that was pulling him back from seeing life through the locals' perspective, which he in fact was part of? Having lived there more than three years certainly constituted as being part of a culture, she figured. It intrigued her when noticing his indifference to anything Norwegian; she had suspected maybe he resented her countrymen. Struggling to contain his boredom and agitation at the Norwegian talk shows and her music selection she adored to lay back and enjoy in his company had been a challenge she pretended to ignore. It was not religion, despite him proudly claiming to be a Christian never had he been to the local church his countrymen congregated to on the weekend evenings. He was well-versed in the Islamic culture and religion as well to her surprise, in the rare occasions he delved into his past. He devoured the pork as well as she did for all she cared. As she had learned through experience, there was a traditional city boy African and typical Western urban black man imitating African Americans. The latter were laidback, cocky if not over-confident souls masking the rage and uncertainty of life yet felt at home. The likes of Teme had that melancholic suspicious spirit underneath the humble tentative manners who always felt like a guest. They both had their appeals to her rebelling soul, who had the propensity to stray away from the Nordic herd ever since her childhood days. But he was on a league of his own in many ways. Matured in some way and so childish in others. Just a wounded child, just like she was; all he needed was time. He sure will take her some time but he will come through, she promised herself, done applying her make-up.

It was ironic though, for Teme she was just a white girl, maybe a mulatto European girl, never an African. She was sure he was in denial over her being half-black, how many a times he had referred to her as you people in a joke.

Why was he so obsessed with the black and white thing, she was not sure! He would look away at times in that stunned realization when she was defending some Norwegian value or maybe criticizing some African tradition that contradicted her own values and principles. The silence that followed short heated exchanges irritated her. Some things were better unsaid or never to be brought into discussion with him, probably confirming his suspicion that the white half of her was running her persona.

Why couldn't he let it go, though the world was cruelly designated in those imaginary arbitrary racial lines for those who paid too much attention to it, life was not always in colors. It ebbs one's energy from within, skepticism and negativity in the air makes one forget the true meaning of life, which was love. She grabbed her purse and her keys from the bed stand, leaned cautiously towards her man and planted a kiss on his cheeks. He twitched and mumbled something and went still. That brought a smile to her face.

Chapter 8

The stench of death suddenly overwhelmed his nostrils. He was perplexed. He looked around left and right, it sure was a packed bus. His heart was racing in his tongue. *What the fuck is going on?* But he was well aware of that smell. The pungency of rotting human flesh. The gut of a bloating human was the most horrible smell he would ever encounter. Open sewers, rotting animal carcasses he was used to despite the gagging effect; human stench was on a whole lot other level. It was dehumanizing reek that attacked the soul. The first sighting scared the living hell out of him. Gagging and throwing up, his head spinning, his knees shaking, he was not ready to witness death upfront, he recalled. The mind was crazy, soon the lifeless stinking thing would stop being associated as a once walking talking human just like him. It would just become a bother one would rather be rid of at once. That lingering rotting smell was so nauseating, at times lasting for hours. The more frequent one runs into a dead mangled oozing body though the senses got used to it. And when that was part of one's job; well, bodies take the shape of tools as in any profession, like bricks to a bricklayer and nothing else. Fucked up. *But that stench, who the fuck could be carrying the stench of a dead body?* Teme was confused. Was he losing his mind? He looked around the white and brown faces, some even noticed the tension and quickly looked away. They sure all looked alive but that stench, he shook his head in disbelief. First it was the nightmares with all symbols and images, then it was flashbacks and now this. The manifestation of his past in a sense of smell, his mind had gone way too far. Suddenly, he felt the urge to break out on a sprint and just run and run and never stop until he collapsed. He touched the stop sign to get off at the next stop. Now eyes were nervously watching him. He was sweating profusely. He got off and ran all the way to his workplace in Bislett.

****

Working in a kebab joint in the middle Bislett was a change of atmosphere he needed. Though paid under the table, it was more reliable income than a temp in storage or cleaning in schools and airports. Besides, the odd hours were unsuitable to his lifestyle. One off day at work or a couple of late show-ups and he was done. The racist fucks were intolerable to his kind. What kind of idiot works at night anyway? The tiny doner, sandwiched between an antique shop and a rival burger and kebab diner around the Bislett stadium, was attended by two employers in two arduous shifts. Running about all day, cleaning, slicing, and dicing the vegetables, taking multiple orders, deep frying and grilling while handling the cash, was a timely introduction into a hectic working environment for Teme. The Arab owner, who had migrated almost two decades ago, was a sneaky boss who tormented his employers, by paying surprise erratic visits like one of those relentless detectives on TV. Whining to keep them on their edge, to the delight of customers, Inspector as he called him was a nightmare to be around. There were times where he would even creep by the doner, in his ugly yellow Volvo wagon, staring with his accusative suspicious eyes, wagging his chubby tiny fingers through the window, uttering something incomprehensible in Arabic and drive off, raising the anxiety level of whoever was sitting at the counter. The sight of a yellow approaching vehicle reflected on the side mirrors of the doner would send frantic attempts to double the effort of whatever task he was handling. Out of paranoia, he often had kept a rag or two stashed in his apron he would instinctively pull out to clean an invisible smudge, just in case he was ambushed. The sight of another black face having a conversation near the counter was the other thing that would irk the edgy Middle Eastern man, reminding Teme from time to time to tell his friends not to bunch up at the doner in fear of scaring the white customers off. He used to laugh at the notion, after he had nodded enthusiastically to Inspector's face; black was just not a lucky charm for business! Back home he knew some who had canceled all arrangements for the day, after the sighting of a black cat so early in the morning! But that kebab joint was the type of job for him where he could negotiate when to work. That was the only benefit. Inspector would bitch about and go on a rant but would have somebody to chip in his place every time he called in sick. Likewise, he covered for the others.

With the thought of death on his mind he could not concentrate on the orders though on that day. The minced meat reminded him of disemboweled corpses. His senses were on a hyper drive that he could smell every sizzling, burning frying meat, every rotting vegetable, even the heat in the kitchen took him back to memory lane in the desert on such a chill mid-winter Tuesday. "Hey man, you overcooked my meat, what the fuck!" protested one young customer. Before Teme could defend and offend the fucker, Inspector cajoled the customer to make him a new one. Then went on venting his frustration on Teme in Arabic. *Puff*, he exhaled every now and then; he was suffocating. He excused himself twice to take a fresh breath and a cigarette to compose himself. But his mind had locked in the past, like a loop in a desert he was barely there in Oslo. A splitting headache was kicking in, his bowels had gone soft, it was only a matter of time before he threw up. What the fuck was happening, he cussed in three languages, drying his face with the inside of his greasy white apron. He watched a tram-full of people getting off and disperse, some hopped in and the tram disappeared. All strangers like in a fucking dream, was he even there?

A couple of customers walked in from the sports bar around the corner for a bite at the doner. They were a bit tipsy and one of them accidentally bumped his shoulder against Teme. It was harmless and the guy kept on narrating some joke to his two friends in an animated manner. Teme felt invisible. All the shit he had to deal with in life and now that, it tipped him off. He waited a couple of seconds but no apologies came his way nor did any of them acknowledge his presence. He cleared his throat, "Hey fucker, do I look like a fucking garbage bin to you?" He stared down each one of them one by one. "Hmmm, you bump into me and you apologize?" The tipsy guy much older and fitter than Teme was taken by surprise. He dropped his cigarette and raised both his hands to claim his innocence. Yet the goatee-bearded smirk enraged Teme even more. He pushed the guy back as sort of challenge and rolled up his sleeve. "What are you going to do about it?" Teme added, waiting for the reaction to go berserk. The stunned trio kept looking at each other. Teme pushed the man much harder the second time, nearly knocking him of his feet.

"You little shit. I will fucking smash your fucking monkey ass." And the guy jumped with both hands to pin Teme to the doner wall. The guy was much stronger than Teme anticipated. He tried to free himself, but the man had pinned both his hands to the wall and they were face to face. "You got a death wish, nigger?" snickered the white man at Teme. Strong alcohol breath overwhelmed him.

Teme was still unfazed though, "Maybe I do you, fucking white monkey." And spat on the white man's face. In a flurry of three seconds, the man punched Teme hard in his guts while Teme replied with a headbutt. His two friends, other customers, Inspector quickly broke in the fight to subdue the tension. The man with a bleeding nose threatened to kill Teme, who was giggling and taunting him.

He was restrained by his coworker, who pleaded with him, "Brov, you trying to get fired, starting a fight with regular customers, what the fuck is wrong with you?" Teme did not give a shit but that headbutt felt so good, even the headache on the buildup had disappeared. The hard punch to the gut was worth it, his mind was back in focus. The two calmer friends escorted their friend away from the kebab joint before the police arrived.

Inspector was visibly shaken by the incident, he was lost for words in Norwegian whenever he was upset. "I don't know what to do with you, Welahi? My good customers, hmmm? Ayyy, you are finished submit your apron and get away from my face. Collect your pay tomorrow, and I will never want to see you again."

Teme almost lost it again. It was not the job but the way he was dismissed. He wanted to knock the fucking Arab out, but Inspector quickly sneaked in behind the counter. With other customers and his coworker between them, he went on an Arabic rant to even bring a smile to Teme's face. His colleague persuaded him to leave, "Brother, if the police come, more trouble for you and all of us. You know, please leave."

Another job lost. The element of surprise as a cashier at a kebab joint unnerved him anyway. Taking orders from fucking rude customers tested his patience. But worse, one just never knew who walked through the door any given day. All grudge and new grudge abundant all over town; it was not cool to be a sitting duck with a silly fucking hat on and that stupid apron, he mumbled to himself getting on the tram headed to city Centre. He had no validated ticket. Any ticket control would face his wrath, he reminded himself. It was just the wrong day to fuck with him. Just too much in his head, but he could not even figure which was which. Just jammed. *Fucking sucks,* he sighed to himself. Fuck it now all he needed was some ganja to mellow him down and no one to talk to. Right timing, the crew called him. His presence was required for a mission. He was all game.

****

Chapter 9

As soon as he arrived at the Tøyen square, behind one of the children's parks the crew was all hyped up. High as a kite but with purpose about them. It lifted and matched his mood. He got the breakdown. A shakedown of a rival group was about to go down. Teme did not even ask who, where, or when? He was in and they loved it. It was like a movie. They were fearless and focused. Of course, they were high but it was more than that. "We will fuck these boys good," snickered the older and much experienced Dave, who often coordinated the shakeups. The twins both had a baklava with a skull on it tied around their necks. Toure, indifferent as usual, rolled a bandage tight around his knuckles ready for a fight. Martin was all geared up with his ski outfits with that dead fish eyes dying for some action. Five other new faces were all geared up with knives, a baseball bat, and one even with a kendo he flipped for demonstration.

"About time, man," one of the twins fired back. They all nodded.

"Killa, we need you to strike first like last time. You good?" Dave requested, hoping for an emphatic yes.

"Yeah, all set man," confirmed Teme, dying for some action.

"You need a bandana or scarf to cover your face, you know the cameras and all," Smokie said, reaching into his pocket for a purple bandana.

Teme took the bandana, but instead wrapped it around his right knuckle. "No, let them see me, I don't give a fuck!"

"We got word they are getting off in a couple of minutes at Tøyen for a meet up. We got to strike them before they leave the station."

All set. Silence fell, just boots trampling with intent.

They all grinned at Teme in satisfaction. Even the people, civilians around them, sensed their vibe and fire and backed off, parting like the fucking red sea when they marched down the side street bordering the botanical garden en route to the underground metro station, where they will ambush their rivals. A lot at stake; their reputation in the streets was on the line. Whoop the Storo boys and they would claim supremacy, and the fame shall spread like wild fire in the underworld. Get their ass beat up and they faced extinction. It was their chance to mark their distinction. Teme had not spent time with his boys a lot after he moved out and started working. Nor was he hustling with the boys, but whenever a muscle was needed, he was just a call away. There was a buzz about what was about to go down. The word was out in the streets, a finale! The face off! They had a bad week, the newspaper documentary about the dangerous teenage gangs in the city had even failed to mention them on their shame list. To add insult to injury, a bunch of nobodies were on the list. Even some of the crew they had crushed for breakfast. That really hurt, a full documentary was conducted, and they failed to make the cut, despite all the noise they constantly created. It was a sham, that was why he never trusted the media. Maybe it was time to remind them of their presence. Fuck every one of them on the list, one by one, then maybe then shall they be recognized. Even the fucking popo knew them by their names. It was the respect and the fear factor that thrilled Teme, never the drug and the hustle anyway. He was just in the game to enforce his presence.

Soon it went down military style. They covered all the exits of Tøyen station and pounced on the Storo boys. No civilian was hurt, and they made their mark and disappeared when the blue blaring police cars closed on them. He made a run for it and jumped on a bus. Switched to a tram and then the Metro to head to Røa on the west side to see his girl. Three minutes of madness was soon behind him, but boy was it a therapy. He kept checking his mobile for the twitter feed of the local police. *Coordinated assault, possible gang rivalry. 1 seriously injured. 3 lightly injured. 3 arrests* read the twitter feed. Job well done for three minutes stint, Teme snickered on his own like a crazy drunk old man before he got off at his stop.

****

69

Chapter 10

Guzzling his third beer with Elise resting on his chest, Teme looked down and caressed her hair. Her eyes were fixated on a documentary revealing the 'appalling' condition of the prisoners held at Guantanamo Bay. She disliked watching movies. According to her, "What was the point in wasting two hours of my life, watching a movie I can predict the end right from the start?" and, "It is not healthy to run away from reality into fantasy world all the time. I like facing reality," she had emphatically announced during their first days.

Hmmm, lucky what do you know about reality except for what you see on TV? had been a reply that echoed in his head, weighing and scaling if she could handle had he handed over his version of reality that he was subjected to in his life. Guantanamo was nothing but a 4-star hotel compared to the prisons he had been back at home continent, but he did not want to bring that up! But what run him ragged in his mind at the moment was not the prisons he had been before but the one he was heading to, head on collision to the brick wall of whichever prison was eminent with the way things were going. Had Dave and Toure not pulled him off one of their targets, he was sure he could have killed him. Smashing the fucker's head on the cement as they said, but he recalled none of it. He had blacked out the moment he launched at the first guy in sight. He was losing his head. He bent over and kissed Elise's forehead, the only thing that was going right in his life was her. His only link to sanity. She knew he had been in a fight but did not ask. But he read her concern for him in her eyes. She was concerned for his safety, not hers.

Chapter 11

The next day Teme showed up at his shrink's office on time. She had noted on the journal that he had begun to take initiative in making appointments and showing up on time. It was a sign of progress. Phase: denial stage breached; understanding the need for help reached. "Can I ask you something?" Hesitantly, Teme looking straight at his psychologist's eyes, "You know like. Stuff happens in life in the past. But then you were not feeling anything. You know when bad things happen. Then after years you start to see things that happened clearly than you can remember. As if someone put it in your memory, you know. Then it was all cloudy."

"Are we talking about your pre-teen childhood experience? Or in the later stage of your teens?"

"14–15."

"Okay."

She gathered he was referring to his Libya excursion. She chose her words carefully as through a string of other teenagers with similar experiences had supplied her enough grotesque pictures to deprive her of sleep for the rest of her days. Scrapping those images, she begun, "You know the mind does not fully develop until you are in your mid-twenties. So think of it how immature and not ready the mind is to make life-altering decisions at when you were 15. And with all you have witnessed in that short span of time, it would be too much for your mind to process it all at the same time. So as you mature, and still developing as you are at this stage right now, your mind tries to make sense of your experience."

"But why does one not fear then, you know? It…ahmm you know when all the bad things going around you. It's like, I don't know." Teme was frustrated at not having the words come out right as he had contemplated them earlier. He huffed, rub his forehead and started again, "You know, why do you believe people who you know are evil people and then they make you do stuff you don't want to do. Then you feel nothing, even though you know it is

71

wrong. It is not like you want to do it, but you keep on doing it and you feel nothing."

She took a longer and deeper look at him. Her heart ached, but she reminded herself to remain objective.

"At that age your mind is so impressionable, meaning you are like a blank page. Like this," she pointed to her untouched page. "When you are lost and at your darkest moment at such a young age, you are vulnerable to believing anything and anyone that tells you things that may sound cool or different. With your young mind disturbed and confused, their wrong guidance feels like support. And their word becomes your bible that shapes or wrecks your life, sadly. By the time you realize the consequences of your actions, it is too late. That is how the mind, our mind works, sadly. And life as we know it for all of us. But that era of your life is full of trial and errors."

"So you are saying even if I have done some bad stuff, it is not my fault so I should try to forget it?"

She wanted to say yes, but her years of education and reason differed. Sadly, to his disappointment, and she felt his spirit deflate at once. She quickly regrouped.

"But that does not mean one is totally free of guilt. We all have our regrets. We all do things we would not do naturally. Thinking oneself as a victim is deceiving oneself, that is even worse. Accountability is very essential. Most importantly to ourselves. Punishing the self is not the solution either. Recognition and admission of one's guilt is a way to start. Then comes redemption, to make what happened not to be a scar in your life but a signal marker, a light at the end of the tunnel for those in their darkest hours. Reaching out to others who can relate to your experience could vindicate you. You have your entire life to make up for it if you wish. Some people pay severe consequences for their actions, you know. You know in America some children as young as 13 who commit serious offenses are tried as adults and sent to prison for life at times. So think of it, you are free and healthy. You have your whole life ahead of you. Go out have fun, set a goal in life and achieve it. What does not kill makes you stronger. Feel blessed and grateful for surviving. Be a role model and never another victim, okay?"

Easy for you to say, bitch! he nearly said but bit his tongue. *What the fuck she knows about life anyway? Sitting behind her desk, with a fucking diploma from a fancy university suddenly makes her an expert in having a fucking opinion. Fucking bitch!* he promised himself to never ever step inside her office again. He smiled and thanked her for her time and walked out.

****

So furious that he barely noticed the black ice he had avoided stepping on his way in. He was flat on his back. Writhing in pain, he cussed the living hell out of everything. An elderly woman inquired to his wellbeing. He shrugged her off and scrambled to his feet. He was still wearing his summer shoes. The slippery sidewalk was torture these days. And that bitch of a shrink should have at least salted the entrance to her office building. And this fucking winter he was getting tired off. A gusty wind stabbed his side. He zipped his bubble jacket all the way up and hurried cautiously to the nearest bus station, he needed a drink. A police van with blue lights blaring swooped by, making him jumpy.

****

Bars around Grønland never inquired for his ID whenever he bought a drink with a stern look anyway. Then he will hook up with his boys and get down anywhere. The last thing he wanted to do was think. Some loud music and something to distract the mind.

****

Guzzling cheap beer under the awning at Star Gate along with laidback much older blue collar heroes after work and whole bunch of unemployed drunks, he felt right in. Gazing at the traffic of people and cars racing about him, Teme tried to make sense out of what the shrink had said. It was all cryptic, sometimes she does it to just fuck with him. Stuff she said that lingered all day and night in his mind. What did she mean about being a role model? To whom? He was barely trying to make sense out of what he was going through, and she was already talking about being a proper idol to others. *What the fuck! It did not make sense.*

A police van pulled up across the street right under the bridge, facing the metro entrance. Two giant police officers stepped out with intent. They both crossed the street eyes, focused on the bar he was sat at. He kept his composure when his eyes met one of the cops who happened to scan the bar attendees. He kept his stare. The two cops instead went to the adjacent bar, to his relief. He sensed the others sitting around him sigh with relief as well. He finished his beer and stepped inside for some more. The tipsy owner was a bit suspicious to hand him his beer but never complained again once he left him a tip. He struck a conversation with drinking buddies, much older than him, getting carried away with his imagination, he entertained them with some spicy suspense-filled stories of his travels. Of course, a fictitious version of events, war stories beyond his years that bamboozled the Norwegians. It was cool to talk to strangers so long one never gets to meet them again, he figured. The tension when new or familiar strangers gather rings alarm bells.

His girl though would rather he spend every waking moment with her, inside, and around her. The inquisition though puts him off. Would not mind opening up but then got to man up. Like one of the big boss in his crew told him '*Got to keep your shit and drink always in, regardless of how hard your struggle. No spills and no thrills, just keep it sealed.*' Indeed! He would have loved to talk to his shrink everyday if he could, even he had contemplated giving her a call in the middle of the night some days, *but she is not to be trusted. She is a paid eyes and ears of the government.* The patient-doctor confidentiality was just a trap to lure the soft ones into spilling beans.

****

Chapter 12

After hours of beers and heavy contemplation, he decided to visit the priest he had met a while back. He took bus 37 and headed to the temple in Helsfyr, where the Evangelical group often held prayers. His body subconsciously tensed when he neared the holy place among the apartment complex facing the highway. With hands tucked inside his jacket pocket, he looked up with utter shame, distraught as if the very church had a long sharp lash to smash his face. He quickly looked away, reminding himself it was just another old building.

After a couple of feet, the question still lingered in his mind. Of all the sins, delinquencies, and atrocities he had committed in his young life, would turning his back against his very faith count as the most irredeemable crime? They call it what apostasy or something, he had read on the internet, but when one's life is on the line, staring at the barrel of a Kalashnikov, with the fume of gun smoke engulfing his nostrils, cold eyes with an itchy trigger finger staring down his, was his religion worth dying for? He just wanted to live, he was young with many unfulfilled dreams; *with life on the line faith takes a back seat. Ambition takes the driving seat, steps on the gas do whatever is necessary, lie if one must until one secures safety.* It was just survival, he was no part of the crusaders or the jihadists as they were portrayed on TV or the movies he watched. He was just a kid, just a kid.

The almost rundown former office block had been turned into the local council community outreach programs, with the church being one of them. The three-room wide prayer hall was empty, with few hardcore ones huddled in groups listening to an animated preacher recanting the verses in hyperbole in one corner. Teme fidgeted around the entrance with both his hands jammed in his jacket, conscious of the beer on his breath, so out of place. He was about to turn on his heels and run but a voice from behind froze his steps. "My son, welcome!" said the familiar deep voice of the renowned priest. Teme avoided the older man's eye and greeted him. Without a word the priest ushered him towards his office for a private counseling.

Teme relayed to the patient priest the recurrent dream that had deprived him of his sleep. The priest gave him an elaborate picture of dream interpretation without delving into the details of his dream, to his great relief. Besides, the priest himself had made the same journey across the desert and the ocean.

"Let me ask you this, would God forgive you for everything you have done?" Teme cut to the chase at last.

"Yes, my son, our God is a forgiving god. Our Lord is a vengeful god as well. But our God always preserves and forgives those who humbly and without question submit to him."

"Okay." He had no idea on how to frame his question, his dilemma, to the priest without compromising himself. But he was besieged with doubt and fear.

"Is it okay, my son, do you have any troubling thoughts you would like to share? Do you want me to pray for you? Or we could pray together?" The preacher pulled his seat closer and extended his long arms to pat Teme as a gesture of support.

Teme subconsciously stiffened and pulled away from the stranger's arm on his shoulder. He was not convinced if the second-hand prayers really worked. Nor halfhearted personal prayers for that matter. But he decided to give it a shot but, "Would our Lord forgive you if you deny him, not meaning to but forced to, you know. But deep inside you still believe in him. Like you lie in a situation that you do not believe in him or like if you accept another religion not by choice for some time, just a hypothetical question." Teme blurted out the thought that had been circulating in his mind all day.

The priest was perplexed but tried to hide it by adding, "If you repent with a full heart and dedicate yourself to being a good Christian for the rest of your life, there is always a way to the Lord's heart. Do you know the story of the tax collector and the righteous man in the church Jesus told his followers, my son?"

Teme was hesitant and ashamed at not knowing the story. He had read the bible a few times, attended church ceremonies, but it was a sort of duty that he tagged along with his granny. He was not well aware of the significance of his faith back then. "No not sure, Aba."

"Well, one day a tax collector and loan shark, who took advantage of poor people, walked inside a church with shame and utter remorse. He could not get himself to look up and face his God;

instead, with teary eyes he prayed to God to forgive him for all the sins he had committed and to please grant him the will and strength to become a better man as he was merely a weak and pathetic mortal soul. Next to him stood a righteous man, who looked down at the loan shark with contempt. After listening to the emotional pleading of the humbled sinner by his side, the righteous man confidently looked up to pray to his God in gratitude for not turning him into a despicable, irredeemable soul kneeling next to him. I will ask you the same thing Jesus asked his disciples, my son, who do you think God will be warmer and closer to?"

Teme was astounded by the tale, he might have heard it before but never had a verse or a story from the bible hit him that hard before. It was relevant indeed to his experience, he thought, but he was afraid to answer the priest.

"My son, only God shall judge, those who dismiss and judge others are sinners the Lord is reluctant to. Humble souls who acknowledge their sins and their weakness and pray for strength to become a better servant are our Lord most welcome to. Besides, you have to be grateful that you have been accepted into the Norwegian community. You have a bright future. Think of the thousands that have died along the treacherous route in the desert and those that sunk in the ocean. Even think of those that made it all the way here only to have their asylum case rejected by the government. They languish in the refugee camps with futures unknown. But you have been given a break. A major break at that. You are young, you can get the best education and the best paying job if you put your mind to it. It is not what you have done that defines you, it is what you have learned from every experience that counts. With God's will and your faith, you must stay strong and put your past behind."

They both smiled, and his spirit was recharged with positivity at once.

No one was good nor evil. He should stop beating himself up. Going to hell sure won't be worse than what he had gone through. Even if he did, he probably earned it. It was only on these stupid movies that people were either on the good or evil side. In real life situation dictated what one does with no regard. Those evil people that had been carved on the back of his memory like graveyard markings fail to evoke any emotion of late. Circumstances might have hardened them. Maybe all those people who were indifferent to his distress and cries of anguish had switched off as they could not afford to empathize. Just like he had done later on, no wonder he barely remembered all the evil things he had done to other people, just following orders, but the cries and screams he was deaf and blind to. He was completely immune, almost lie in a trance-like state, transported to another peaceful place while his body obliged in doing harm to others in order to get by. *Survival rules change people, at least for a while that is.*

****

Getting back to the metro station, he decided to cut the night short and head to his girl's place. He texted her to ask whether she was at home. She replied at once, like she always did, to let himself in, she would come later. He was glad he met the priest, he made more sense than the shrink. She was all talking science, which did not apply to him. Maybe religion was what he needed to calm the spiritual waves disrupting his days and running havoc at night, he figured. Looking left and right at the platform, he waited for the line 3. It was dangerous stepping inside an underground station on his own these days, better take the bus, he reminded himself, as he might run into an ambush. Retaliation was and always part of the game he had coming.

****

Chapter 13

A few days later, Elise woke him up from deep sleep.

"You were talking in your sleep, babe…"

"What? What was I saying?" He jumped quickly.

Noting his nervousness, Elise contemplated playing with him a bit but she did not want to risk it. "It was just gibberish. I think in Arabic you were flailing your hands as if to push someone off you or something. What was that all about?"

"Hmmm. Nothing, babe. Hmmm," Teme looked away, feeling his damp forehead. The nightmares were back. He should definitely avoid spending the nights at Elise's, he reckoned. He might say something to freak her out.

"Are we ever going to talk about this?" Elise requested with a genuine concern in her tone while wrapping her hands around his bare chest.

Her warmth was so comforting, it soothed Teme and he almost let it slip out and screamed, "God, I love you and I love being with you. You are the only comfort, safe zone in my life right now," but he held back. No emotional attachment. Instead, he held her tight as they both drifted into the night.

****

Moments later, he was churning his mind to replay if any of the scenes earlier was indeed part of that same recurrent vivid episode. If indeed they were, there sure must be a message behind it, like the priest had mentioned. But his memory would not cooperate in recollecting the scenes from his recent nightmare. It was almost like it was a whole other entity in control of his dreams, nightmares and black-outs. His conversations with the therapist and the priest flashed in his mind, one after the other in sort of inspirational boost to remember. Indeed, the therapist was right, the mind was a weird thing. But the priest was perhaps more elaborate in his approach. His reluctance in approaching the priest and that lingering fear of being bewitched disappeared the moment the priest warmly accepted him upon arrival, without firing away multi-layered questions.

The traditional priest renowned for unraveling the mystery of dreams had laid out in general terms the mystery of dreams. Recollection of a past event in a dream, if recurrent, was a message or a warning one should consider seriously. It is a sign of unfinished business or unlearned lesson. *It is the spirit of ancestors warning you in your dreams of an unfinished mission*. The other type of dreams was symbolic vision of events yet to happen. The shaggy bearded older man had inquired thoroughly without asking for details if there were any significant symbols that stood out in his dreams. He had said to him to note any mystical symbols. Was there fire? Water or smoke? None of it was present in his dreams. Was there any act of breaking, sinking, shinning, rusting, swelling, or burning? Yet the problem with his dreams was mired with the vivid images of the past and a mirage of events and faces all happening at the same time at times. It was confusing to put a time frame on it or to point out which had indeed occurred in real life. Some of it he had no recollection of, yet in his dreams it was vividly recounted, and he was sure it happened. Like something in the back of his mind was recording it while he was just surviving, oblivious to the chaos. His mind was numb for some time as if he was somebody else, but fuck the mind had seen everything. But the symbols he should start paying attention to, though still reluctant that drowning image of his older-looking self was the most disturbing.

Of all the gore and violence that flashed in his imagination, be it awake or sleep, it was his own face in different phases and forms that freaked him out the most. Repeatedly, he had seen himself drift in a misty, muddy water, with no one on sight but the nagging feeling somebody was out there watching and waiting, as he tired out and drowned in a slow protracted motion. In real life he could swim. Nor had he ever been stranded in a misty, muddy water. The Mediterranean tour was he along hundreds of souls, drifting, almost sinking. Alarmingly, once the boat flipped, the head count had halved in seconds. It was that fast, *once you go down, you can't swim, you stay down*. There were no screams, that look though right before the bobbing sinking head disappeared in the abyss of the saline mass will remain for the rest of his life. The moment of realization, the doom, the last flicker of light from the candle of a departing soul was what he read on his older, much older self in that misty river. What the fuck was the symbol of the mist and the sinking and the older self? He should get back to the priest. He was not a prying person like that therapist as well. Teme readjusted the pillow behind his head while trying not to stir the peacefully asleep Elise off his chest. Her welcoming warmth he so much needed to keep undisturbed. She sighed over his movement but made no protest as he moved her head more central, her temple aligned to his heavy heart. His right arm arched on the pillow, supporting his head, he drifted back to his drumming thoughts. Oh, where was he? After a moment of frustration over yet another lapse, he recalled the subject and indeed he was thinking about his shrink. All that talk about the consciousness, sub-consciousness what the fuck ever she was talking about was all confusing psychology jargon. Something she said about the recurrent dream and the hypnosis and the trauma episode in life running in loops in the memory bank until addressed made some sense. He will try to read about it from one of the books in the library or fucking google it. The problem was he had to fill in the entire story, spill every detail for her to do her job. She just needed to get to the bottom of the story. Why couldn't she just break it down in a common language, the psychology as she knew it; he just did not understand her. Was it curiosity or was she prying to fish for the government, who knew? "She was just too fishy," he whispered again to himself, "Just too fishy." he shook his head once again, aware his girl was sound asleep on his chest. He has to be careful in reading his thoughts aloud as well. *Too many ears and eyes around, man.*

****

She had referred many books beyond conventional means more to the esoteric genre rather than standard Freudian school of thought that she relied on in her psychoanalysis. What she was dealing with was beyond scientific, she needed to back it up as a counter with a mystical and more appealing manner in her next session after the last fiasco. That disconnect between her and her patients was at times due to reliance on more scientific methods, she had noted. Patients lose patience over that indifference of scientific approach and reproach over their dilemmas. With superstition rife, especially with people from a more religious background, psychology indeed became a gray area testing their faith. At times even insulting or blasphemous to their perception of the world as they knew it. Threading that line of objectivity to earn the trust of the patient into opening up had always been a learning process. One patient was always different from the next. But some always stood out, as a sort of challenge to her profession and often times to themselves. Uncrackable walls surrounding a dormant dome of volcano inside. Waiting and brooding, unseen to the rest of the world. Mistrusting and condescending to a learned expert in the field for the presumed lack of field experiences over the trauma they simplified and defined while sitting behind a desk was communicated in a spark or a look down. As of young patients with traumatic past and a vague grasp of their psyche and the gravity of the burden they carry day in night out, esoteric methods were more appealing. But then it was a thin ice to trod in order to accommodate the patient with a common ground of human contact while still maintaining the patient-doctor relationship and therapy. Otherwise, one undermined science inadvertently if she acknowledged some version or all of their superstition.

Teme, no names, patient number 4587 had sought after alternative means of guidance she had gathered. Unconventional spiritual guidance to be precise, even though he had not admitted it, as vague as he always was. The emphasis on symbols was evident. It was a good sign that he was reaching out, meaning recognition of his predicament. It was progress that he started to pay attention to detail. Categorizing his dreams into vivid recollection of the past and vague visions of the probable future was peculiar but interesting. His dismissal over her prying into the faded cloudy phase of his life, yet clearly running in a loop in his sub-consciousness, was now the hurdle. Despite a more or less similar circumstance with patient number 4261, who had opened up at will, 4587 has turned out to be very complicated. The dreams being the manifestation of the lingering spirits of the ancestors' hidden message was a bit farfetched in her profession. If he was willing to accept ancestors having access to one's mind that all events in the past in one's line of family would be somehow connected, thus she would be forced to make all the major events ever since one's childhood as well relevant to his present psyche. Thus, delving to Jungian school of thought was more appropriate to navigate that common ground. That underground dark basement of unconsciousness, where the wisdom of our forefathers was retained and passed on innately, maybe the answer as Karl Jung had referred. That had been a test of her scientific objectivity as well. Dreams were riddle at times, poetry or prose some other times. In few and far cases, the language in dreams are universal in their interpretation. To make matters worse, not all the details are divulged by the patients. Subconsciously censored, details too vague or cryptic to comprehend or essential chunk intentionally left out on self-preservation mode, the reasons are plenty. The censorship applied in dreams are never universal, she concluded to herself. At times, cultural norms and taboo determine what the consciousness labels as perverse or inappropriate for the notion to feature any air time in our imagination. But then war-time rules of engagement and civilian law and order life experiences can never be set on the same bar. But most importantly, the mental age of the individual has to always be accounted for.

Growing up in a very superstitious environment, reading and contemplating mystical research material brought up all the suppressed fears, doubts, and coincidences in her life she thought she had gone past once dedicating herself to the field of psychology. But indeed, she was like she had always feared, that unfinished haunted house with ghosts hibernating in the dark basement sealed beneath. But every time she travelled abroad in contact with local people distant from Western ways, she was stunned to find that common answer to the absurd and unseen mysteries of life almost everywhere. The oneness that binds humanity was evident and confirmed again and again. Unscientific unadulterated perception told in many different symbolic ways and means yet arrive at the same conclusion. The unanimous belief and worship of the silent force of nature at work, not religion but natural. Of course, she never diluted nor applied her hunch or finding in her studies and research papers back at work or in seminars; she was purely scientific. But at times she wondered if she had wasted her years studying the human psychology on paper rather than learn from people and culture, mystery and folklore and personal experiences perhaps would have broadened her psychological horizons much better in addition to the studies. The misogyny in the ilks of Freud who assumed females as a mere retarded extension of the established male figure used to infuriate her while cramming for exams. That was why she knew it was her calling. Enriching therapy and counseling from a non-Western feminine's perspective. '*Time will tell,*' she told herself, getting ready for bed, realizing how late it had been. Her poor husband already snoring in bed while she sifted through pages of the pile of books on her bed. Regardless, she was now ready for patient 4587. In fact, she was looking forward to it. Like an onion she would peel his wounded psyche a layer at a time. Even if it took forever, she would get to the bottom of it and perhaps release the ghosts in her basement at last as well.

Chapter 14

A couple of weeks later, they were on the third floor of Oslo city mall, the entire crew checking out girls and new outfits for the coming season. Spring around the corner, the mall guards were keeping a close eye on them as a recent flurry of shoplifting incidents caught the police and media's attention. Of course, the rowdy unaccompanied teenage migrants were to blame, but it was the white local boys and girls who snuck in and out of the stores undetected with the loots. "You check out the blazer hanging by the door, want it bad," remarked Smokie, pointing to a spring collection by Urban clothing store behind him.

"Get Sandra to get it for you. She is good at it," replied one of the twins.

"Oh, ya Sandra. Our Sandra?"

"Yeah, that chic can take off with half the clothes in the store and no one would notice."

"Ahhah! Break it down for me, how?"

"You keep them distracted, changing clothes and acting all suspicious while she does her thing; of course, we were born suspects, it is easy."

Soon they were bored as they made their way down the escalator. On their way down they were face to face with another crew they had beef with on a basketball court in Tøyen. Couple of exchanges, gang signs, and threats were reciprocated equally. Guards intervened and they were escorted out of the mall with a threat of a ban. They were kept apart but everybody was watching the scene, mad attention they were getting. Especially the girls were awed, filming the encounter. They felt like stars as they made their way to the Gunerius Mall across the street, disregarding the red-light to the ire of the honking cars. They were mall and traffic stoppers and nobody could fuck with them. All hyped up, they were up for anything.

The other crew had caught up with them as they neared the Grønland metro station by the south end. Perfect location to set a mark. No whistles, no referees, they were all ready; despite being outnumbered they were up for it. Cycle locker chains were swung. Punches and kicks exchanged. Some knocked to the floor. Onlookers glued to the spot. Blood splattered on the ground. Painful moans and grunts. It took only two minutes, but they were swarmed by ululating police vans from three directions. The mark was set. The crew had made a statement and they split. One giant fit cop caught up with Teme while cutting in the side streets towards Tøyen mosque. He dashed inside a grocery store. Amid hundreds of immigrants protesting and throwing insults his way, the unfazed cop cuffed and hauled Teme towards the police van that pulled up at once. Resisting arrest, he drew more attention to the growing crowd that the backup police had to restrain. "Leave him alone, you fucking pig!" screamed one. The crowd was protesting for his release since he was injured, he had a cut above his right eye. "Look what they did to him, these fucking racists!" Another one added, "I saw him punching him, fucking cops! He is just a kid let him go!" Hoping somebody filmed that incident, Teme relished the attention, maintaining a brave face. The bike chain must have connected right before he ducked. But he had made up for it. The fucker was stumped for good. He was satisfied with the effort today. Very satisfied, it was worth getting busted for.

The police escorted him to the emergency to get his injury treated before they escorted him to the Grønland station for interrogation. It was the first time he was escorted hands cuffed to the archaic movie-like Grønland prison. He was booked and thrown inside a cell until he would be called in for questioning.

****

Chapter 15

Sitting on the mattress, facing the steel door, the gliding and slamming of heavy steel doors, the shuffling of police boots on the yellow tiles was the only sound coming through. Pacing around his cell, Teme was surprised how lightly he was seeing the turn of events. His being arrested meant nothing to him, but deep inside he had this feeling something worse was in store for him. All the noise was the silence before the real storm. It was all exhausting existence, he lamented, collapsing on the mattress. Life was just happening too fast. Just a couple of years he was just a child who knew nothing about the world except his grandmother and her garden. His childhood memory had become a blur. Born on a border town on an isolated patch of land on a hill, it was simple living. It was just him and his grandmother for most of his childhood. Helping his grandmother, on the tiny plot of land they planted vegetables, potatoes, tomatoes, and spinach. He used to run around herding the two dozen goats and sheep they owned. They struggled at times, but his grandmother made sure he was fed every day. School, to which he walked half an hour back and forth across a hill, was nothing spectacular but he made friends. The school was often disrupted by the eminent bloody conflict that erupted whichever side of the border. Tension was rampant on the radio, the school, and the market near the school, but he was too young to comprehend the heat. His isolated grandmother was a neutral that never brought politics or tribal talk into their conversation, all her talk was God. Even when war broke out, they were barely touched. Bombs and bullets rained around them, but his grandmother's prayers kept them intact. Despite rudimentary education level, his granny home schooled him in fables, folklore, and the bible whenever the school eloped into enforced hiatus. But once he become a teenager and his grandmother started ailing, he realized he had to get out. Becoming a man was a threat in that part of the world as one risked being conscripted into the army. He escaped, though as luck would have it, it was from one tense war zone to one full blown-out intercontinental battlefield and he was just a kid. Not anymore though; staring at the high white cream concrete ceiling, Teme soon dozed off. A much-needed nap in yet another detention center.

The clanking of the steel door startled him from his sleep. The same metal on metal sound that brought a chill into his young mind back in Libya. After reorienting to his surroundings, he breathed easy; he was safe in Norway. A clean cell all on his own, he reassured himself. And they always had to disrupt the nice dreams, it was just not fair. Teme peeled off the thick black wool blanket and stretched his hands from the mattress, startling a spider to scurry past his outstretched hands and race towards her intricately constructed cobwebs at the end corner. He was fascinated by spiders ever since he was a kid. Their agility to hang on a roof inverted, watching the entire world upside down, probably thinking how crazy the rest of the world was. The two pedipalps and eight legs pedaling so dexterously across any terrain, Teme wondered if spiders ever tripped on one of their legs, clumsy as he was, he imagined how he would have been with eight limbs! The world was crazy, he was thinking, drifting into the world of the spider that he observed niftily made her way to her own web as if walking on sand, before a female officer burst into his cell to bring him back to reality.

It was his time as he was escorted to the interrogating room. Teme was defiant all along. He was trying to rerun all the episode in his head in slow motion, to recall all the heroic episode he shall recount to his crew and their admirers once he gets out, perhaps with a fine. Two cops sat on the other end, waiting for a moment with him. He felt very important.

"Sit down." One of the cops with a sarcastic grin on his face began the talking.

"Why?" Teme pulled on a brave front

"Let's not do this now. You are not under arrest. And you have none to impress, so let's have a talk man to man. Can we do that? "The other cop was still silent, just studying him.

Silence.

"Okay, I take it as a yes. You want coffee?"

Shake of the head.

"You want warm milk?"

A disgusted, offended puff erupts from Teme's lips. "How about you get me some drink? No ice, please."

"Ha-ha, no ice, please. You are very funny," snickered the good old cop studying Teme.

"How is school going anyway?" the younger one inquired.

"I'm done with school," sniffled Teme, avoiding eye contact, realizing at once these were the same two cops who he had been running into a couple of times. They knew him.

"Yep, big boy now. To cool for school; how do you manage to make a living then?" The younger cop continued, his giant hands resting on the table like two fucking eagle wings ready to engulf Teme.

"What is this parental guidance or an investigation?" The fronting continued but his heart was pacing double the usual rate, but they had said there were no charges against him.

"Easy, this is no investigation," replied the younger cop, then continued, "You are lucky no one else was arrested nor anyone filing charges against you. In fact, you were the only victim. The only one who was bloodied. We could charge you with disturbance of peace and violent gang-related act, but since you are banged up we think you learned your lesson. So relax, kid, we are just making conversation with a troubled kid. Are you not comfortable talking to the police?" The giant young cop was sure enjoying his moment to impress the older cop, who kept a stern glare on Teme. Uncomfortable penetrating look that was.

Another sniffle and the cockiness was back. "I have seen worse, police, prison, you name it. I'm not afraid of anything anymore."

"I am sure you have." The shaggy bearded Viking-looking old cop studied his young face, imagining the hard times he had been through before proceeding with his conversation. Pivoting right on to the case with that look of this kid meant business. Critical sense of innocence had along been knocked out of this one, he had reached his analysis. Realism might sink in better, he figured. In a grave tone, the cop muttered, "Listen, kid, I have been keeping an eye on you over the past weeks. I don't like what I am seeing, you hear?"

Silence and a deadly stare was on the other side.

Muffling a snicker, the cop continued, "You might be the man right now, but where do you think you will end up in a couple of years, hmmm?"

Silence, the resolve in the kid's eye was still there. "Stubbornness will lead you to your demise!" The cop was relentless, "The gang you are hanging out with. Do you know what they do?"

Silence.

"Do you realize you are into serious trouble?"

Another silent blank stare was the response.

"Maybe it was just fun to fight and show friends how tough you are. But this is not a school fight. This is gang on gang related violence. Do you know how serious of a situation you are in?"

Indifferent blinking was the response again.

"Listen, kid, just a reality check. The people you call friends are working for hardcore criminals wanted for serious crime all over Europe. The fights you pick up in the streets is for them, over territory, you understand! The big boys that you never meet are somewhere in Spain or Brazil in a fancy hotel living the life of a rockstar out of the sweat and blood of street hustlers like you and your friends. The soldiers is that what you call yourselves, fight each other over territories, you hunt each other, one gang with the other like natural-born enemies. But the bosses are friends. So long there is competition, they get more money. The young ones like you when you join fresh, you have something to prove and show off like you do, and you think you are invincible. You think everybody out there is afraid of you. No, no, the game in which you are dying to prove yourself is a short-term affair. They make you and then they are all after you, to destroy you. So watch yourself. And you think you are getting away with all what you been doing? Think again, we have the witnesses, we have the CCTV footages of your delinquency. You keep messing around, we know you turned 18, so you will be tried as an adult. Even get deported back to the country you run away from. Do you want to go back?"

Another bout of silence was on the other end. But the message had sunk in. The cocksureness was wiped away. Doubt and fear were evident in the frequent blinks in an attempt to compose his nerves. '*Nice try*,' the cop thought.

"So this is your life." The old cop continued his reality check pep talk. "Think about it. We are out there watching everything you do. We know you are not involved in the drugs. But don't think you can get away with all the disturbance and violence. You are just lucky because no one has filed charges so far. Don't think it will last forever. It is not us you should be afraid of more, it is the very streets. How long do you think you will last? How many of those you know have really profited from it big time and made a career out of it? Hmmm, none! No one makes it! The game is rigged and never in your favor! Stop before it gets too late, before it turns ugly, kid! Think of this as a fair nudge! Our next encounter will not be this cordial, understand?"

Silence. Shifting in his seat. But barely managing to maintain eye contact. Teme finally mumbled, "Am I free to go or you still got more lessons for me?"

The cop no longer entertained Teme's comebacks, "You are free to go, but like I said, watch out!" and gave him a firm stare of authority.

The police station felt heavy on his way out. Like all the cops were watching him. Begging to keep him in. He could not wait to get out. "Fuck cops," he muttered under his breath and rushed out, hoping not to run into anyone witnessing him leaving the slaughter house.

His knees buckled. *What if they deported me?* he questioned himself. *They could do that?*

Chapter 16

Next session at his shrink's office. But Teme's mind was someplace else.

"Are you okay?" she referred to the dark circles around his left eye, the stitched up patch on his forehead and the bruised knuckles.

"Yeah," he smiled back in that cocky way of his knowing what she was referring to.

"Were you in a fight?"

"Sort of."

"You want to talk about it?"

"No, nothing to say. Shit happens."

After studying his face intently, she begun to probe with caution.

"Do people provoke you sometimes?"

"Yeah, they do, and they get what they deserve," he answered empathically, giving her that lethal stare that scared the life out of her. He at times enjoyed watching his shrink, shrink.

"Do you often have to defend yourself if you take offense?"

His feet shifted, his eyes rolled, and the smirk was back on his face. "Shit, you have to if you want to gain some respect."

Silence and analytical stares exchanged. "How do you react when other people, people you don't know, are provoked or attacked?"

"If I know them, I defend them. If I don't, fuck them. It's every man for himself."

Empathetic and protective, she noted to some relief. But she quickly turned on the objective self.

"How about if you see vulnerable people picked on by a bully?"

"Depends. The thing is what goes around comes around. You just got to let it be sometimes."

"What do you mean?" She was perplexed at how mature his reasoning sounded.

"Like when I see people that have done evil to other people or me, let's say suffering or dying, I would not lift a finger. In fact, it gives me, you know. Not that I am happy about people dying, but you know," his voice died down.

"A sort of karma, you know what goes around comes around feeling," she added to keep him going.

"Yeah, like that, those people got exactly what they deserve sort of feeling. But not the women and children," he quickly added, not to sound like a psycho. Although everyone out there can be so cruel at times.

"It is natural, you know, to feel that way. That does not make you a bad or an evil person."

"Yeah, I guess!" He wanted to tell her more, perhaps all of it, but he came unstuck like that pause one took when running into a dead end after a long drive before cussing and making a U-turn. He wanted to tell her sometimes he felt like someone inside his head made him do things, evil things he was not in control of. Like he was held hostage in his mind at times. But the words could not come out.

"Do some faces on TV, I mean the news remind you of some of those evil people?"

He was taken aback by her question but nodded emphatically, recalling the deadly resemblance of a dead mutilated militant to that of that evil fuck of a ring leader of the militias that had kept him captive. The fucker, if it was still him, had that signature smirk on his face despite him being dead. How was that devil so adored by his followers and even the locals who worshiped him, specially the ladies and children, he had no clue. Teme's blood boiled every time he thought about that man. Bloodthirsty fuck deserved to suffer for all he had done. Death was a swift relief not a punishment for men like him.

Noting his demeanor being transformed, probably gripped by some flashback instigated by their conversation, she waited patiently, not even lifting a finger until he came back. He looked so vulnerable and shriveling old, the fear and fright of a long suffering old man was all revealed when he was in a trance-like state. He finally snapped back, jumpy, wondering, unsure in case thinking out loud for a second. With an assuring smile, she changed the subject, "So how is the new job?"

"Pfff, I might be soon looking for another one." He lied, he was unemployed at the moment. But he had been promised an opening at bakery packaging unit. He cracked up, boyishly covering his mouth.

The boy was back, she smiled back, "Ha-ha that bad? Is it physically that demanding?"

"Hmmm, not that demanding. But boring routine. And the droning of the machines keeps going on and on even after I leave work. And my back and my feet are fucking killing me standing for eight to ten hours straight."

"Uff, that must be hard."

"Yeah."

"So where else are you thinking of working?"

"I don't know, maybe inside a delivery depot at one of the docks. I hear there is plenty of openings. Night shift, I think." He rubbed his chin, caressing his baby hair goatee he had been working on, she noticed. The race to match the old mind…

"Night shift, interesting."

"Yeah, maybe I will take the dozer fork lifter training and get the license. Easier to get a job then."

She was proud of him. He is making a tremendous progress. For the first time he has a long-term goal. Instead of the usual rushed easy fix.

"I wish you luck, and I know you can do it. Stability at home and work place plays a significance role in your state of mind, you know."

He nodded in agreement.

"So how is your girlfriend doing?"

"She is fine."

That was a back-off retort, she noted. The line not to be crossed. She backed up.

Checking at the time she noticed she had a couple of minutes left. She contemplated ending it on a high note, sensing he was opening up.

"Can I ask you something? Don't consider my question intrusive or offensive, but do you ever consider harming yourself?"

"No. A quick one at that."

"Do you ever have any suicidal thoughts?"

"No, I am tired of living. Feel hopeless at times, but I don't want to kill myself. I just feel trapped and want to move. I just want to forget about what happened."

"Do you feel like hurting someone sometimes?"

"What, are you the police now?" He literally wanted to tear his hair, just felt claustrophobic talking to her. It felt like he was being interrogated. *When will the fucking sneaky questions stop? Fucking bitch*, all these questions were all geared up to get him to confess.

"No, I am just worried about you," she replied.

"Hmm, I read the confidentiality pact you have with respect to the government. If there is any threat, you are obliged to break the rule and notify the police."

"NO. No, no, you misunderstood."

"Stop lying! You are always fishing to find out if I am a threat to others. You never cared about me. And I say yes, I want to hurt somebody, next day the police will be at my door. You think am stupid?"

Lost for words, with a weary smile, she waited pensively for him to calm down.

"Why can't you just write me a medicine like a sleeping pill so I can get some sleep? If I sleep well, I will have a better day."

"But I am trying to help you overcome the sleep deprivation by tracing the underlying issues, so you could face them and address them instead of taking a pill. That does not solve your problems. Besides, I am a psychologist and not a psychiatrist, you know I am not allowed to give you medication. My job is counseling and therapy."

"No, you just want to listen to my sad story, so you can feel good about your life. I know how you people are…" And he stormed out.

This is not what she signed up for. Her hands were still shaking, and the slam of the door was still ringing in her ears. What she had learned and been practicing was beyond application in some cases; if she could she would dedicate her time to a sole patient. For mutual benefits of science and relief of the significant other. Like it used to be, before being commercialized and recognized as a profitable profession. Back then it was just for the scientific thrill, the in-patient and the ever-learning inquisitive recruit discovering the mystery of the deep ocean and wide deserts of the mind, layer after layer. At times she felt like a prostitute fronting to listen and relieve the pressure of every crooked soul stepping into her office. Indeed, it was prostitution when one never chose their patient. Like a whore her door was open for a stranger pimped by the state.

It was not easy working with these damaged teens. Not the kind of job she switched off and leave for home. It lingered in her mind constantly. Reading yet another teenage refugee committing suicide unnerved her. It barely caught the attention of the public or the media. It had become an obsession, more like an obligation, to try to help them. Ease their pain at least if not heal them. The invasion of able-bodied young men, the crime wave, and the radical

Islamization of the youth and, of course, the threat to the Norwegian way of life dominated the attention span of the public, obviously. The suicide attempt of the healthy-looking but traumatized minds far outnumbered the threats they posed to society, the fact remained. But like their deaths, their suffering was undetected and untreated, often met with silence and bafflement. According to some studies, migrants pass through similar phases before successfully assimilated into the host society. The awe phase, where one marveled the glamor and glitz of aesthetic value of the city they arrived in. Afterwards came the shock phase where all the minute and giant cultural, social, regional and religious different traits with the locals emerged into the magnifying focus of the mind, halting progress. Then enter do or die stage, where one's character, ambition, moral ground, and expectation was tested upon immersing themselves into the host country. Which then eventually led to the changing room phase, after trial and error, where one learned what to compromise in order to fit in. Finally came the recognition stage, where one accepted the compromise and begins to call the place one lived home. However optimistic, the theory outlined the different phases a productive migrant might go through; in her opinion it failed severely to outline the stagnation phase, where most never advance. Stuck in the middle of nowhere. These traumatized kids were never represented by any of the studies. They had been on a volatile vicious cycle of progression and regression right upon arrival. Growing and shrinking at the same time. Misunderstood and underestimated!

Left to their own devices or among themselves, she felt helpless and useless watching it unravel. Fresh ones withering before they blossom. Young men and women who never had the chance to be boys and girls. Too late to regain the lost manhood brutally taken away from them. Men not ready for the world, trapped in the past, the future terrified them. Misconceived sense of manhood denied them the option of seeking out help unlike their female counterparts, who embrace and purge themselves of their past to start afresh. The girls by far gravely traumatized and victimized, despite their early reluctance, opened eventually and rehabilitated into a productive life, but the girls were far and few when compared to the massive influx of underage boys that had braved the deserts and seas. The boys were impenetrable. It was at times a lost cause. She questioned at times why even allow them if one could not handle them properly? Handle them not like a child not as an adult, but special cases that needed to be watched from a far as well. They were ticking bombs!

Chapter 17

On the 13th day a lorry arrived in the dead of the night. All containers were emptied, and its occupants filed in, pushed, and shoved, kicked, and punched and at times spat at the three dozen refugees climbed up the lorry. They were transferred to another militia, arranged by the ringleaders in Khartoum and Libya, who had deals with most tribes along the path to guarantee the passage of live goods, at least most of it, if not intact. The women were missing among the group perhaps as a part of the deal but none complained. They kept their cut and passed them forward as joints. The new band of militia had lighter complexions and were even more notorious in their approach, they were rumored to be the Toubou tribe protectors, who controlled the south-eastern part of Libya. They barely addressed them; it was communicated through their sticks and the back of their Kalashnikov.

In the nearby hills, a constant exchange of heavy gunfire could be heard. They were indeed at the midst of the battlefield; the tension was evident in the eyes of the militia men that accompanied them. The lorry braked abruptly every now and then to assess the surroundings. The armed men jumped off and on the truck like hares in a graveyard. The passengers sat still with heads buried in their hands, praying for a safe arrival. They were only fed dry breads that clogged in their throats, only to be washed down by kersoine diluted water jug passed around every now and then. All their belongings had been stripped away upon departure.

Another day and night went by with no incident. But their pace was slowed down by constant stops at checkpoints, negotiations, and breaks only the militia were allowed to take. Every time they entered another tribe's territory the negotiations got dragged and the face-off intense.

Teme had a good feeling about the journey though. Sure, there were glitches along the way, but he was almost there.

Three days crisscrossing the Libyan Desert, they were barely let out to stretch their legs and relieve themselves in the open plains under the watchful eyes of the paranoid militia. By then they had already convinced themselves of their status as prisoners. The deeper they traveled to the heart of the uninhabited desert, the faster they drove and the gunshots and heavy artillery blasts receded as well. With the high partition of the truck covering their visibility and partially curtailing the scorching sun and the constant dust, most slept through the journey.

It all went smooth until the second day, when the lorry begun to slow down, intermittent checkpoints and the exchanges and the negotiations became heated. It must indeed be unfamiliar territory for the militias as they had assumed a more pleading tone, their menacing authority had vanished. Taking it all out on them, their prisoners always paid the price. Kicks and punches were thrown at them for the slightest of provocations or the lack of a quick response for their curt commands. The denser the settlements and the towns they were closing in as well they realized with the gunfires intensifying, the lorry was skillfully avoiding the epicenter of any battlefield so far, slowing and assessing the ground before cautiously proceeding. There sure were some close calls, when heavy artillery blast would blow up a crater on their path, showering them with dust.

The third day nearly at dawn a rattling gunfire against the hull of the lorry startled them from the deep sleep induced by hunger and thirst. It must have taken the militia men by surprise as well and the response was lackluster and panicky. They shouted for a surrender and negotiations but whoever surrounded them fired back in defiance. The driver and the three passengers, after holding their ground, finally succumbed. The motor died and the shots closed in on the back. The guardians, with hands raised in the air, surrendered disembarking from the back of the lorry. They were all shot on sight. Four dark military fatigue dressed young men in their twenties climbed up the truck with guns aimed at the shell-shocked prisoners. The older man who seemed to be in charge scanning the faces asked who could speak some Arabic. Three hands were raised. Then asked if they were headed to Italy. They all nodded. The man smiling notoriously, with his finger finally relaxed off the trigger, pronounced they were now under the protectorate of the local Jihadist unit. "Relax, we will not harm you, you soon shall be on the way to Italy," he pronounced. Then with a grave tone, he pointed the gun at the one older guy who was having a fit, sobbing uncontrollably, incanting some prayer of sorts. The rebel pointing the muzzle to his head asked if he was a Muslim. The man hesitated to reply. Then it all happened fast, boom and the back of his head was splattered all over their faces. Panic struck the back of the truck.

Another shot went up in the air, another man climbed up from the side with his AK 47 slung over his shoulder. He was smoking a joint. "All our Muslim brothers on the left and the kuffars on the right," he demanded. Six of the twenty-four stepped to the left while the rest with heads held down moved to the right. The Christians were then shoved off the lorry, herded to line up and frisked one by one for their possessions. Soon they disappeared from Teme's view. One by one the six were asked their full names in Arabic, their nationalities, where they were headed, if they had money on them and if there were any doubts of their faith, they were asked to recount random verses they recited during prayers? Two stumbled to answer the questions. One regained his composure to recant the Morning Prayer in Arabic with his eyes closed like a muezzin would. The second one messed up his name and had no idea about the Arabic language nor the faith; for his blasphemous act he was shot right on sight. Brain matter was once again painted on their faces. Things were happening too fast to process in his young mind. It was like a movie, but then he could see, smell, and hear death happening right in front of him. Not once but twice someone who was alive and well a minute ago was lifeless, headless, and dead. Blood everywhere, the stench of a gun smoke plus the human blood was nauseating. He could not take his eyes of the brain matter that was plastered on his shoes. *It belonged to someone's head a minute ago, how was that possible?* he questioned along with thousands of unanswered questions flying in his head. But he promised not to end up that way, not die like that. He would go to Europe and become a football star one day. He would not die there. He was no longer shocked, his mind was all focused, all in a survivor's mode. Soon his turn came, he told them his alias, Nasir Ahmed, and he answered all the five pillars of Islamic culture: shahada (faith in Allah and only Allah, salat (the daily prayers and rituals), zakat (charity), sawm (Ramadan fasting) and Hajj (pilgrimage to Mecca) confidently. As a bonus he recounted his favorite verse from the Quran as he had rehearsed in proficient Arabic. They bought it. He was off the hook for now.

Moments later, while they were loaded on to a truck, another pickup was departing, transporting the bloodied unbelievers with a sullen defeated look on their faces farther away in the direction they had come from. Teme's eye followed them all the way until the dust trail became oblivious. He felt guilty at abandoning his faith, denying his God, his almighty maker, but he did not come all the way here to die, by any means necessary, he reminded himself until he made it across. That was the moment he became a man. His mere 14 years' mind matured overnight to process the grotesque life of adulthood.

****

The next few months were a blur. All happened to fast, too gruesome, and never any breather in between. As a sort of initiation into the squad, the recruits were tormented and tortured upon arrival. Kept in an underground bunker near the town of Bani Walid, the militants took turns in breaking down the resolve of every newcomer. Every bit of information about their upbringing, family affiliations, and resources were tortured out of them. Once they ascertained Teme was incorporated into the squad, the makeshift camps and hideouts they constantly switched became a routine. The fighter jet planes dropping on their trail like migrating birds pooping simultaneously, the wounded and mutilated was just part of their days. War was going on, the whole world had its eyes on Libya. Nations were rallying in alliance to vanquish the rotten radical seeds that had run rampant in the desert, of which he was counted as one. But in the eyes of the young Teme, life had stalled in a perpetual state of chaos that had surprisingly numbed him. He never questioned, nor stopped to think, he just followed orders and got by. Militants against militants and, of course, against the government aligned forces was still ongoing then. At the meantime, the migrant wave was on an all-time high, trying to reach the unpatrolled Libyan coast. Those intercepted awaited cruel fates. The five weeks instant military crash course and the Quran studies barely left them time to think or fraternize among each other. But all the recruits from different cultures, though some had joined voluntarily, had one thing in common, shock and fear, which soon gave in to automated indifference and almost fearless subordination.

Deep inside the fear lingered but constantly watched, they had better step in line and blend in. Prowling the ever-changing desert territory, the notorious disorganized but tight unit terrorized any encroachers who trespassed their authority. Government troops and suspect supporters were executed on sight, but the non-Muslim migrants faced the worst wrath of the militants. Most on the way to the portal city of Sabratha, had been intercepted and forcibly detained and guarded in open storage compounds that used to be industrial hangars. The women, kept separately, were constantly raped and tortured. The men were given three options; pay a huge amount of ransom for their release, convert to Islam and join the ranks of the militants, or have one of their organs harvested or worse be tortured to death.

After his training Teme, with his alias Nasir Al Habesh, was posted as a guard on one of those industrial warehouses hosting the captives. Constantly smoking the hashish gratefully numbed his mind as he followed orders nonchalantly. The largest hangar housed the congested 950 male detainees while the dormitories built at the other end of the compound housed the women, and the guards living adjacently conveniently kept an eye on them. On the few occasions he ventured inside to distribute meager food and water rations, the stench overwhelmed him. The sweating unwashed muddied bodies, overgrown hairs and emaciated in tats and rags huddled in corners in clans, all timidly following his move like hens in a chicken farm squirming in fear of not being plucked out of the crowd for execution. At times he pitied them, then there were times he resented them for their helpless state, their depravity and their tolerance to take in the pain and still hope, reserving no hate for their captors. Bizarrely, they all had accepted their fates as more of a difficult phase they shall persevere to make it to the last stretch, the dream trip across the ocean was just miles away, they could smell it in the air and still lacked that fire or rage, no will to fight back across the last hurdle. All had succumbed to their dreams, dreams for which some were willing to sacrifice the dignity of their children, their wives, and people like him religion and his soul, all for a dream. The brave or the fool ones, his young mind was not sure what to make of, had their throats cut for not obliging. It was confusing at times kicking his way across the stinking human maze to refill the hostages' rations while his own captors kept a close eye on him guarding the entrance. Dreams fuck up reality, he had reckoned in retrospect.

The storage unit farther up field inside the vast brick-walled compound, strategically built underground in the back of the hangar, was where the torture chamber was kept. The underground chamber was unnaturally darker and cooler than the rest of the compound as if death resided inside. Greasy heavy tools and machinery parts were hanging on the racks in all corners, clattering once in a while to a chilly effect when one brushed past them. In the middle of the chamber was a rusting steel high table with hooked steel chains protruding from above. It looked as if the place was designed as a perverted torture chamber. The stench of heavy air, corrugated metal, and burned-out oil inflamed the nostrils when one stepped inside. When the chamber was operational, the sound effects brought the entire compound to silence at times. The sorrowful moans and screams were constant music to their ears by then. The bloodied bodies who gave in to the excessive experiments were buried in the backyard dug by a tiny China-made crawler excavator. The lump of uneven soil all over the yard told the horrifying end of the migrant story.

At first some of the hostages believed he was one of them, the one who would be kinder to them. Some tried to speak to him in his native tongue, but he maintained dead ears, curt Arabic and a kick was always his reply. That worked in his favor in winning the trust of his superiors, especially the fuck with an ugly scar and a smirk he would never forget but will never mention his name aloud ever. Being aloof to the captives and indifferent in his approach had killed of their attempt to win over his empathy. The young girls that were raped right in front of his eyes in broad daylight, soon he was numb to it, watching from a distance.

Then one day, with a gun pointed to his head, he was forced to rape one girl his age. Her hands tied by a rope, her naked body lying on a dirty mattress, her bloodied expressionless face looking at the grenade-ridden holes of the wall in the room of the guards, but he could not do anything. He wanted it to stop, he contemplated shooting them all right there and then, but his finger would not respond. The sight of her exposed body aroused him, he felt ashamed at himself. Gripping his Kalashnikov tightly, he whispered for one of them to stop it, the girl had enough; the guy snickered and brushed him off to assume the position and take his turn to relieve himself. Teme could not take it anymore, and he begged them to stop; the four of them, including that devil incarnate began to exchange glances over his agitation. Their suspicion grew to concern when Teme threatened to stop the first militant from going on a second round of pleasure ride. The girl was barely heaving, submissive she had her eyes closed by then as if her soul long departed her body. Three of them jumped Teme and subdued him when he pointed his rifle, shouting aloud, condemning their behavior as not Islamic by quoting a verse from the Quran. But to no avail, they had taken away his rifle, and the Scarface with the devil's smirk on his face ordered him with a gun on his head to rape the almost lifeless girl. "Take your pants off and have your way. It is a God's gift. A reward for a warrior." He resisted for a second, only to feel the gun smacking his temple hard. Almost unconscious, he had looked up to meet the smirk and the hollow black emotionless eyes gazing down on him; he had given in to lower his pants. His penis let him down though, unwillingly it had responded at once. "God forgive me," he mumbled in his native tongue before entering her passive inside. He trashed inside, her eyes tearing up, he avoided her eyes. That was the day darkness descended upon his soul.

That was the day it all sunk in, that he had indeed become one of them. They had triumphantly applauded and congratulated his limp self, right after his loud orgasm. "Now you have become a man. A real warrior, my boy," Scarface had celebrated, patting him on the back.

The girl disappeared soon though to his relief and grief at the same time. Her ransom had been paid by her family abroad and she had been transferred to the shipment yard unit of the militants to await her spot on the dinghy boat across the Mediterranean. What would he say to her if he ever was to run into her? Her face appeared and disappeared like a mirage in a city jungle once in a while to send chills up and down inside every now and then. Regardless, new faces were better to face than those that keep remind one of the ills one had been forced to perform. However, there was no room to sympathize or fraternize there when eyes were constantly on him. Young boys were torn from their mothers' laps and abused; one or two had disappeared, sold to older militants in the battlefields who craved young fresh boys. He had heard them joke, "Nothing like a squealing boy after a stressful day." To the sick fuck Scarface, many of the young boys were at his mercy whenever he was stoned. There were those deemed surplus for their inability to pay the hefty ransom sum or the money for the boat were sent to another unit down the port for medical purposes. On one or two occasions, the ramshackle filthy surgical unit where most injured militants were operated was also where they harvested organs. The victims of the botched kidney surgery by amateur doctors the likes of him buried when the sun set, which Scarface oversaw from a distance with that smirk plastered on his terrifying face. The smell of rotting human flesh became the norm. Battered skulls, gaping mouths, shattered bones, open torsos, and that nauseating odor, the green flies buzzing about it. His mind was for some crazy reason numb amid the unbearable desert heat, almost shut down and not registering any of the horror scenes the eyes witnessed on a daily basis.

The horror continued inside the compound, burials were a daily task he underwent around dusk or dawn. He was soon escorting some of them to the chamber; in the beginning he could barely look at them straight in the eye, just cussing and hurrying the timid souls, the hundred yards would be the dark carpet to their judgment day for some. The Scarface especially took tremendous joy and pride in tormenting the flesh and soul of his captives. It was like his hobby, and he enjoyed it even more when Teme was right there watching him as he used all his improvised toys of torture. Melting plastic dripping on the bare back of the bound and gagged bodies was his favorite routine that brought a rasping glottal laughter out of him. When Teme refused to join in the fun, the same fate had befallen him as well, took weeks for the infected wound to heal. At some point he stopped caring for any of what was happening there, to him or to others, realizing if he wanted to stay alive he had to stop thinking, play along and shut up. *Every man for himself.*

Chapter 18

The kitchen rat existence. As the darker the shade of the skin tone, the closer one was to the oven was the unspoken rule. The lighter skinned southern European and east European waiters glided in and out of the kitchen carrying orders cooked by the Arabs to the blondes, while the dark souls do the dirty job, concealed in the background. The constant piled up dirty dishes were a Sisyphus-like task of a mountain they had to constantly demolish yet never to clear up, alternating between manual and machine assistance, until check-out time. The pay was good, but the opportunity once again for an unskilled worker was to be relegated in the long line of temps, waiting for the skilled ones to get sick. After a short spell in Rica hotel, in the Helsfyr center, Teme was the closest he ever came to a luxurious environment in his adopted hometown, sneaking in and out of the back door of a hotel he never had a bite of. Maybe it was his destiny, the destiny of black souls left to tough it out in the gutter to eke out a living. '*Crazy*,' he thought, changing his street clothes in the wardrobe; despite the chaos he missed some moments in Libya. When not supervised he was the top dog, man with the gun all cowered to and feared. He was the law. Now he was invisible, working his ass off in the kitchen. He logged out to sneak out the back and hit the road. He probably should have taken a shower, he figured, sniffing his fingers and his armpits. "*Fuck this life,*" he mumbled. He was getting tired of everything as he hurried his step to catch the bus heading to the city center.

He hopped off at Hausmansgata and lost his bearings. Fucking cold, sniffling and watching his step he turned on his heels towards Tøyen. His job had taken a lot of time off his crew. They were probably chilling at the bowling center or shooting pool at one of the bars, he figured, while making his way towards Løkka. A black BMW pulled up just around the curb, cutting him off. Shiny and brand new, the bass was bouncing with some hip-hop jam. Tinted windows, he thought it was illegal down there as he arched to see through the passengers. Everyone had their eyes on the car though, a proper showstopper. The windows finally rolled down, and the bass echoed along the entire block. It was Big Boy who smiled at him from the white leather seat. Two others who he was not familiar with were behind the wheel and on the back seat, "Step in, young buck," he signaled for Teme towards the back seat. He did not hesitate as rolling with the big boys in a bad ass car made up for a drab week he had. He greeted the duo, who barely nodded at him.

"This is Killa, that kid I was telling you about. Bad ass nigga," Big Boy made the introduction. The other two grinned and bumped fists as a sign of respect. Teme felt proud, people were indeed noticing. Despite the fucked up state he was in, at least he was getting some respect.

"We need tough soldiers like you in the streets, Killa. Proud of how you holding yourself," said the older one sitting next to him. Teme barely nodded.

The man behind the wheel chipped in, "I heard how you handled the cops when they came by for a shakedown. Man, you got some balls," and they all cracked at that. Soon silence ensued as they rolled around the city with their eyes on the city and the city on theirs. It was surreal moment for Teme, just chilling with the shot callers with no regard to the law. They circled around Grønnloka, cruised around Tøyen, Galgenberg, and back to Grønland. With the hardcore rap blasting from the bass speakers, he felt like he was in one of his fantasies. Watching American gangster movies, his imagination would construct scenarios with him the villain and the hero. His own boss with the entire neighborhood paying respect and taxes. His fantasy was cut short though as blue lights zoomed from behind. Sirens blaring out, they were signaled to pull over. Two cops closed in on both sides. "All the passengers step out of the car, please," was the curt order. Another police van joined in with a police hound on a leash panting his way towards the car. Car registration and license checked, IDs inquired for the passengers.

It sounded like the boys were used to these stops as they nonchalantly responded to the inquiry, "We got nothing to hide, Officers."

"Where are you guys heading?" one of the cops asked.

"We were just cruising around town and looking for a place to eat," answered the driver.

One of the cops though was paying way to close attention to Teme, inquiring, "Hi young man, so what were you doing in the car?"

Teme snapped back, "What are you, my foster father? I am 18 and last I checked, it was legal to hitch a ride back home. Nobody is doing anything illegal here."

The policeman cracking a smile at his audacity interrupted, "You watch your mouth, young man."

Teme was having none of it, tsk-ing in disgust, "Don't you people have other job to do than harassing black people?" His boys giggled with satisfaction. Another point earned, he figured. "But if I do something wrong, Mr. Officer, I will make sure I call you in advance so you can come and pick me up, I promise."

Even the cop was smiling at that. "Smart ass." Looking back at the other police a crackle of coded messages came on the radio strapped on the shoulder. It sounded, 'All clear'. "You guys are free to go for now. But the tinted window has to go! This is a final warning," he fired a stern look at the driver and Big Boy.

They soon dropped off Teme around Munch Museum with a wad of cash for his bravery. "You earned it, young buck, stay strong, the streets need you!" And Big Boy bumped his fist. Jubilant Teme begun calling on his boys to assemble for a party. He first thought he should treat himself with some new sneakers and then hook up with the boys later. While walking down the quiet street skirting the botanic garden, he contemplated. There was something that made him uneasy about hanging with the big boys. It was not fear, he was not intimidated by them. But it frightened him in a weird way like a déjà vu, back in Libya in some ways. He was on the side of the outlaws, not by choice but this time he had a choice. He was not in their game for benefits. He was not their employee. He hustled from one shitty job to the next, paying tax and all. He was just in it to let out some steam. So they owe him nothing. And that cop, why was he staring at him like he knew him well? Something fishy about the way he was studying him, were they on to him, he questioned but quickly dismissed it. "Fuck them and fuck the police too," he mumbled to himself. It was a mild weather and not a bad day to have some fun!

He thought about taking a stroll inside the botanic garden and get lost in the history and geography of plant world. With all the flowers and trees from all over the world available in display, it used to fascinate him, walking around reading the labels, the weird scientific names and their geographic origin. In the tempered glass houses all those exotic flowers from Africa, Asia, and Latin America were fascinating. But these days walking around alone inside a park was asking for trouble. With all the cliques they had beef with, it was safe to be out in the open for fight or flight reasons.

Mind racing everywhere, his feet kept up towards familiar ground around their hangout and council towers. Their corner was occupied with drunk old heads and the omnipresent junkies. Three black and brown boys along with two Norwegians were doing tricks on the skate ramp. He felt offended, it was trespassing. But they all lived in his block. They were all dressed up in the same skinny tight faded jeans, some colorful vans and white t-shirts. Even the black boys had their hair relaxed to look white. You will always be black, he cussed in his mind. He gave a sneering look towards the black boys. They knew who he was and succumbed to his stare, freezing in silence. He cherished the moment, lighting a cigarette he eyeballed them one after the other. One of the brown boys nodded at him with respect, "What's up, brother, all good?"

Teme had to put him back in his place, got to highlight the hierarchy, "You don't fucking know me, you hear," he pointed his finger at him. "You talk only when I talk to you, understood?" They were all shaken and nodded. He felt sorry for them for a second, but he despised them as well. *They were spineless niggers yet to find out who they are.* It would be a rude awakening once they grow old to find out there was the designated native pie and crumbs and leftovers for everybody else. He wanted to torture them a bit but maybe some other time, as he skipped past, eyeballing them one last time.

Frustrated, his feet were back on the tarmac towards the prison. For some peculiar reason he often found himself circling around the penitentiary, subconsciously drawn to it. Skirting the vast expansive walls, he would cast a glance and imagine how it would be like for the inmates. It was a strange place right in the middle of the old part of the town. Almost invisible giant, sucking in the rotten souls society deemed harmful. Unlike the prison he knew, no sound ever came out of it, no screams of agony or distress. Eerily quiet it was, only police vans with tinted windows creeping in and out of the belly of the huge silent beast. The guarded gates would glide open and closed while he glared inside for some curious reason for a peek into the life behind bars. He would at times lock eyes with the prison guards, who were intrigued by his interest. Maybe they will send him an invitation one day, who knew, to satisfy his curiosity. He indeed had been to the holding cell but yet to make it to the big house. Ducking the stare of a police van that emerged from the heavily fortified gate whose occupants happened to glare his way with that cocky police way, Teme scurried ahead back to the metro station. He hopped in on the first line heading to the Oslo city mall. Shopping time it was!

****

His crew was incognito for the afternoon. But fuck it he treated himself with some brand new Jordans. Blood red with black features, his favorite color combo. Rocking his new J, he called Smokie. "You, where you at?"

"The crew wanted me to back them up on some trip to the Swedish border. We will be back around eight. All good?" Toure inquired, dying for some action.

"Yeah, all good. Party is one me tonight hustled some dough. Catch up if you can," Teme assured his good friend.

"All right," the buoyant Toure was thrilled to meet his friend back in town.

"Yo, buy some bottles, I pay you later."

"I'm broke man," protested Smokie.

"Come on just borrow some and buy drinks and cigarettes for later."

"Can't you vips (transfer) the money, man."

"All right, will do some. But better buy the shit. No excuses, you hear."

"All right, Killa."

He was restless again. He could go to a bar around National Theatre, where he could most definitely get in without ID. '*They play some awesome music down there*,' he thought. But wandering alone in unfamiliar neutral territory was not a wise choice. He opted to head back around their territory. On the way back around Brugata, a familiar bass coming at out a bar stopped in on his trucks. After contemplating the risks, he stepped in. He met two old school mates and joined in. Often the moment the drumbeat, that monotonous peculiar beat to that part of his world he was born and raised in, refreshed his spirit like the sighting of an oasis to a Bedouin or a trafficker. It brought all the good memories back in warm flashes one after the other. It had always been a source of joy. But not of late, these days all it was, the sound of alarm. Monotonous blaring ululating sound of alarm, his nerves begun to pick up, vigilant as his eyes scouted his surroundings as if he was in an enemy territory. He thought the feeling, the jumpiness might go away, but it sure did not. His appearance had changed dramatically;

he had grown chunkier and taller, his hairstyle slicker, his moustache and beard bushy and his brown skin lighter. It was not easy to recognize him from three years ago. But then it was the sixth sense, they sensed each other from a distance. The hair at the back pinged erect at once before the sighting of one or many witnesses of them dark days.

Teme tried to keep cool with the baseball cap donned halfway to his temple, with a corner seat next to so-called old friends. One thing in common though, despite the intoxication, eyes remained vigilant on every corner, comings and goings along their threshold. That collective nerve unsettled him. Then two individuals set their eyes on him, whispering to one another, something sinister it looked. Teme could not place their faces at all. He kept his composure, locked eyes with both of them for a second, then they all casually looked away in unison. His heart dancing in his heart, his face maintained that cold blank look, though he swayed to the beat in a laidback mode. A moment later another man child took a second lingering thorough examination towards their table, that animal instinct of recognition noted Teme. The blaring music was now becoming unbearable as he signaled his friends that he would be back and stepped out.

On the front step he lit a cig and casually looked inside. Maybe he was being paranoid? Maybe they were just measuring up a new face in their territory? Maybe they knew each other in the former life, who knew? Why push it, he asked himself and began to walk away down Brugata towards Hausmansgata, passing a huddle of swaying junkies in their silent junkie prayer in slow motion, waiting for some junkie whistle to wake them from their trance. His mind was still vigilant though, retracing the faces that were paying him more attention. He causally looked over his shoulder for the eighth time before crossing the red light in a hurry, definitely sure he was not being followed but one never knew? *The past will always follow you.* Better head to Tøyen, where he felt at home until his boys came to town.

****

He eventually ended up walking his new J up and down Løkka strip. The guard at Memphis looked bored, he noted. With a stern look on his face and a phone on his ears, he walked past the guard without a hitch. It was all about confidence, he patted himself on the back. From the wooden long balcony in the middle of the oblong bar, the skeptic mid 30s waitress handed him his order, "There you go, and here is your change."

"Thanks sugar," he replied and left her a healthy tip, "and this is for you," he smirked with a cocky wink that brought a crooked smile. How many times had he been turned back from this establishment at nights, only God knew. As if he was not ready to have some fun. Had they known what he had done in life, he would get a pass anywhere. Too early though, a lot of empty seats, a bunch of honeys in their skanky dresses. Some lone figures occupying the benches facing the window overlooking the busy street. He took one next to a lone black man older than him. That humble exchange among Africans was nice to have in those hostile times. Soon he struck a conversation with the man, looking in a world of pain and sorrow.

"Speak Norwegian or English?"

"English, please, brodda."

"Okay, you new here?" asked Teme, sipping his beer.

"I live in de camp, my friend."

"Oh! Okay, still waiting for your asylum case to be processed?"

"No man, de already rejected me. Mtsee! Twice." The man let his head down in shame and disappointment.

"Sorry, bro!" Teme was genuinely touched; he could not imagine still living inside a camp.

"No, we still alive, dat is what I am most grateful for, I guess."

"Yeah, I hear you. So what's the next move then?"

"No school. No job and no rights to travel anywhere, we just wait, man, till de either deport us or maybe if our case reviewed," the man replied, looking away and around the bar while bobbing his head to the music.

Teme felt really sorry for the man. And he felt disappointed at himself being ungrateful as well. He should consider himself very lucky indeed. What would have happened if he had been rejected? That would have devastated him. All the sacrifices paid along the way, all the pain and sorrow would have been in vain. He could not even imagine how he would have coped had he been in this man's shoes. And now he was throwing it all away, messing around, taking it all for granted. If he kept it at it, he might get his permit revoked as well. Puff, he wished it was easy though as his actions were mere impulses of his raging state of mind.

"You made it across the Libya, bro?"

"Yeah, all dat for dis, I tell you life is bullshit. Mtsee," he gesticulated in that African way." All de sacrifice for nothin', nothin'."

Teme instantly headed to the bar tender. Moments later he came back with another beer for his new friend. He handed him the drink that instantly brought smiles on the man. "Fuck it anyway, man cheers to being a survivor." Teme patted his new friend on the back and raised his drink to cheer him up.

****

Chapter 19

Missing the cultural link during the informative years, the mid-teen unaccompanied minors exhibited certain traits that were common among them. From the adults that had embarked upon the treacherous journey through the desert and the ocean had at least processed and evaluated the risks. The survival odds were on their favor 7–10. Good odds for any desperate gambler. But above all, the formative years of identity construction and mental capability had been developed in their motherland. Most had conceptualized the setting, had metabolized the hardship and the threats they faced first hand. Be it economic, political, or personal had been tested. Most important of all, most that had fled war zones had seen the evil human nature and seen death firsthand. Thus, fear for their lives. Despite not fully developed their young minds, they had a vague understanding of the workings of the world and human nature. In other words, they had lost their innocence before they left their country. With the ways and means of their homeland engrained in their system, they were reluctant and very cautious in acquiring new skills and methods. The informal education that had developed and heightened their instinct was overwhelmed by fear in an unfamiliar setting. They struggled learning a new language or the ways of the host. They, however, tackled traumatic experiences better. Their mental capacity despite being strained did not shelve those sorrowful experiences. They instead immersed themselves in their work to rebuild their lives, seek spiritual guidance, were reluctant towards scientific methods but at least sought out help in an invisible comfort zone they created, secluded from the host country. The hardship and the trauma they accepted as the sacrifice for a brighter future. Most seized the moment and redeemed themselves while few succumbed.

However, the early teen unaccompanied migrants exhibited a raw brute courage that was thoroughly missing from their older mates. Their underdeveloped instinct due to the lack of exposure in their original setting inadvertently shielded them from the fear of attempting the unknown. Their innocence somehow tainted, at times severely dented, still allowed them to adapt to new settings more easily. They were often impulsive and quick. They acquired new language easily and learned skills remarkably well. Thus, the digital technology in the Western world they tock to as a swan to a lake at ease, unlike their older skeptic and hesitant mates. However, all the massive, intensive traumatic exposure to violence that had shaken their worldview along the disastrous journey to the West remained shelved for a while. What was more appalling and astounding was the prevalence of rape among the boys. Though not open about it, unlike the girls who were proportionally abused, the boys exhibited those telltale signs. Sexual disorientation before they even began exploring. The concepts of manhood, sexuality, and faith brutally introduced and tested in the middle of the desert had left them reeling and confused. Despite growing up fast, the concept of death, evil deeds, right or wrong became meshed and molded. Instead of perceiving the actions and consequences, they made up their own version of reality. Thus, give one the impression of untouched, unfazed totally functioning teenager. Yet all that was shelved in the vault begins to seep in to the surface like a leaking sewer from the unconsciousness once they reach 17–19. Twenty the latest case she had studied. It had become a disturbing pattern. With some cultures lacking even a substitute for the terms trauma, psychosis, or schizophrenia in their language, or worse were taboo themes, these kids were in for a battle. All the progress done upon arrival suddenly hit a skidding halt. Regressing at an alarming rate, they could go either way. They became moody almost as if possessed by a foreign force. Their sexuality in upheaval, their identity mangled, they were in for a tough battle. The shelved phase of their lives running in a constant loop, they just need guidance to allow them to break free on their own, wrote the psychologist as a summary of her observation of the year so far. A soft knock on the door reminded her of the next client. The enigmatic Teme showing up late.

****

After exchange of pleasantries, she tried to open Teme up, but he had that look, opaque. His reply was curt and to the point. His attention in disarray, she noted, as he barely paid attention to her behavioral theory and how people his age react to trauma. The passive yet resilient tight-lipped empty look blinked once a while in front of her. There was no option but to divert her probing from a different angle.

"Do you have any plans for the summer and the season after?"

"What do you mean?" Teme was perplexed.

"I mean you know, like a new year's resolution. Make a list of things you will be doing or the things you will stop doing for the summer, just like you do on a new year. Like start training or stop smoking or read one book a week. Go on a vacation and come back focused to work hard for the rest of the year."

"Hmmm," Teme thought about it for a minute. Funny, he thought, how white people always got to plan things ahead when people like him had a whole lot of challenges planned out for him as if he was on some reality show, "not a plan like a concrete plan, but I always wish for positive things I want to happen in every wish. Just a wish, otherwise it is tough to follow through."

"Yeah, it is tough for everyone, honey. I mean, Teme," she corrected herself at once, "but it does not have to be perfect, you know. Like a doctor prescribes three tablets a day for six months and just because you forgot to take your pills last night does not mean you have to quit at all. Just pick off where you left off. No matter how many off days and night you may have, keep going. The keeping on going is what makes people successful, you know. So it is wise you know to make a plan, a flexible plan," she smiled.

****

Later on Teme and Toure were chilling at Teme's place, watching a movie.

"That is a bad ass slave man," Teme snickered in awe of a renegade slave who slaughtered his slave masters with no disregard on the movie *Django* that the two of them watched. It was the third or fourth time they were watching the movie, it engaged them. The desert scenes, the slavery, brutality, and the lawlessness they could relate to, unlike any other movie or even more than any movie watcher.

"You thinking what am thinking, Teme?"

"Libya," replied Teme with a hush after a moment of hesitation.

They were both in a marijuana haze. But their minds were clear and the images processing in their minds were working in tandem, re-running their days back in Libya.

"Shit, people think this is just something that happened in the past, man," said Toure with a blank smile, trying hard to fight off the memory flashing back.

"I know."

"Sometimes I think it all as a dream, like a movie I have seen way back."

"Ahha, yeah living here it feels like it happened a long time ago."

"Crazy shit, man," Toure shook his head, overwhelmed by the scenes the movie instigated in his memory.

Another moment of silence ensued. Their eyes glued to the movie, they followed Django marching forward on horseback, annihilating all that stood in his way to pursue and rescue his enslaved wife. But what were the two chasing all along?

"Did you ever think in your life you would end up living in Norway?" asked Toure, rolling another joint. The tobacco and ground marijuana leaves were all separately held in his right hand, along with a Rizla. His steady dexterous fingers could roll a joint amid a hurricane, as some had said.

"No, man. I never dreamt of going anywhere, to be honest."

"Well, me I always dreamed of going to UK and becoming a professional footballer."

"Ahhaha, how is that working out for you, man," snickered Teme.

"Fuck you, man. Life happened, as you know it."

"Yeah, I know."

"Do you think about the future? Like what will you be doing in 10, 20 years?" he quipped another question while giving a final nip and tuck to a perfectly rolled joint.

Teme thought about the question for a long minute before replying, "No man, I just can't picture it. I try sometimes when people ask me and all. And my mind goes blank. Like I don't see myself living that long, you know?"

"Same here, man."

"Halloo," they heard Elise rising from the dead. She stretched her arms and lazily slung her right one over Teme, who barely responded. They had long forgotten about her as she dozed off while they were watching Django.

"Want to play FIFA?" suggested Toure, who was often uncomfortable in Elise's presence for some reason unbeknown to her.

"Hell, ya," responded Teme with enthusiasm that irritated Elise.

"Don't you guys get tired of it, just tweaking your joysticks all day like fucking robots?" exclaimed Elise, getting ready to leave.

"Naaa, it's better than talking. You just let your fingers do the talking and you almost stop thinking."

"Thinking about what?" asked Elise, wrapping up her scarf around her neck, waiting once again for Teme to explain himself.

Teme and Toure exchanged looks. That look of exasperation when questioned. He shrugged his shoulders at her to face the TV. "You know, life." Toure switched on the play mode and connected the PlayStation. The FIFA music on, Elise knew it was her cue to leave, otherwise not a peep would come out the two for hours now. With the rap music playing loud over the speaker, the two would be in another world, not just competing but escaping. They barely celebrated nor showed disappointment when they played each other. They were in synch. When one game finished, they smoked their cigarettes in total silence and then were back to another game and on and on until they were knackered.

But inside they were both reeling. The painful memory of Libya had just lapped back and forth in their intoxicated mind right after watching the slave hero movie. Anything to keep their mind from thinking would do!

****

Chapter 20

Toure took on a different route to Europe. Teme's dream rose like the sun from the east while Toure set from the west to the black hole of the desert, where many dreams were vanquished. After a horrendous chain of events that had disrupted his childhood, he and his cousin had made their way to Agadez in the heart of the vast Niger country. They had both saved through months of hard labor at small jobs across all the towns they had passed. They spent two nights in Agadez along with more than two hundred other dreamers from all over West Africa. The dusty bustling desert town where everyone was on the move. At times it looked like a bus station. The smugglers had a lorry and four Toyota pickups lined up to make the six-day trip across the desert to Libya. From Agadez, on a dusty humid night, they set out on the back of a pickup, he and his cousin along with 31 others. The smugglers were curt but courteous in the beginning as long as one paid upfront the 275 US dollars for the trip. With ski mask or scarf covering their face from the dust, the desert trip was success. On the seventh day they were intercepted or rather handed over to the more organized militia across the border, a powerful Tuareg clan. That was when they ceased to be humans rather properties sold and bought with disregard. They split them according to age, gender, religion, knowledge of the Arabic language, and physical strength. He was separated from his cousin as he was shipped to a remote farm to the east of the southern Libyan town of Sabha.

His Muslim background despite him not ever practicing it properly along with his boyish look worked in his favor during the labor draft. Herding goats, tilling and watering the land, nine months flew by under the watchful eyes of an Arab who was relatively generous towards him. Learning the language and the customs, Toure later found out he was indeed sold to the gentleman on the cheap. *Not many slaves know their status under duress.* Survival being on the mind, one had barely a moment to reflect upon human rights and privileges. He was soon allowed to accompany his master to the Sabha town market every Saturday, a privilege earned for his loyalty, he figured later on. The bustling town where everything was on sale, even his brothers and sisters, he would find out. He was unable to locate the whereabouts of his cousin but he prayed to Allah every day for his safety. As soon as he had a rudimentary understanding of the language, he was horrified at what the locals said about them. Watching black Christians being paraded like slaves in the movies in Sabha almost made him be grateful for his own master. The muddy, emaciated, ashy, haunting faces devoid of hope and life being herded like the very goats he tended to everyday shook him up pretty well every time he accompanied his master on the beat-up Suzuki pickup packed with their fresh goods for sale in the market. He avoided eye contact with the poor souls, who perhaps were on the same pickup from Agadez. Despite not being paid he was never in shackles and he was well fed. Through snippets of conversation he overheard the fate of other slaves. He was terrified to the core upon hearing the lynching of runaway slaves or disobedient ones being spoken in a nonchalant dialogue.

While escorting his master, no one was rude to him or abused him. But their veiled hatred was unleashed on his brothers and sisters. It confused him though, some of the very people participating in the trading of slaves were as black as himself. His master taught him how to pray properly, taught him how to cook, and operate some electronic gears that were unfamiliar to him. Some Arabs were nice to him, even cooperative, when realizing he was a Muslim as well. There were some visitors of his master who humiliated him on purpose, some white Arabs. There was this one-toothed cripple who used to kick him while he was doing house chores. Apart from that it was bearable as long as he never disappointed his mild-mannered master. The trick to maintaining the peace and order was to never question the master and fulfill all chores and always pray. During the lavish EID feast, his master bought him a brand new traditional cloth and every visitor showered him with gifts. "You are like my son. It was God that brought us together," he had said to him. He was allowed to enjoy the festivities as an equal. It was a fond moment as well, splayed on giant carpet the family and friends in flashy white attires congregated under two conjoined tents. The food bonanza, the laughter, the traditional music played by paid musicians he had taken part with, none showing him any superiority or hatred. Toure was conflicted at times like that.

Bidding his time and gaining the trust of his master, Toure struck out on a lazy Sunday after nine months. He stole 967 Libyan dinars, worth about 800 US dollars at the time from the hidden stash behind the prayer room and took off. From Sabha he hitched a ride to the northern shores. For five days and nights he used up all his money to lodge, dine, and hitch any ride up north until he was intercepted near the coastal town of Sabratha by the infamous dark horse militias roaming that part of Libya. By then he had improved his Arabic and the Islamic customs and prayers, which saved his skin. While being escorted to the desert hideout of the militia on a pickup, he first laid eyes on his future best buddy Teme. He was by then in charge of the escort, with air of authority and a Kalashnikov slinging over his shoulder he sat leaning on the rails of the pickup while keeping a vigilant eye on their captives.

And the welcoming committee never wasted time upon arrival in their secret hold-out. It all started with a bang; the executions, the rape, and the humiliation all in day one.

Chapter 21

A trip to Hollemenkollen with his girl, perhaps subconsciously the words of his psychologist swayed his resolve. He was very uncomfortable carrying the ski bag with all the gears like a blond teenager. He felt the eyes of first generation migrants on their way to work condemning him. He felt like a traitor. He took of the ski goggles and shoved it inside the bag while hanging on to the pole in the center of the metro car. Two boys affiliated with his crew gave him a condescending nod as if they had caught him snitching. Elise, excited to have finally convinced her boy to join her on a joint typical Norwegian excursion for once, held on to his arm as the number one line to Frognersenter stopped at every stop. Teme, conscious of every eye from the platform they stopped at, was on alert as if waiting for anything to happen. Once the metro passed Majorstua and deeper into the western affluent part of town, his nerves calmed down with the knowledge of the lower probability people he knew running into him.

Leaning on to him, Elise stared at their vague reflection on the sliding doors. He was tense as usual, scanning cautiously like a cat every eye that looked his way. She had wondered at times if he was subconsciously uncomfortable being in public or was he ashamed of being seen with her. But he was genuinely stunned at her doubt and dismissed it with a hug and a kiss. Sure he was fresh out of boat African not used to public show of affection, but there sure was something to it, he was way too alert when he was out of the house. She had followed him a couple of times just to confirm her doubts. He was an anti-social freak and way too conscious of his skin color as well. His discomfort level stepped up a notch at the presence of or when overwhelmed and surrounded by white faces. That vigilant mode was activated, waiting for what she was not quite sure.

Straddling the bag, they got off at Hollemenkollen along with hundreds of ski enthusiasts. Despite summer approaching, the temperature slowly rising, snow kept pouring, especially in the mountains that season to the delight of the natives. Teme noticed he was the lone African among the crowd. Way out of place he told himself as he timidly tagged along the animated Elise down the ski resort with the high jump in view. Picturing himself jumping off that ramp made him crack a snicker. "What?" she asked nudging him gently like she always did to get him to talk.

"No, nothing. Been a while since I last went out for a ski."

"It will be fun, come on," she held him closer and ushered him towards the check-in cabin to get their locker.

Soon all geared up they were gliding, well she was while Teme cautiously slipped and slid across the white open field packed with joyful young and old mostly white faces. He soon forgot the cold.

On the highest point of the hill, music blaring from their boom boxes, intoxicated locals sat in huddling groups dotting the hill overlooking the city. '*Beautiful view,*' he thought with the magnificent afternoon haze of the setting sun over the horizon, the city he liked and loathed from afar. Albeit a couple of curious stares towards him at the beginning, now no one was paying him any attention. He was quite awful at skiing but he had picked up some skills while he was living in the underage refuge reception centers upon arrival. He was quite keen to learn skiing but then could not recall how and when he had suddenly lost the appetite; he just quit showing up at the group training for refugees one day. Drinking his hot chocolate in his sealed paper cup, Teme tried to pick up his girl from the ocean of white faces. She was white from afar anyway, inside of her was white with the slightest drop of chocolate, as he called it. Not skeptical like other white people he had known thus far, but she was enduring, warm, and open like old Africans. '*She was special*,' he thought, finally locating her with her yellow ski mask slaloming down the high jump effortlessly. She was a natural at it. '*She looks so peaceful and beautiful,*' he thought. *Why couldn't he say that to her*? That would complicate things. Besides, once he sliped that, she would want to hear more and often as well. He did say it once in a while in a heat of a moment anyway, he figured that was fair. Better let it be, he reminded himself. He waved back signaling her maybe it was time to head back. But he would definitely come back. The peace of mind in a crowd was a rarity these days that he so needed. Wait till he told his psychologist, she would be proud of his effort. But then why tell her, it was not like she was his mother. Had he become dependent on her? He should even skip the next session, the last thing he wanted was recall all the tragedy she kept tracking back relentlessly. At times he wondered if she was a detective of some sort, like the CSI or something. He had seen their silky moves on the movies. They first win your trust, then they smooth butter down that line of *you are not to blame, it is not your fault* so you could spill the beans. He was not going to fall for that! *Never!* he convinced himself, keeping an eye on his girl with a smile to his face

The Amphitheatre-like structure with the jump tower dissecting it like a birthday cake knife shot up the spring clear sky, 144 meters up. Sitting by the jump tower café, underneath the pillars of the protruding steel structure, he leaned on the bench sipping his hot chocolate. The amphitheater-like seats were occupied in flocks, all rowdy and animated. There were a whole lot of tourists from all over the world, he was surprised to see. Mostly European and some Asian, mostly Japanese and Chinese, he suspected scanning the crowd. The city panorama he had been looking forward was sadly obscured. He was in fact staring at the back of the city. Still elevated, the pine woods that encircle the popular ski arena were a change of air, green was reclaiming back the surroundings. He had his doubts going there but so far he was not disappointed.

Noting his desire as she always did, hand in hand they trekked down the step path towards the café down the street, an open wooden castle, less crowded and offering a better view of the city. He had a peaceful look about him. "You like it, don't you?" she chided, leaning close to him.

He held her closer, looking around and sighed, "Still white people stuff but not bad." They both laughed at that. They grabbed yet another cup of hot chocolate.

Noting his excitement, they made several stops on their way back, to take in the night from a bird's eye view. Oslo in full view dazzled him from the Besserud metro stop. "Wow, I never knew it was this big! The lights, it's beautiful," Teme got animated.

She was delighted that he was enjoying himself. That brought her more joy, making him happy. Besides not very often had he uttered words of praise for what she loved to call home. "I know I used to come here and just watch the city from this station all by myself back in the days. The metro lines coming and going every now and then remind you that you still live in the city. Otherwise, it is so quiet and beautiful, right?" she clung to him, waiting for a kiss. Kiss reciprocated.

"I know." He smiled, eyes still locked on the panorama.

"It is even more beautiful to share this view with the one you love, you know babe. That is real romance."

He bent down to plant a wet kiss on her always waiting pouted lips.

"Someday I will take you farther up the hill to show you around the entire city, if you want to."

He nodded enthusiastically.

Chapter 22

After skiing and sightseeing they had some dinner at an Indian restaurant and went to her place. It was a wonderful day completed with an intense lovemaking. But at night the recurrent dream had disrupted his peace, *after sunshine comes the rain*, as the saying went. Now watching his favorite documentary on DVD, he tried to rerun all the images that were flashing in his dreams. The Scarface had never appeared in his dream in a vivid manner. Last night he had owned his dream like a superstar, steering his dream into the valley and the shadow of death. Teme had felt the greasy, hairy, sweaty, and filthy body of that evil man pressing on top of him, he could not fight him off, even in his dream. Hands tied, his limp naked intoxicated figure wriggling in terror, trying to fight off the inevitable. Scarface had playfully giggled, time and time again knowing he was in full control. That disturbing empty giggle echoed to scar his soul more than any pain his body endured. How the hell would he ever be free from that, he questioned himself. His girl was getting dressed up to head to work. As of work he would be on the lookout as well. "*Fuck work*," he hissed in frustration. Sending CVs and putting up an ass-kissing face all day to get nothing but fake smiles and dismissals was disheartening. But it was either that or seek the social welfare. Despite being legible for a welfare handout, he had promised himself to never step foot in that office. It made him feel like a handicap when waiting for his queue number to blip on the monitor along with young, old, and all races unemployed or sick wallowing in shame and desolation. The empty contemptuous look on the faces made some impression on him. Besides welfare handout meant staying at home, sleeping odd hours and, of course, meant a whole lot of time to think. The last thing he wanted to do was think, be it the past or the future.

If it was suffering, better be on his terms; it was not like he was going to starve in Oslo. One of the Kurdish twins had promised to put in a nice word at a restaurant where he used to work. Would have been nice to work, dish washing with less communication, he fantasized, not realizing his girl had stepped into the threshold watching him, "Oh, is it another Ronaldo documentary?" she asked, pointing at the TV.

"Hmm no," Teme shifted in his seat, knowing what came afterwards; the nagging.

"The same documentary. Boy, you got either a man crush on him or that guy must really inspire you."

"Man-crush, pmmmff," his face screwed in disgust. "He is the greatest player in the whole world, you know."

"Yeah, he might be. But he is too cocky, you know. A put off." She raised an open palm in the air to pronounce her claim. "He is just too overconfident. I don't like him."

"You think he cares about what you think? Besides, you are a nobody." A vicious unprecedented lash-out, he knew.

"Ooouch! You defending him, wonder if you would ever defend my honor like that when one of your friends talk about me." His comment really hurt her, like a stab on the side, a hard jab. She waited for him to continue. He knew the damage he caused, he avoided eye contact and remained glued to the TV.

"I watched his documentary too, you know?" Elise begun after deliberating on what to say to break the awkward ice. "And boy, his dedication and discipline is off the charts. That you could learn something from, you know. I guess you can afford to be that arrogant when you are that good. Because you know how much work you put into it."

"Yep!" He nodded without looking her way, impatiently waiting for her to leave for her schoolwork or whatever.

"He might teach you something too, sugar. Patience, hard work, and discipline is what got him to the top, you know."

"What do you know about football anyway? You watch one documentary and you are suddenly an expert, fuck," he snapped at her, throwing a cushion with venom against the wall.

"Fucking asshole, was just trying to make a conversation. Fucking grow up, will you?" Her tears were dying to burst out to the world. "I am just..." she broke off, fighting off her tears cupping and pinching her nose and mouth to somehow regain her composure. "Forget it," she said at last and begun to straighten her hair and sighed, trying to forget what just happened. She was flushing with anger but no need to start something and spoil her day. She grabbed her keys and purse, glanced at the mirror by the front door, and marched out, putting on her coat. She did not even want to look at him anymore. She screamed towards him, "Lock the doors on your way out," she paused for a second and no reply came before she slammed the door and flew down the flight of stairs. She was still raging. "Need a coffee perhaps, to cool off," she told herself. Why was he doing this to her? Torturing her. *'He was so sweet all night, charming, and all funny and then wakes up blank, soulless, heartless, stone cold fuck. Can't keep this up,'* she got to cut him loose as her friends and family unanimously advised, specifically her mother. He was dragging her down, sucking her energy. Elise started her car and drove of the driveway, tuning the radio for her favorite radio talk show to mellow her down. She was late for work anyway.

Chapter 23

It was at a birthday party thrown by some rich kid she knew in high school that destiny brought Teme into her life. She showed up tipsy from another pre-party with some girls as she often did on a binge back then.

The other campers welcomed her and some dug her laidback style. She felt at home already, taking her place next to two lookalike mohawked Africans in a corner sofa of the cramped living room. She looked around, her eyes searching for her next new love. Not many potentials, she noted. She saw one candidate walking back down the stairs into the corridor and smiling at her. Maybe the night had something to offer, she figured.

Booze overfilled the table in front of her. A half empty Absolut vodka bottle passed from hand to hand, filling up the plastic cups. A full Jägermeister bottle, a quarter of Bacardi, half a dozen sweating Mack beers, two opened red wine bottles, Zero Coke, bucket full of ice and a bag of peanuts scattered all over the table stood welcoming. Noticing her hesitation, one of the Mohawks poured vodka and cola in a plastic cup and extended to her, "Hey pretty girl, don't be so shy now."

"Thanks, that is sweet of you," she replied with an infectious flirting smile.

"The pretty face got a name?" added the other Mohawk.

"*Ja Jeg heter* Elise Marie Torbensen," and extended her hand as introduction.

"Nice to meet you, Marie Elise. They call me Sleazy and this is Mason," introduced the one sitting close to her while shaking her hand. He quickly added, "You new in town, right?"

"Ja. Just moved in town today," she lied while rocking from side to side with the rhythmic Azonto song from Ghana blasting from the giant speakers reverberating mysteriously from all sides.

The party bored her. She shot back one Jägermeister. *Loneliness in a crowd is the worst form of torture* she had read once on a book. It was killing her, was she unlovable? What was she missing? She glanced from one bouncing happy couple to the next. The eyes fall on the very thing the mind sorely missed to torture you even more.

She sighed and watched the good-looking chocolate man with a cute tiny nose and restless big beautiful eyes she loved. His crooked lips quivered when he talked while he pulled at his invisible beards. She was mesmerized by him. Licking his lips in a sexy manner that had already wetted her inside, he embraced every guy that walked past him but he barely nodded, leaning over the corridor's white wall. Throwing a quick line or two he would move on and never engage with a long conversation with anyone in particular. Most players craved the attention of the ladies, laughed, hugged, glanced, and winked towards the ladies, the smooth-talking and the comforting buttering lines were mostly for the display. And he smiled and winked at her before embracing yet another girl. Next to him was a quiet one she mostly avoided but had heard of a couple of times. The boy had one of those commanding eyes buried under thick questioning brows. He seemed to be respected by most. Girls paid him a lot of attention but he merely acknowledged them. He was either too cocky or gay, or maybe he just did not give a fuck but the guy had some dark force that put her off. The boy was definitely younger than his friends as well but did not seem to possess any of those player attributes all flaunt at will. He was just distant to everyone around him yet vigilant in some way. *Those mysterious types are the most fucked up* that her mother had warned her to stay away from as she analyzed. She kept her cool but she kept her eye on the player as well while sipping her second cup of vodka. Boredom setting in, she emptied one cup after the other. Time flew by along with her consciousness.

Sometime after one at night, numb but fearful she stumbled to the bathroom. It was all vague, the faces and the wall and the music was loud but fading. The walls moved. *Oh God,* she prayed to make it to the bathroom. She would lock herself in and fall asleep if need be. She fell right at the edge of the bathroom, somebody must have tripped her. But she had no energy to look up and see. She heard a giggle, perhaps it was directed at her. Uff all the hungry boys would have a feast on her, panic set in with thousands of violent scenes from movies coming to the fore. She gathered all the energy she had, humiliation was not in her mind at all, survival and salvaging the last bits of her dignity was all she wanted. She made it to the toilet. But there was somebody following her, she tried to push that person but he slid inside before she pushed the door and locked it with all she got. "Nooo," she barely protested. The face was a blur she could barely make out. A deafening noise rung in her head, constant beeping like an analogue old-school TV losing signal, she could barely stand still. Leaning on the porcelain white oval sink, she struggled to lift the faucet. She mumbled something inaudible even to her, willing her body to obey. She looked up to meet her reflection on the mirror above the sink. Her eyes could barely focus, but there was a shadow of a figure behind her, nibbling at her neck she could barely feel. Both his hands groped her breasts. Yet she was oblivious to it all as if it was happening to somebody else. But she finally managed to shove off the stranger off her back and leaned down, she felt her bowels moving up. She wanted to throw up but was afraid of losing consciousness afterwards. Instead, she opened the faucet and splashed cold water on her face. Her hands were cold, the water cold, and her face numb as if it had a metal coating. She looked up but her vision begun to get hazier, her mind was irresponsive and then she slipped.

She heard a giggle of excitement behind her. She then felt a hand reach and fumble for her crotch. She felt her pants being peeled of her in haste. Words of protest would not come out. Hasty hands lifted one thigh and a cold wrist wriggled its way past meek resistance to savagely penetrate her. She moaned, "No!" but to no avail as the fingers trashed between her. She was dry inside, his fingers burned. Elise was drifting in and out of consciousness by then. Unbeknown to her she was naked lying on the floor and the boy crouching behind her was half-naked, struggling to put on his condom. Her eyes shut again, about to drift off, when a savage knock awake her.

The bathroom door was nearly knocked off its hinges, someone was demanding to get in. "Open the fucking door!"

"Not today please," she begged to herself.

The boy finally opened the door. An argument ensued, "You fucking bitch ass!"

She passed out, the new voice was charging at the half-naked boy, who was protesting indignantly, "Look man, will let you in once I am done. I swear she was asking for it all night," begging to be left alone to finish his business. She then heard a loud smack and somebody falling onto the shower cabinet. A loud moan and then other voices entered the bathroom. She drifted away again.

When she woke up an hour later, she was alone in the bathroom, her head leaning on the wall behind a dirty clothes basket. Her underwear was put back on, the other way around. Her top was lopsided. Panic set in amid the splitting headache. She immediately felt her vagina. She was relieved. There was no fluid. She looked around, there was no sign of a used condom either. She felt no pain inside as well, thus meant she was spared. She bent down on to let her throbbing head rest on her knees, and she cried for fifteen minutes.

Then the door keys begun to move from the outside and the door slid open. She reached for her skinny jeans, trashing her feet to put them on in time. It was too late though. A figure stood on top of her. "You okay?" It was the voice again but she was relaxed, something about his inquiry assured her. She nodded without looking at him.

Barely restraining a sob, Elise mumbled, "I think I am cursed. Every time I fuck up, every little mistake, every minor lapse of judgment, and I get punished severely. I don't know what I did to deserve this."

"You will be all right, girl! You got away this time though." She looked at him, it was not a dream then, he had indeed fought the opportunistic lowlife of a player and saved her. She smiled at the thought of having a guardian angel. The last person she expected, the dark force with the mean reputation, whom she never would have thought to possess a tiny thread of morals in him, had come to her rescue.

"You want me to call you a taxi; can you make it home by yourself?"

She nodded, finally managing to zip her pants. She adjusted her top and rose to her feet, stumbling. He steadied her. She looked at him again, calm, stony but alert eyes were locked on her.

"Did you, hmmm, did you dress me after your friend tried to rape me?"

"Listen, first off he is not my friend! Second thing, nothing happened, okay. No one raped you. We all chilling, partying, and everybody is drunk. But all good, no talk of rape or police needed, you hear?" he reminded her firmly. She nodded, startled by his gravely tone.

She washed her face while he lit a cigarette and patiently waited behind her. Eyes firmly set on her reflection.

"Did all of you see me naked?" she asked, the shame of facing the rest of the party on her walk of shame to the taxi ringing in her mind.

Silence and a stare was a reply behind her but there was slight hint of a suppressed smile on his face.

He finally fidgeted in his stand to pronounce. "Listen, I got Johnny, you know him, right? He will drive you to your place. Will give him a call now." He reached for his phone, "You got some cash on you for the taxi?"

She nodded and quickly added, "It is a pirate taxi, is it not?"

"Yeah, got a problem with that?" he questioned, offended.

"No. No, it is cool." She dried her face with her top, ashamed at revealing her belly while doing so.

They walked out together, the party was receding, with most having left. The remaining ones barely paid attention to them. All faded and groggy. Some lying on the floor of the corridor. Some passed out on the sofa while other sipped and nodded to the beat in stupor. A few were still standing and dancing on the balcony smoked the last of the joints. Teme ushered her inside a room. Two drunk girls and a boy were passed out on the bed unnaturally. Teme almost slipped, stepping on the vomit by the door. Disgusted, he cussed and faced her. "Listen, stay here, will come and get you when the taxi arrives." He quickly slid out the door. She wanted to ask him a couple of questions and thank him but he was gone.

****

She had to wait for two weeks to talk to her guardian angel. When she finally ran into him in another day party at the balcony, with all his boys smoking cigarettes or whatever the funky smell it was she had no recollection of, she confronted him upfront.

"Why did you do that for me the other night?"

He just stared at her. Blank, disinterested, with a slight hint of irritation and conscious of who else might be overhearing their conversation. She understood it was challenging his manhood in public, so she pulled him to the side away from prying ears and eyes.

"Hey, answer me."

When he looked away, she waved her hands at his face to get his attention. That was a wrong move that instantly ticked him off. From cool zero to a steamy rage in a fraction of a second, his entire facial expression had transformed. A snare of an old man in place of the cocky, crocked smile of his. Those icy steel black eyes though were on fire. His nose twitching, he finally spoke, "Don't you ever do that, you hear, bitch?"

"Or else what you going to do, hit me huh?" she snapped back in his face, deep inside though her heart sunk in fear.

"No, I never hit women," and he walked away.

She caught up with him, putting her hand inside his jacket pocket. He broke his stride, annoyed.

132

"Leave me alone, will you?" But she was not put off as she had caught his bluff. Smiling defiantly, she stared back at him.

"What do you want from me?"

"Answer my question, why were you nice to me? Protecting me when I was down and out, and now you barely want to talk to me now?" Her face contorted. She studied his face for a hint.

Unsurprisingly, he looked away. Taking a reply. She knew then he was just a boy who bottled his feelings, all the good and the bad. She was not to let him leave, stopping him right on his track, standing his way, staring right into his eyes. Both her hands on his shoulders, she forced him to face her. "I just want to thank you, okay? Nobody has ever been that nice to me, ever." This time she was dead serious. Her face closed in on his, he was obliging that time around. Her lips connected to his gently. Sparks flew. He was responding as well. She kissed him again, passionately and longer. He returned the favor with his hands around her. Time stood still

They soon left the pool table and all the noisy clique. Hand in hand they walked across Young Torget along the statue-lined bridge and headed towards Grønnloka. Comfortable peaceful silence enveloping the couple. They both felt the bond right away. What a magical kiss it was. If kisses could change lives, that did it.

Later on sitting in a Starbucks sipping their café lattes, she asked again, "You still have not answered my question."

"What?" He was puzzled, thinking all was settled.

"Why did you save me?"

He answered her question with a question, "Why do you drink so much anyway? You know what's up when you are all faded like that with the crew. You all game."

"Yeah, that is why I asked you why was I not game for you then? Don't you find me attractive? Am I not hot for you?" She accentuated it with a raised finger and sway of the neck, like Hollywood actresses do whenever they seduce their victims. He smiled at her attempt.

"Seriously, are you gay?"

He was stunned. The smile froze like he was offended.

"Do I look like a faggot to you? Did you not feel anything when you kissed me?"

"Even if you are, it is not a problem, you know," she joked.

He did not find that amusing. "Whatever!" She reached out over the table for his hands. He quickly withdrew them out of her reach.

"I just want to say that I am glad you stood up for me. Am glad it was you. But listen as well…" she broke off, waiting until his wandering eyes met hers, "whatever you heard about me, partying and all it is not the real me. I drink sometimes. But I am not alcoholic or something. I party on the weekends and stuff." She wanted to add that she would stop drinking if it made him happy, but it was giving in too much right from the start, she figured, but she would!

His eyes studied her but his lips were tight sealed. She continued, "But been thinking these couple of days. I mean about you. The way you talked to me that night triggered something. And that kiss earlier even more."

Silence still on the other end. But she had gripped his attention, she was sure of that. She was amusing him even. "You were dead drunk though," he questioned her theory.

"Still, a girl knows," she broke him off. "It is a female intuition thing, and I listened to everything you said. Besides, I like you, okay? But no pressure, we can take it easy, okay?"

Silence! This was all unexpected to him, she noted. To her surprise he finally said in a measured calming voice, looking away towards the window, "I like you too, girl. And no stress, we got time."

The way he said it was when she started to fall for him. Despite all she heard about his tough reputation and his weird disturbing silent treatment, there was still a man she could count on, a boy she can invest in to be a proper man!

Some minor adjustment to the key theory maybe, she had thought then – '*It's not about the first impression of the key but how well the key stays in the lock.*'

As of Teme, his entire existence reminded her of an airport. Always in a rush. Ready for the next flight. Always vigilant. His apartment, despite making progress, was a sham. She did not think he was ready to move on his own. It was not the lack of taking responsibilities that scared her it was his lapses that cost him a lot. He was severely punished for his mistakes, like her. He was one of those marked people her mother always talked about. When they blossom, they were the most radiant and exuberant, and when they collapsed they were the most hideous and pungent. Either way they were conspicuous, thus an extra pressure for them to maintain. Teme had always been on survival mode. His shared apartment felt like a motel. Just the basics were enough for him. Two spoons and one fork. Two knives, two glasses, and two pans were all he needed for his culinary improvisation. One extra set of bedsheets she brought him as a gift and just one pillow set on his single-sized bed. Just a bathroom, utility room, and a balcony to share with another quiet

Norwegian kid, but somehow Teme failed miserably. She cringed seeing the dust piling up on a corner the few times she paid him a visit. Not wanting to start a fight she would keep a tight lip. Despite handling himself in the toughest streets or the desert from the impression and snippets of stories and heroics she picked of her man, he still was a baby to her, who needed cleaning up behind him.

Chapter 24

A couple of days later, Teme had booked an appointment with his psychologist for an emergency session to get some stuff off his chest. The nightmares had become more vivid and some details he had no recollection of were now being replayed in his dream. Was that even possible? While standing by the sliding door of the bus, with one eye on the ticket control trolls, he ran the list of questions to raise to his shrink. But then the nosy psychologist would start poking around for the details. Teme tried to figure a way to formulate the questions without the need to divulge into details. At his stop, he hopped off rehearsing his made-up story of a recurrent nightmare he would describe to the psychologist. Right when he was about to step into the building, he froze. The person standing in front of him on the way out had the same shock on his face as well.

"What the fuck you doing here?" snapped Teme at Toure.

The shock and mistrust still visible on his face, Toure blurted out, "You are seeing a shrink too?"

With a smile to hide his shame and embarrassment, Teme shrugged his shoulders a couple of times, "Just like you, bro." He quickly added though, "I thought shrinks were for pussies."

"I guess I am a pussy too," broke out Toure in an uncontrollable snicker that finally lightened the fury Teme felt momentarily. "Ya, you big pussy, I bet you cry your heart out inside like bitch. And front the gangster mask on us."

"Just like you, bro. We are on the same boat." They both broke into a loud giggle on the corridor that caught the attention of the receptionist. Indeed, they were on the same boat all the way to Europe, until they were rescued by that Italian Navy ship. The receptionist gave them a weary smile, a sort of reminder to keep it down.

"So you are on your way in, Killa?"

"Yeah."

An awkward silence ensued. Thousands of questions raging inside their minds. Both wondering what the other might have divulged to the shrink or if the shrink knew if they had known each other since Libya. Lots of unanswered questions as both stared and weighed each other. They eventually waved to each other in a weird manner like a gulf had suddenly appeared between them. Just two strangers, like the first time they met.

****

Teme raced to the shrink's office without being called in. The receptionist could barely look up to signal her protest when he burst in.

"What the fuck! So what were you up to then? Tell me how come you never said my best friend, the one I sure mentioned a couple of times, was doing here?" His eyes had the ice coldness about them. Pitch black laser-sharp focus all set upon her.

Her knees were shaking, underneath the table gratefully. Her face probably gave off her nervousness, she figured. She did not try to mask it with a smile. That would aggravate it even more. She waited for his rage to subside before raising a calming palm towards him, "Who are you talking about? I have no idea what you are referring to."

"Stop acting dumb. You think am a child? Some stupid kid you keep lying to. Of course, Toure, who just walked out of here."

"First off, no more of your tantrums in my office, you hear me? I am a professional psychologist and not your cousin or one of you buddies. I don't know your friends personally nor I have the right to share any of my other patients' information with you, just like I will never do to yours, you hear me?"

He was recoiling for a retort he had rehearsed and versed his thoughts in a foreign tongue on his way. And all the doubts and resentment he had about her was flushed in her face. *Bitch was good*, she threw him off with yet another psychological trick. That confidentiality rule was indeed her great escape. Wish he could use that code in the streets. But then how come Toure was surprised as he was when he ran into him? If she never told him about Toure, not even a single instant about his friend that means the same is true for Toure. Maybe this bitch could be trusted, he concluded. He smiled over having her worked up for a second, having ruffled her feathers for a bit. She was ashamed at having revealed her true personality. *Bitch was good fronting the shrink, impenetrable objectivity as she calls that flat face. But can't front for life, girl.* He owed her an apology but then *fuck it she is getting paid by the hour*. He looked

137

up again, that quick though her steel gentle composure was back on, the courteous Nordic smile plastered on her caramel face. She said in a soft, measured voice, "I apologize for raising my voice, that was truly unprofessional of me." He kept silent. But avoided her genuine apologetic look. For some unknown reason his instinct told him she was a great mother.

"You have every right to question and demand answers, but you as well need to address me with respect. But you have nothing to fear, if you wish I can make sure your sessions with you friend would never coincide. Or if you wish we could end our sessions, and you can seek for someone else to be assigned."

"No, no, the cover is blown already," he interrupted her but in a more calm, reconciling manner, "but one curious question, has he been coming for counseling for a while, I mean with you?"

"You know well I can't answer that question."

"Did not ask you about some juicy details," he protested.

"Like I said, all remains between me and him. I would not encourage you to ask him about it either. Let him have his counseling and you concentrate on yours."

"Ya, ya, okay, that confidentiality rule again." He gave up but with less belief he finally pleaded, "So I never ever came up in your sessions with him?"

"No, no, and No comments." She was defiant.

"I mean it never even slipped up?"

"Never, let's move on now!"

"Come on," his eyes were boring into hers like a lie detector machine, predatory like for tell-tale signs of any lie.

"Shall we begin our sessions now then?"

"Come on but you did know we were friends, didn't you? All along?"

Not a peep coming out even if he tortured this wicked bitch, he said to himself with an ounce more respect to her professionalism. "Yeah, we can now begin our session," he finally said with a smile and upstretched submissive gesture of his hands.

The shrink showed some slight clue of relief before rearranging the neatly folded files on her desk. Plucking out what was his, she placed the rest in the file cabinet under her desk. "Listen, I never said I was perfect. I never judged you. I am not trying to fix you; this is not a car garage, you are a person with issues. But I am a professional, always remember that."

"You made it an issue, not me," bellowed Teme accusatively.

"We all have issues, Teme, and we all need a hand, guidance so we can figure it by ourselves in the end. You need to open up though. I know what you are going to say… I don't need the details, just trying to help you connect the dots. Help to release the tangle, the knot in your past, so you can move on, otherwise I am not interested in your personal stuff. None of my business at all."

You know I even refer you as a case number, she wanted to add but held back, that would definitely freak him out even more. "My concern is your wellbeing, okay?"

He nodded trying to decipher the professional bullshit from the genuine concern. For the first time he felt that motherly subtle concern look on her face ever since he started seeing her. Indeed, there was a heart behind that wall. *'Damn, maybe this bitch cares,'* thought Teme. But still it might be a slip up. Just to get another bite of that sensibility out of her, he snapped, "What do you know about what I am going through or what I been through? Huh? You are just some spoiled Norwegian chic who knows nothing about pain, real pain, I mean the one that lasts for days. What do you know about starving for days, when a crumb of bread becomes a distant memory or you forget what a real food tastes or smells like? Hmmm! What do you know about dying and rising from the dead and then almost dying again while your friends never rise back and just rot beside you. Hmm, tell me?" He glared.

She was taken aback. But was ready for this tirade this time.

"I never said I have experienced everything you did. What you have gone through at such a young age breaks my heart as a mother and as any human. But now that you survived, you deserve to hope and have a better present and future."

She wanted to recount all the hardship she had lived though, the cloudy teenage years she had persevered through, the numbing painful past stinging her at every step; she wanted to tell him all the sacrifices at such a young age she had paid and all the challenges she had to go through to get to where she was. She wanted to tell him how it would only make him stronger if he made it through the rough patch he was stuck in but *'Keep it cool, stay pro this is not about you,'* she reminded herself. Instead, she cleared her throat and said, "So let's clear the air if we are to continue our sessions, dear. For one thing, I was not born here and you know nothing about my life to assume I had it all, a posh, perfect life as you put it. Second thing, we have the same skin color; mine might be a tad lighter than you but in this world you are sadly either black or white, no in between! So it is not that hard for you to imagine the challenges I faced as a black person like yourself."

Wow, a sort of recognition stare followed. He realized at once what he had suspected all along. All he needed was a confirmation, indeed she had a rough time growing up, but damn he had thought ordinary white people problem perhaps. He had assumed she was second or third generation migrant, maybe even a half-caste Norwegian with an affluent background. But that look, the hard knock graduates glimpse said it all. She was one of them, one who started from the bottom and broke through the ranks against the odds. It was not about the color but the experience, and she looked to him as an African for the very first time. But that glimpse also revealed what had been gnawing him all along. She most definitely knew what he went through but not only that, she related to it as well. It was just his instinct to detect a dark dormant sorrow like a buried treasure hunter.

****

After the feisty session he had the sudden cravings for some burger anywhere. He took the next bus number 20 to Majorstuen. He dropped by McDonald's across the metro station. He ordered a double Mac burger with bacon and cheese deal.

Munching his burger, snapping his fries in a causal mode, Teme looked out the town, his work was late shift. He was in no mood to show up to work and listen to some orders today. Drying his hands on a napkin, he took his phone and wrote the simple message and called in sick. Instant reply came for a speedy recovery from his immediate boss. With a smile Teme dived on his burger. That shrink though had him going. She almost had him but bam, he got through her skin and reversed the role for a minute. Got her all wimpy and confessing about how hard it was growing up. "Fuck that!" he mumbled to himself. *What the fuck she knows about hardship*? But thumbs up to his instincts. Maybe he should consider himself becoming a detective. Like the ones on CSI or he could become a badass cop like Denzel. Interrogating crooks, they would be spilling their guts under his pressure. Silent pressure, he imagined himself just staring at a suspect, just drilling him and then asking unrelated questions to catch them off guard and then never lightening up. Ha-ha that would be fine, Teme entertained himself watching trams and buses, people and bikes invade his vision from all direction across the square. He finished off his burger and left, looking left and right.

Always take caution, you never know who you run into! With the mind occupied for now with that detective episode and who else, the macho smooth Teme Killa as the star, he was rolling, patrolling. He decided to head off, play some pool, buy some drinks, and kick it with his clique today. Just chill, *fuck responsibilities*. The rent was due as well, *fuck it too*! In the back of his mind though, he was plotting scenarios on how best to confront Toure without compromising his story.

****

Understanding the historical significance along with the roles of the omnipresent parties at play was essential. The hierarchy was dictated by desperation of the times and roles were reversed. Despite the passage of time, once blood was spilled, vengeance remained in the back burner of the collective consciousness, just waiting to be triggered by some incident or manufactured as an excuse to profit with clean conscience.

Ever since her involvement with the likes of Teme and Toure, her perception and imagination had expanded to reading materials written about the regions involved. The same drama was played all over again. Apart from technology, people had been bought and sold like cattle for centuries. Andalucian women, spoils of war and wandering Europeans like the character of Voltaire's classic novel Candid were paraded for sale in the Mediterranean lands, then sold and resold from one human trafficker to the next. It was just acceptable way of life back then. West African slave trade was well-documented, distorted yet well imprinted in the psyche of every human on earth. Though not widely taught and depicted in movies, the East African slave trade was massive, stretching along the coasts of Massawa, Mombasa, and Zanzibar, the trade was active for at least half a millennium. Mostly run by Turkish sultans, Arab traders, complacent or even collaborating local tribes, the trade was devastating yet profitable. Leafing through Turkish personal accounts of the human trade of centuries gone by, it was remarkable how vicious and cyclic human nature could be. Young boys stolen or sold were castrated and shipped to the Arabian Peninsula rich families as eunuchs. It had gone on for centuries, uninterrupted.

Both the slave trade on the Libyan coasts and the Horn of Africa was put on hold by the brutal colonial power of Italy. One of the few positives of European invasion. However, it was the forced conscription of natives into Italian army that entangled the natives of the three Italian colonies into a vicious bloody cycle of inconvenient codependence.

Used as a buffer during the colonialists' attempt to squash all resistance, they had inadvertently became the front of the brutality.

Thus it was not the first time East Africans from the Horn crossed the Sahara, nor flooded the Libyan coastline. Nor never the first time the Libyans took to arms, even the passive Italians got involved in the plot. Just roles reversed, the setting remained, the hunted became the hunter, the colonialists became the humanitarian saving their face to make up for the past exploits. Vengeance and guilt in play, the complex web of violence was entangled even more with more blood spilt. How she had wished to break it down to both of them, that the vicious cycle had been in play forever. That they were not the first, nor the last victim, but how?

Chapter 25

Later that evening, after a wild party at some of their peers who had seen through their education and graduated, Toure and Teme had avoided each but finally came face to face. Both had something to say to the other. Not jealousy but they both had felt the odd men out watching others in glee and euphoria. The two soon decided to retreat for a much-needed man-to-man talk. They walked in the summer night rain in silence as if all the guilt and sin from their past was being washed out clean by the heavenly powers.

Though exhausted, they could not sleep. Avoiding each other's eyes, they talked about the wild party and the chicks before the empty conversation regressed into an uncomfortable deadly silence once they arrived home. Then suddenly, Teme decided to break the ice.

"Do you ever think about it? You know all we have seen, done, and were forced to do; you know it was just too much," fidgeting and scratching his forehead asked Teme almost in a hushed tone.

"We were boys, man. It is even too much for big men. So it is all normal that we talk to shrinks and all. It helps process shit like she said, but did you know her…?"

Teme broke in, "Yeah man, but it fucks you up, you know?" It came all in hot flashes in his mind.

"Yeah man, but it was not by choice. It was forced, so don't mean a thing," Toure shrugged, avoiding Teme's intense eyes. Always studying him. His eyes were worse than those Arab torturers.

Teme wondered if they would ever raise the subject unguarded without the induced state of ganja again. It was now or never, "You ever get weirded out when you are with some other guys, sometimes you know thinking about what happened and all?"

After long considerate minutes deliberating with intent all the pros and cons of continuing the subject in his young tired mind, he mumbled in reply, "I was never enjoying it then, you know, when that fuck…" he broke down and stifled a sudden sob. "I just closed my eyes and thought about something else. You were not enjoying it, were you?"

Teme was stunned and pissed. "Fuck no, man, but it confuses you, you know."

"I know."

"Why did I come when it happened?"

After a long silence, "It is normal, man. The shrink said during penetration, even rape, it happens. She said even when doctors are testing your asshole. That is natural even when you are not into it. Even after it happens though, it does not change who you are." As calm as his voice was his eyes were watering up. Silence ensued as they exchanged the blunt. Intoxicated but lucid, they both processed their conversation. Not often did they raise the subject.

"You get weirded out afterwards, you know when you see other guys naked, you know. Shit like taking a shower in the gym with other guys there makes me fucking nervous. But then I look at any naked man and I feel nothing. I even went to this gay bar once, just you know to see how they are and act. But I knew I was not into it. It is not me."

Toure shrugged. "I avoid that scenario."

"Look, all I know is I like pussy. What happened was an accident, just forget it. Why you got to think about it, man? Uff!" Toure was suddenly in a distress. The wall had given in.

"Forget it? Am I the one who confessed everything to the fucking psychologist? To a government employer." Teme was by then glaring down at the shrinking Toure. "To a fucking total stranger? You big pussy telling me to drop it, we are just talking."

A sudden fact was revealed to Teme out of the blues, he had never seen Toure with another girl. He sure talked a lot about chicks, like all of them. But never pursued a girl. Something was up with that, infuriating him even more. Enraged, he lit another cigarette. His shaking hands barely obliging

"Okay, but it helps, man. Talking to the shrink about it. It makes sense, that psychology stuff clears the cloud, man. Besides, I only told her about me being abused, nothing else, relax."

"Still, I can't believe you told that woman about it."

Toure just shrugged, avoiding the raging red eyes of his friend and shook his head, a tear drop escaped his eyes. He quickly buried his face in his arched elbow to wipe it off.

The intermittent bout of uncomfortable silence amid the intense exchanges was becoming unbearable. Both vanished in a black hole of sorrow.

"You know there are plenty of people like us who are living through this shit like us."

"What the fuck are you talking about?" Teme was billowing in rage, "Forget that shrink bullshit. What the fuck I care about others? What you want to join a club, now to talk about what happened to you to a group every Sunday? Get a hug, a group cry-it-out session? How do you feel, tell me about it? Tell me, is that what you want to do?" Toure's head was still buried in his hands, no response coming, yet paying attention to every word."

"You know I was thinking about ways to kill that motherfucker slowly. That fuck, I think about killing him every day, you know?" at last blurted out Teme what he always wanted to say in a cool voice.

"You know, it is funny but there are plenty of guys thinking exactly the same about us. You know, thinking of killing us. For them we were the worst as we were one of them."

"It's not the same." Teme dismissed the notion at once. "First thing, we were forced just following orders. Second thing, we did not kill anyone nor did what the sick fuck did to everybody out there. We," his voice quivered before continuing, "he was enjoying it, man. We were just scared to death. Everybody knew that."

"Not everybody, Teme. We know what it felt like because we have been on both sides. I hated you as much as I did with them at the start. Then you saved me, man. You did and you did not have to do it too." That brought a glint of hope in the dark eyes of Teme. Toure added quickly, "You know what fucks me though, some of the faces when we were ushering them to that underground pit for some beating. We were walking them to their graveyard. Burying them afterwards, their eyes still watch me, man, in my sleep. Those who survived I am terrified of running into. That sick fuck is the least I think of."

"No, my issue is him," Teme was adamant. "Even back then my mind was blank. All I was thinking about was escaping and killing him, man. He was the devil."

"Got to let it go, Killa. I see it in your eyes. The anger. Talk to that shrink about it, man, otherwise it will kill you from the inside. It helps, she won't say much. But it helps us process as she says, you know. They got this psychological theory about trauma…"

"Fuck you talking about…?" Teme burst to interrupt his friend. But Toure had regained that icy composure again and luckily, no longer reacted to his outbursts. Cool as ever, Toure glared back at him to instantly chill Teme back to his senses.

The dissatisfied and pissed Teme at losing the momentum stared back before blurting,

"You ever told her about us or me, man?" His eyes glared back with fire, studying his adversary's face for the degree of truth in the response.

"You know it don't work like that. I do mine and you do yours, man. Chill man, you got to let it go, man. You ever wondered why they were hard on breaking you down back then, man? You got this swag, you know this pride about you that you never can never hide even when you were hurting."

"What the fuck did you tell her then? Magic psycho hubla and you started spilling, ain't that a bitch! You miss your mama? Did she give you a hug too?"

"Yo chill. I did not say shit!" Toure protested, not liking where this confrontation was leading to.

"What else did you say then? Did you tell that they tied you up and rammed you in the ass and it felt so good?"

"No, no, stop it!" they were now all square facing each other. "I told her I was abused, yes. You know what she told me about victims' mixed feeling afterwards." Toure was back on the sofa. "Some punish themselves over the guilt. Some punish others as revenge, but they never heal so they keep doing it. Hurting others and the cycle continues. But it is never about pleasure, it is all pain."

"So you are saying you are the victim now, huh! First time you were a victim, like all of us. But then remember when you were laughing off others' pain, as they screamed in agony and fear, man. Just like I did. Did you tell her that too? That is what fucks me, man. It is maybe in us is what scares me. We were twisted from the start, and they just woke the evil in us, not made us, you know? Maybe that is why they chose us." Teme was at a brink of bursting into tears but choked it twice and held it back.

"Don't say that, man. It is just survival, man." Both hands covered his ears, it was just too painful to hear let alone consider it. "It was either that or suffer every day. The fucking beatings and the fear and the darkness, with hundreds of soon-to-die friends. The stench, the flies, and the cries, man." Tears dropped freely undisturbed on both cheeks this time as he continued, "We survived the violent scenes of Libya, survived the sinking boat and, man, we can survive this."

Yet the flashes of scenes came in too fast to shrink his mind at once. He felt a sudden splitting headache on its way, "You think? So why do you think of all the hundreds they chose us? And used us against our own kind? Why did they choose us unless they saw something, man? Game recognizes game, man. Evil same man. That is what fucks me and that I can never say to the shrink, feel me?"

"Teme, please let it go, it was survival." Toure had had enough of this conversation. "We were angry ourselves, you got to let it go." Toure begun shivering. Shaky hands fumbled through his back pocket for his weed bag. Supply was dwindling. Had enough for two blunts, he figured. And begun bussing himself to roll on with some dexterity.

Teme's eyes following the quick fingers of Toure and he almost whispered, "You know I thought about killing that fuck a lot. But I never had the chance. And he knew it too. He used to tease me about it. Like waiting for me at all times. I still think about him, sometimes I see him lifeless in the news or my dreams, and sometimes I want him to never die, just get badly injured. So he can suffer for a long time or until I get my chance to finish him off."

"Let it go, man. The anger will never heal the pain, it makes it worse."

"Look at the shrink boy talking!" snickered Teme. "You know what I am angry about, not what he did to us. It is what he made us do to others and then what we ended up doing without even being told to. With that fucking smirk watching we did what we did as if we enjoyed it." His blood boiled every time he spoke about that evil incarnate in the desert.

"You don't talk about that. I just want to forget it and let it go. Why you think I get faded every night?"

Teme was unforgiving. "You cry in the daytime to your shrink mommy and then smoke at night and then front like a real man. You fucking disgust me. You fucking faggot."

"We both faggots, remember?"

Deadly standoff ensued. Teme erupted finally, "You fucking son of a whore! Maybe you were asking for it, who knows? I never seen you with a fucking girl, anyway."

"Don't you ever talk about my mother like that again, man. Maybe some of us still have one, you know."

"Fucking cunt, I'll skin you off. I should have let them kill you right there in the desert." Teme threw up his hands and wrapped them both on the thick neck of Toure, pinning him to the wall. Toure obliged but his body was vigilant and tense to defend himself if things escalated. They held stares for a long, long minute, until Teme released his grip. He stepped back, holding his head in admission of guilt, "Sorry, man."

"Ain't nothing, bro. But you are losing it, psycho!" With that Toure left the room toward the kitchen to roll another blunt in peace.

****

The next day they woke up in that fuzzy, dreamy state of marijuana hangover. They barely looked at each other nor said much. Like a long-time married couple, they went their ways avoiding each other. Teme had his shower, ate some crunchy muesli with sour milk for breakfast, while Toure rolled yet another fat one and high as a motherfucker was glued to his Xbox plugged on his giant TV screen. Teme left for work after mumbling, "See you," towards a non-responsive Toure. It sure will be long time until the dust settled and the two would talk to one another eye to eye again. But the past they share was a bond too tight to ignore, regardless of how painful it was. Toure was the only one who knew what was eating him inside.

****

Chapter 26

From the first time the two of them met in the desert, on different side of the spectrum, Toure was terrified of Teme. He was as brutal and curt in his ways as the rest of the captors. He had the air of authority about him, by then he had ascended into ranks with some locals even under him; his word was final in that warehouse in Bani Walid. Any dissent was met with flogging with a hand-carved stick he often carried in person when escorting the prisoners, unlike the others who kicked and punched them. Teme acted like a veteran militant with no empathy. There was no sign of his young age in the way he carried himself. But unlike the other older militants, who fraternized and played with their captives, Teme kept his distance. Not just with them but even when he was among his compatriots, he was a recluse. And that intrigued Toure, and he was all set to impress the young guard for earning some favors. After relentless few days of effort and some resistance, Toure finally made the impression on Teme, and soon he was delegated a few routines like food distribution and being loyal emissary to Teme in relaying orders to the captors in French, Arabic, and English. His loyalty soon elevated him from the class of prisoners. He gained some freedom and wandered within the compound and was better fed. He, indeed, had to work his way up to earn the trust of the other militants, but it never would have happened had it not been for Teme endorsing him and vouching for him. Had it not been for him, deemed worthless and penniless, Toure was disposable goods and would have been dead and buried in an unmarked mass grave in the desert he at times used to dig for other victims. Perhaps he would have had his organs harvested or been tortured to death for just the thrill of it as often it happened whenever the militants faced setbacks in the battlefields, their humanity plummeted among their subjects.

Why did Teme beat himself crazy with the shit that happened Toure did not know? He sure did make good things than bad but he never paid attention to it. They all fucked up but not with choice, reckoned Toure. But it was not the guilt that ate Toure inside, it was more of what he had seen repeatedly with indifference all the atrocities on a daily basis that showed up in his dreams, magnified and more vivid than they had happened in real life. Almost like the dead were coming back to reenact their final episodes... Toure shuddered every time he thought about it. It was those thoughts he openly shared with his psychologist. Through her, he had been able to put things in perspective. Sure, there were some moments that still confused him, every man that did evil things to him or others had somebody doing the exact same thing to them, at some point or the other. Like the shrink said, it ran in cycles. The only way to break the cycle is to forgive and never forget, she had said. Teme had been brutal to him in the beginning, but then he had been his savior as well. Scarface, in turn, who was equivocally brutal in his ways toward everyone, had specially enjoyed tormenting and breaking Teme's resolve. Ironically, Scarface cowering and all timid towards his superiors was a rare sighting but reassuring in some way, now that he looked at it in retrospect. He had seen the pain and hatred Scarface had for his superior on one occasion. It was the same feeling everyone had about him. Everybody out there was following orders. A cycle of pain and fear was all that was. Trapped in a cell of tormented souls, nothing but pain could be a common ground. But he was not sure if Teme had been able to see it from a broader perspective.

But had it not been for Teme, he would not be alive right now. He bailed him a couple of times. Once from the trigger-happy fingers of Islamic militants and the second time in the Mediterranean Sea as their boat sunk. That scene was still fresh in his memory bank. When Toure had tired and almost gave up, beginning to sink, Teme had reached out yanked him into the makeshift raft of the boat's debris. They had drifted along for ten hours as their compatriot dreamers' heads disappeared one by one, sharks circling, one boat or ship teasingly appeared like a mirage in the open sea before disappearing into the distant sea that kissed the sky. Their voices hoarse from screaming for help, the fear and panic had long evaporated, with the hope replaced by a blank resigned look in their eyes. Death was in the air but for some reason, Teme did not give up, he had that fire burning in his eyes. Then moved in the cold night, blanketed by the darkness the only sound was the lapping of the ocean waves but somehow, they felt the heads disappearing one after the other into the deep belly of the ocean. They had drifted hanging onto the debris, sleep sneaking in like a shark from beneath; Toure had almost slipped a couple of times but

Teme was wide awake and steady right beside him all along. He kept whispering in his ears, courageous words that lifted him up and to never give up, that they were close. There was even a second when he cracked a joke, "I can smell a McDonald's burger nearby," that had brought a smile amid the cold sea shivers. What a long night it was, but his mind was remarkably blank, he recalled it as one suspended awkward moment. The spark in Teme's eyes never died until they were picked up by the giant Italian coastguard boat patrolling the waters at dawn the next day. Less than two dozen had made it that night. Toure did not care what others thought of Teme, for him he was the ultimate hero and true survivor.

Chapter 27

A couple of days later, Teme rushed to the metro line, to head to Elise. There was a suppressed hint of panic in her voice when she called him, "We need to talk in person was all she said in a weird trembling voice." What could be so alarming, he ran thousands of scenarios in his head. He sure had pushed her too far over the edge, it would not surprise him if she called it quits on them. In fact, he was on survival mode, contemplating how he would cope without her. He had come all this way this far, he convinced himself. Deep inside though the fear of losing her might destroy him. Like a loose thread keeping him sane in these turbulent times, it sure would be tough. His crew were just a distraction. Kicking it with them looking for trouble until God knows when, he questioned catching up in time the line to the west side.

He took a seat next to a fidgeting old white man. The way he dashed through gap right before the gliding doors closed, panting for breath, collapsing on the nearest available seat, must have alarmed the old man. *'They always assume the worst of us anyway,'* he thought. Running the list of all his misdemeanors, he figured maybe the man was right to be nervous. He smiled at his own conclusion, which further drew a tense glance from the old man. That was the reason he enjoyed living on the east side. Since the white folks were almost outnumbered, they kept their prejudices in check. But on the west side the condescending look away, grabbing their purses too close, or checking for their valuables every now and then infuriated him at times, regardless of how hard he brushed it off. Torturing the man into further discomfort, Teme snickered all by himself like a lunatic and kept a wild eye on the old man. On the next stop at the central station, the man scurried to find another seat away from him. In his place a white thick lady reluctantly sat in front him. Teme lost interest in her, his mind racing back to Elise, *what could be the drama that was cooking in her place?*

On the fourth stop at National Theatre, the line going on the opposite direction grabbed his attention on his vigilant scanning mode. The preacher he looked up to with a woman, not for the first time with that intimate lock of eyes; Teme felt betrayed. It was a different woman every time he saw the preacher with. No one could indeed be trusted. They were all liars, just words about the good deeds, otherwise every one of them out there pretending to be good were crooked, he concluded in a fit of rage. Even worse, living in denial and deceiving others. What was even worse was people like him, blinded by their own burden, seeking the advice of these fake righteous souls for guidance. *Fuck them all*. Teme was raging. Even fuck that psychologist, he concluded, having already decided to skip his next session without notice. *Keep it all to yourself and you will always be safe.*

****

Elise looked pale. That was not a good sign, he thought, the moment he walked into her flat. With those pink sweatpants that accentuated her figure and the white t-shirt with a bear picture, cuddling a pillow like she was constipating, she awaited his arrival. Taking off his shoes, he timidly joined her on the sofa. His nerves tight-knotted. He was fearing the worst. Teme no longer felt panic. It was just self-preserving strategy of embracing bad news gracefully, as numb as a painful blow to the guts with a chin up.

"I was sick, you know; I was not feeling well of late, right?"

He nodded, trying to free his hands from the tight clutches of Elise.

"And I went to the doctor for a check-up."

What is it HIV, cancer? Girl just throw it at me, can't take it anymore! the voice within screamed while maintaining a cool composure.

"And don't worry, everything is fine." She must have read his worry; she waited for a long moment before finally saying, "But I am pregnant, six weeks."

Teme was stunned. He was not expecting that.

Expecting that kind of reaction or lack of any reaction, Elise tried to reassure him,

"I will take care of it, relax."

"What, ahhhh, what about the pills you were taking?"

Pensively fighting back tears and shuddering over the lack of support or any show of compassion for that matter, realizing she was all alone, a high-pitch cry betrayed her. Shuddering in front of a boy-

153

man with no emotions broke her. Accusations now of all times. Was it her fault? She never skipped on the pills, it was just fate.

"No, babe, you know I take the pills on a regular basis. Sometimes the pills don't work."

"But we, I mean I can't…" he pulled away from her grasp and put up that defensive wall she would never scale.

"I know. You think I want to have a baby now? Are you serious? You think I fucking want a baby now? Sacrifice my future and my studies to have a baby by another baby?" She regretted the moment she said it.

Scuff of a grunt followed by a shake of the head was the response.

"I still have many weeks to decide. You know abortion. It is my body, I decide, you know; this is not Africa, I don't need your permission."

Teme was in no mood for a discussion or an argument. He was suddenly hit by a splitting headache. His mind was just blank. Too much in his head, yet it felt heavy and empty at the same time. This sure would sink in and hurt, like it often did. But the very thought of his being a father had never occurred to him nor ever featured in his wildest fantasy.

"You should have seen the picture from the ultrasound. You know like there is a little person made by me and you growing inside of me."

He was in no way going to let his imagination picture that. No way, he switched off, her words bouncing of his ears like a foreign language.

Wiping off streaming tears, Elise reached out to hug the irresponsive stiff figure standing in front of her. A fucking stone-cold animal, selfish, not once had he even asked how she was feeling. How it had affected her well-being, what was she going to tell her mother?

"I know we have not planned it but it is a gift, you know."

No response. Stiff as a mummy with a nauseating headache, Teme was just weathering the storm dying to get out and get faded. '*Puff 99 problems but baby ain't one,*' he smiled at the thought. No way he was going to be a father.

"You want to see the pic of our baby, the ultrasound pic?"

After a momentary pause and careful deliberation, he calmly stated, "You have to take care of it. We are not ready!"

He pulled her arms off his shoulder and walked out. She threw a fit behind him. Throwing something that almost hit his head before he managed to sneak out. Her piercing cry as painful as it was to hear deterred not his flight. She would get over it for the better, for the best in fact, for both him and her. He was doing her a big favor, he consoled himself. He was not fit, though she would make a wonderful mother. It would destroy her to father a child by him. She was probably right, he was a baby!

Chapter 28

A week went by since he last had a talk with his girl. He had his own shit to figure out. No job offers so far, he was enjoying the end of the summer. Party wherever available. Anything to stop him from thinking.

After a binge of five days, the crew ended up in yet another party.

"Yo, been hearing something about your bitch," whispered Toure while dubbing to the hip-hop beat.

"What?" Teme's ears were perked despite his intoxication. The weed was indeed good.

"Yo, they been talking about who used to tap that ass and all." Toure nodded, staring deadly at him yet with some concern. "Thought it was just rumors but your girl used to get around a lot while she was in Tromsø town. Like with a lot of niggers out there."

"That was before I met her."

"Yaya, I know." Toure cut in getting closer to Teme's ear and whispered again.

"One of them dudes that goes by the name D was in town a couple of times, and she let him hit it is what I hear. Not sure but some niggers saw her leaving another dude's place together, real close like they, you know..." and let it trail, allowing Teme to finish it with his imagination.

Fury built in. Teme guzzled the vodka and juice, trying to connect the dots. When could it have happened? Were they fighting then? Or was she like the rest of them bitches, not trustworthy and all. Just could not trust anyone these days.

The music was good. Mike the Superfly DJ was in town from Trondheim, showing off his skills and tricks with his mixtapes. Everybody was chill as fuck while he mellowed into a numb state of uncool. After the recent baby drama, he hears of a news about her fucking other guys. She moved on that fast! Trish and Celeste, the two mixed girls from high school, loving the attention, were twerking in that tiny apartment, knowing all eyes were upon them.

Long had Teme a thing about Trish but never had he pursued it. His aloofness kind of drew some of them, it scared some of them as well. His explosive reputation indeed did not help. He had heard some chicks called him the psycho behind his back. But now watching Trish with her tight mini flex dress swaying and twerking in front of him, exposing her light caramel thick thighs was a delight. He suddenly wanted her. He got up with a swag; his crew cheering him up. The two Kurds sitting close to each other as always in their identical outfits on the sofa bed, Toure's cronies sitting by the table, the DJ sitting on the windowpane playing with his iPod playlist and whatever he was doing, lost in his music. The rest though watched the two girls teasing and twerking for their audience, and now Teme stuck like a fried burger meat grinding the willing Trish, suddenly the rage he felt earlier was gone. *Fuck that bitch!* he declared and grabbed the slithering sexy Trish by the waist and moved along, bump and grind.

The party went on through the evening, until the place was packed. Familiar faces dropped by. Teme dazed passed on the joint with merely a puff. He was faded by then. The beat sound different, Trish sitting on his lap, his other hand caressing her soft big-toned thighs Teme sang along to Weeknd and Future's 'Low Life'. *Shit, should have been in the US. Would have been a proper gangster there. With the life I had, I sure would cut it,* he contemplated to himself. Drifting once again to his fantasy land, where he would make it in the cutthroat underground world of New York or ATL or LA to rise in crime and grime all the way to the top. How many conversations had he had with all the big names, Jay Z and 50 and all. The newbies all showed him love and respect in that fantasy land. At times he would be baller, at times a rapper, or just a common gangster running the street to cause havoc in the city all day. Trish brought him back from his dream with a kiss and a whisper, "You think too much, you know?"

He smiled and just stared at her. She was sexy, more than most girls he knew, but shallow as fuck, he told himself. He said nothing though and just kissed her passionately. In the meantime the rest of the boys were catching up with the latest gossip on the hip-hop world, who got beef and who got dope or duped and all that. Mike the DJ, the self-appointed expert, gave his analysis on who is hot and who is not. Most agreed, none dared to face off the DJ. "Migos got the game on lock, I tell you," he was repeating to a resounding yeah!

The music blazing, joints and drinks passed around, all faded they stumbled their way across the lobby, dissing and hissing. Trish clinging tightly to his side, they took the bus from Tøyen till Grønnloka. They strolled about Løkka for the word, the hotspot for the night. The downside to the city of Oslo was their age severely limited their options of a nightclub. They tried a couple of places 21, Memphis, and a couple of bars. The stretch was yet to fill in. The music too mellow and the fucking guards too restricting. His phone rang a couple of times, but he knew it was her, *that fucking slut*. He ignored her. She kept calling, he put his phone on silent. Trish noticed, she knew his girl but did not bring it up. Perhaps they slut together, who knew, Teme did not give a shit. Let everybody fuck each other. "The music is too slow in this bar," he complained to his crew. Besides, they were low in cash. Sharing the four beer glasses among the bunch in a dead pub irritated him. Toure tried to hustle but came away with none. The Kurds were having an off day, and most started playing with their phones, taking selfies and lying their asses off on Messenger and snap. Finally, the two new girls, white girls he knew in high school, got the word there was a party in Storo but they needed to bring some drinks or some weed to get in. Toure and the two Kurds ran off to fix the joints to last them the night while Teme swapped saliva and sweat with the lovely Trish. They were all over each other by then.

In Storo, the place was packed. Most with older college-looking boys, sausage fest who ogled when they walked in with five women. The inside was packed, so they made it to the garden and sat by a broken dusty table and a slab for a chair, facing two drunk blondes arguing or conversing or whatever. Teme was in the fuck it all mode but somehow alert of his surroundings to jump if anything set off. They were indeed in the enemy territory. The music was all white people music but trendy. The light beer was suitable, and Trish was something else. In their corner suddenly it was tense and quiet. Teme noticed on the other side a certain crew were sizing them up as well. His crew was nervous and outnumbered. Toure whispered in his ears that one of the guys whose ass they whooped three weeks ago in west-side party was there. Teme nodded to reply in assurance to all. "If they try anything, we fuck them up good. Anything. But just don't start shit up. You hear?" All nodded in agreement, but he watched their relief and that pumped his adrenalin. He stared down their rivals. He zoomed on the bigger and older the better the challenge, the big guy held the stare. A blank dark stare flashing on Teme's eyes. The guy flinched first, giggling to look over his crew and say something like *you see that little kid*. But Teme measured him, he was just a punk. He would have him for lunch any day. He waited once again until they held the stare, and that time Teme spat on the ground viciously. Sending some standing between the two tense crews scampering back inside. Teme's crew was all cocky at once. The enemy was ready as well. But not all of them.

Soon the tension was resolved with a pep talk by the owner of the house, "Come on, guys. Let's keep it cool! Let's just have fun. Hey, Killa, come on let's just party. Home alone, parents out of town, no need for trouble here." All good, the party continued. The incident inflamed Trish. His phone vibrated again and again. He ignored it. Let that bitch suffer. Back inside DJ Mike Superfly took over and the twerking ensued.

After midnight, after many missed calls and dozens of messages, the phone went quiet. He read a few of them. *Have I done anything wrong?*

Will you just say something, anything?
Are you okay? Okay, don't say anything, just tell me you are okay, so I could get some sleep. We are still cool! Just come home.

He pulled Trish before anybody snatched her off his grasp and took her to the bathroom upstairs to the protest of the owner. Wow, wow, the chubby white boy stood in his way along the corridor, no go zone, parents, bla bla bla; Teme pushed him aside. He did not remember what color the bathroom was, once they were in they got down to business. He tore off her top, panties while she worked on his jeans. They could not wait for long; the buildup and foreplay had been going for ages as he shoved his hard lingham inside her with her thighs resting on his strained arms. No protection and no protest from her either. Just live for the moment. A couple of hooks, sighs and moans, scratch on his back of her long nails, nibble and bite on his earlobes, he kept going but he felt his knees bucking not after too long. She begged him not to stop, but he was not in control. His strokes slowed and he squirted his juice inside with one final hard hook that went deeper, drew a deeper moan. His knees buckled as they both slid to the floor panting. She was not done as she kept riding, pinning him to the warm bathroom tiles. She was beautiful, no question, he admired the firm breasts bouncing on top of him, her snapping neck rolled around until it froze, her body clenching, tensing, she went quiet for the first time. Peaceful almost then erupted, spasm like shivers running through her, sighing and breathing hard, she finally collapsed on top of him.

"Oh baby!" she screamed. Long, long after he was done. '*Women*,' he thought. At that instant though the face of Elise flashed in his memory on how after every sexual encounter she would look at him in gratitude as if she was doing it for his sake, as a sort of duty used to give him chills. But who knew she might do those favors to a lot of niggers. Rage and every dark thought erupted within. Trish must have sensed it as she quickly stood up and begun gathering her clothes, avoiding his glare. "You all right?" he asked casually.

She had that look of somebody delivering terrible news but she replied, "Yeah," and hurried, putting back her clothes. Admiring her figure maybe for the last time, Teme lit a cigarette and puffed the smoke towards her. She did not even look up. Reapplying her make-up and her hair over the bathroom mirror, Trish asked with a worried tone, "You fuck raw all the time?"

Teme wanted her to suffer for a little while as he hesitated before replying, "I only hit raw with the fine ones," and broke into a giggle.

He literally saw fear vanquishing her soul as she snapped, "I am not fucking playing, man. Are you... I mean are we safe?" She was almost in tears.

Still giggling, he waited until she looked his way, "Take a chill pill, girl. We good."

"You fucking psycho!" she must have mumbled before she stormed out.

They barely talked nor held hands afterwards downstairs as if the transaction was complete and all part. The music was blazing, the woofer nearly shaking the roof. "Ooow there is our playa!" His boys received him downstairs as if he was the rapstar on the way to his limo.

"Look at you, acting cool, as if nothing happened, hahaha!" Toure nudged him playfully.

"Yo sure waste no time, Killa boy!" tapped him the Kurd boys, one of them handing him a plastic cup full of a lethal cocktail punch. It stung like hell but was well-deserved, yet not good enough to wash off the tiny scrap of guilt he felt.

"Fuck that righteous bitch of yours. She thinks she is too good for us anyway," Toure said at last, seeing him all quiet. Everyone seemed to agree that Elise was no good for him. He was surprised they all hated her.

He knew she was reserved towards them but hatred, damn! Maybe they were right! "I drink to a beautiful night, boys," and he raised his plastic cup. They all cheerfully raised their drinks in unison, "This is to the loco, boys, wooo! And if anybody wants to fuck up our night, man, you chose the wrong day as well," Teme added in a chilly tone. His crew cracked up, some nervous looked away, others looked down but most just noted his intention and avoided him or his crew. From then on the remaining of the night was just a blur.

****

Chapter 29

"Yo, what's up!" a familiar soft voice of Toure inquired.

"Wagwan," replied the groggy Teme, with a throbbing hangover splitting his head.

"I called you like 25 times, why don't you pick up? You still asleep?"

"Yeah kind of… what? What's up?" His eyes were still closed.

"Shit, you tell me. After last night, ha-ha, you crazy motherfucker!"

"What do you mean? It was fun, huh," Teme was confused, trying to recollect the events of the night.

"Damn, man. You went all psycho at the Tøyen station, man!"

"Psycho?"

"Wow, you don't remember or you what they call that condition where you forget stuff?"

"Amnesia, hahaha yeah!" Teme then suddenly had a flash of smashing heads, blood, and gore, the scream and the punch in a sort of a blur. His knuckles were bruised too. Must have cracked the left ring finger as well, hurt like a bitch.

"Pfff, was crazy, man! You fucked up one of the boys real bad though, man." Toure was shaking his head, whispering on the phone, looking all paranoid on the tram heading away, as far as possible from their hang out. Toure finally jumped off at Bislett to head down to the gym Fitness Xpress to let off some steam and lay low.

"That bad. We all good?"

"No, man. Check the news. They already looking for us. The headlines, everybody talking about it. They even posted the CCTV footage on the website. People calling us savages and shit."

"That is cool."

They both cracked up.

"Anyway, Amit, you know one of the Kurd boys, has been busted. I don't think he will snitch on us. But you never know. They drop deportation shit on your face and you be dropping names like rain in Bergen all day, man."

Silence was on the other end.

"You there, right?" Toure was trying to hide his paranoia.

"Yeah, I am listening."

"Why, you scared?"

"Shit man, you know me." Teme giggled at that remark. "Not the first time to get locked up. After what we been through, what the fuck will these cupcake cops do to us here?"

"I hear you. You cold ass motherfucker. But they are thinking of making an example over us, bro. Even the politicians commenting on it on Fb and all the media, man. CCTV image is everywhere. Brace yourself. They will sure pick us up sooner or later."

"Don't sweat it, man."

"You crazy motherfucker. Ha-ha proud of you though, man. Went all psycho on them bitches, and we were all in. But you got to control yourself, man. Sometimes you just got to stop. You know, otherwise you delivered the message very well. It was worth it!"

"Yeah, man I am a reliable messenger, ha-ha," Teme slowly remembering the vicious episode in fragments.

"Ya, catch you later, man."

"If they don't catch us first," Teme replied, knowing Toure was scared shitless.

"Hahahah! Let me hit you later, am about to hit the gym, Killa."

"Aiight, man."

Teme hung up the phone and immediately checked the digital local newspaper on his phone. It was not hard to find, they finally made it to the front page. The most viewed article of the day.

Headline – Teenage hoodlums run amok in the train station in Tøyen. Two injured, one severe head trauma undergoing surgery. One suspect under custody. Five suspects on the run.

Chapter 30

Donning thick glasses and a baseball cap all the way down to his eyebrows, Teme finally stepped out of an old friend's apartment in Tøyen, not far from where he lived after three days laying low. Took the bus to Grønland. The police were hot on their heels. Toure had gone AWOL, most probably arrested. The other Kurdish twin, Toure's friend, and even Trish were also busted. The police had been to his apartment twice. He had switched off his phone, fearing they would track him. The last call he received was from Elise, who called him all the insults she could muster amid the crying. She said she knew he would end up that way. She had a gut feeling all day that he would be in trouble. Bullshit, he had been doing the same thing for a year now, nothing could change the situation. *Shit just happens!* An ululating police van swooped by, nearly driving the spirit out of his body. He felt like everyone was watching him. Like in one of those movies where a fugitive on the run in an action-packed drama all day. He should get some proper disguise, he mused to himself, imagining himself as Jeremy Renner in the Bourne Legacy thriller.

To get the down low on the events, he rushed towards a barbershop, where Toure used to come by down in Grønland, a stone throw away from the prison. He knew he was the butt of the joke or the hot topic through the silence the moment he walked in. A quick swipe at who came in and all had fallen quiet. Smiles disappeared nor did he bother to greet any one of them fuckers anyway. *'Fucking pawns, just clowning and stroking each other's ego to get by. Fucking pathetic!'* he roared inside his head, eyeballing every one of them, one by one. None held his infamous glare for far too long. *Fucking pussies,* he muttered under his breath. He nodded towards his boy, "Just a trim, my man." His barber nodded. Despite a faint protest, he snuck past the queue, and the barbershop bums lined up on the sprawling chairs meant for potential customers, loitering and staring at each other, then at their own reflection, before getting conscious of others' stares to deflect their wandering eyes by following the constant droning of the clippers running up and down nappy headed Africans as if it was the golf club lawn getting mowed. Teme almost laughed. It was often one of those sassy barbers that often instigated a rumor or a debate that energized the clique before wallowing into that redundant long ass boring silence. Funny thought how pathetic everybody was there to talk about other people, who either must have something going really right or something fucked up to conquer their unanimous attention. While mounting the barber chair like a presiding king, Hail, all eyes on him, he questioned what must have he done to own their attention. He hoped he was doing something right. Obviously, not all await your downfall!

"Your boys locked up, you heard, right?" the barber whispered in his ear.

Teme nodded, watching over the mirror as did everybody else. One of them probably called the cops on him, he figured but kept his cool.

The barber kept on trimming the hairline as Teme wallowed in eerie silence. He knew it, that silence was the calm before the storm. With the music from the TV and speakers blazing the cheery barbershop mood soon picked up as if nothing happened.

"You should lay low for a while. The cops were here asking for you," the barber notified him along casually.

Teme nodded.

"They got your pictures on TV and the newspaper. Today, you know," he whispered while dusting off his hair. "Not clear pics but everybody here knows it's you. Besides, one of your boys will eventually crack," applying the final touch with a pinch of gel, the barber brushed Teme's hair.

"It is what it is, man," he replied defiantly. All eyes were on him once again and most liked his reaction. So far no cop car showed up, a testimony to their loyalty, he figured.

Bumping shoulders his barber swatted off Teme from paying, "Your money no good, cuz, you need it."

"Stay safe," sounded another on his way out.

Bus 31 to Helsfyr showed up right when he stepped out. He got on and not a minute later a police car with blaring blue lights stopped in front of the barbershop. Two cops raced inside. Nobody had his back, it was every man for himself. It deflated him.

Chapter 31

He woke up from a deep sleep, a heavy one at that. He had the weirdest dream that lasted all night as well. He looked around and he was on his own in the flat in Grorud. Stretching from the sofa, he ran through the events of the night before. Card game, heavy smoke session, and a cocktail of drinks and drugs he never heard before that knocked him out cold. The owner of the flat was out as usual, running dope. Dude was a heavy runner. But who cared, he had been the only one to welcome him under the circumstances. That he would always be grateful for.

However, there was a disturbing dream that ran on a loop all night. Not the usual rerun of the desert and the ocean episodes. This one was different; it was very vague more symbolic in a sense. He felt like he was wide awake and alert of his movements while sound asleep. *Fucking weird!* In that dream he had this unimaginable pain in the stomach, right around the navel area. As if some alien creature living inside was trying to push its way out. But all was vague, even he himself did not sound or act like himself. There were no faces in the dream. But there were hands, a lot of hands, and blurry faces that faded in and out his vision. The crippling pain soon receded. Trying to compose and recount the dream while wide awake staring at the ceiling in the morning, Teme contemplated the meaning of it. But the first thought that popped to his mind the moment he woke up was Elise. Of course, Elise and the baby growing inside her womb. For some weird reason his instinct told him there was no longer a baby. Was she getting an abortion while he was dreaming? Had he become somehow psychic and telepathic? How did this dream thing work? He was all confused. There was just no time frame in it, just back and forth, how was that possible? Like the day before a vivid image of a long-forgotten past was replaying in his dream and now he could foresee the future or the present what was going on in his head? Where was a shrink when he needed one to interpret the dream? Even that fake preacher/lover would have been handy in deciphering the dream. But as of then he was on his own and the dream was the last thing he should be worried about. He was living a nightmare. He had been kicked out of his apartment by text. His property was in the storage of his former flatmate in two black garbage bags. His girl had finally given up on him. She cared for him, but she would not harbor a fugitive and she will only cooperate with him if he surrendered himself to the police. So much loving! His friends were total disappointments, none would answer his call. The cops had finally got his name and were looking all over the town for him. He was all on his own. And the only friend who was willing to let him stay with him was a hardcore criminal himself. Life was a two-edged sword at that moment. As of Elise, he had put her through enough, contacting her again would only prolong the torture. Let her be, he decided, hoping she came through untouched.

****

Chapter 32

He was back in Tøyen, without a disguise. Walking around the council towers where he once lived. He sat by Tøyen square bench overlooking the bustling cafés, the library, the boutiques, where people mind their own business. He was aware of the glances but he did not care. The rain was pelting it. Not even a raincoat to keep him of the autumn rain. The gloom was returning to town. Maybe it was a sign, he figured. While walking aimlessly behind the square past the council recreation center, familiar faces nodded at him; he skipped past the children park, envying the children running around wet oblivious to the rain. Slow pace his eyes scanned the murals of the council brick walls he barely paid attention to before. The pigeon birds in midflight and the squirrels, charming animals that were vibrant, he was not even paying attention to his surroundings as he often did. He was worn out. Staying on guard 24'7 to evade and prolong the inevitable. He had the craving to talk to someone who would just listen. He took out his phone and ran through the contact list. Not one he could think of right then. He switched it off back again. Could not trust that shrink either. She knew too damn much. That bitch probably had connected the dots and been playing with him all along. How could he face her, she probably would call the police on him, he contemplated. If it helped talking to that shrink, how come that Toure was still fucked, Teme questioned himself hard, replaying the image of his friend stoned on a daily basis. He was still the same, if not worse. '*Shit, what good was in talking to that shrink if you couldn't get your shit together?*'

Right when he reached Sommerfly Park, where they used to rule in the dark, a police van rolled past him. He was not even nervous. He was sure they had paid extra attention to him. He casually crossed the park, stepped inside the Kiwi store. From the inside, he glared out to see the van roll past. They were not into him, just paranoia. It was not like American movie, where an APB of his profile is broadcast to every police vehicle to be on the lookout. Or even his mean-looking photo displayed on every news channel, begging for the civilians to tip for the apprehension of a violent offender. *Reward for cooperation! Dangerous criminal on the run! Do not confront, just call 113!* What would be the bounty on him, he smiled at his own wild imagination. They had a CCTV image of him on the newspaper and once on TV, but they barely resembled him, the pictures were mostly distorted. He bought a pack of cigarettes just to buy enough time and went outside, cautiously. And all went down so quick, he was swarmed by uniformed police, all screaming at the top of their lungs to "Get on the ground!". The corner was sealed by two police vans, keeping the anxious locals away from the scene. The crowd was already gathering, curious and agitated at the show of force, with phones set for caption. All that drama for him. "Get on the ground now!" screamed one more cop as they closed in on him. Teme obliged. One giant cop pinned him to the ground while the other secured the cuffs. There was no protest nor any show of emotions.

The local youth, some of whom he knew, were cussing the police on top of their lungs, "Leave him alone, you fucking pigs! You come only to our neighborhood to arrest someone!"

"All this police to arrest one child!" added an older lady. But seeing the resigned, guilty look on Teme's face, it was a halfhearted protest. In fact, he was relieved it was over.

****

Chapter 33

Oslo prison was a stone throw away where he was. Arraigned and placed in a cell.

Back to D block for the routine registration and officially charged for the offenses he perpetrated. After 24 hours in a D block cell he was officially denied bail, and as a flight risk he was transferred to A block cell to await his court date. With his violent past, and his gang affiliation, he was in the isolation unit, where he spent most of his time in his own cell. Sentence was likely to be from four weeks to six months, his public defender had casually notified him. If he could play his cards right and show remorse and reform, he could get out five to six weeks tops, he figured.

After one week he was escorted to the courthouse. A brief court appearance, where he pleaded guilty, with a public defendant on hand. The prosecutors had built a formidable case on him. Witnesses and evidence of his repeated delinquency were presented. Even his friends had gave him up, rightfully so. Stoic Teme watched it all happen like a movie. Resigned his fate was behind bars, no need to fight. The legal procedure was quick. After some deliberation, the judge handed him 18 weeks of prison sentence, 6 months' probation, and a mandatory anger management course for an entire year.

****

I have been in worse. This is like a hotel. 18 weeks get away anytime of the year. Piece of cake, he had contemplated with a cockiness he had displayed since he was escorted to his prison cell. On A block. The stern dead green fish look of the humongous guards did not faze him either. He had scuffled with the guard right away to show his intent that he was not to be pushed around.

What the fuck do they know about prison anyway? he figured. After two other prison guards subdued him, he was escorted, rather carried, to his cell. For his troubles he was denied the luxury of being with the general population. With the sight of the neat and cozy 4×4 cell with a toilet and bathroom included. Teme winked and giggled at the indifferent elderly authoritative guard, who shoved him to his room like a bored real estate agent. The bed, the TV on the corner, a reading table by the window with a view of what a looked like the wooded hill behind his old hangout, what a perfect white vacation he much needed, he figured. He needed to get away to reflect anyway.

****

He settled in at once, flipping through the dozen or so local channels, leaning on his bed stand.

Three hours later, after his lunch was slid into his cell, a decent meal that is, boredom trickled in gradually. He muted the TV with a discovery channel of Alaskan snow hunting documentary on. Pacing back and forth, the cell suddenly felt smaller, the high walls seemed to have shrunk at once. He ran the image of the shipping metal container of a cell where a dozen African men was locked in, forgotten in the searing Saharan Desert heat, with no water and a leaking, reeking half of a barrel at the corner as the open sanitary zone, they were numb to the pungency of their own collective excrement and puke by then. Sweating profusely, the slump figures barely talked for hours, except for painful grunts and moans in the dark, day or night, shuffling and shifting bodies over the hot steel-covered floor with taters of clothing, blankets and pieces of shipping carton matted and glued to the surface with multiple layers of sweat, blood, and urine. The bugs that crawled on their bodies, the stinging flies that hopped off their lethargic dilapidated bodies, they barely fought back by their second week. After a while the darkness beds into the system, and soon they had begun to narrate their stories to one another, different cultures, same crime, being born black!

But the first week, still in a state of shock, decorum was collectively observed; they all waited. Time was not theirs to count. But the days they dreaded from the humidity and heat surge throughout the day, peaking in the midday, hard-boiling, slow-burning furnace grilling their inside, from the sporadic wind that blew the sand stirring like a cyclone inside their trap, then the heat peaked, and finally set the sun to their relief. And the night from momentary relief from a soothing calming cool breeze that builds up to a frost by dawn that they longed for the sun to set the frying pan of a cell back on fire again. Time was a foreign notion then, when all life was in someone's control, it was no use to keep account

171

of the time. The sporadic visits of their captors, the random beatings, they were numb to it by then. Silence in a crowd was a weird feeling. But silence observed in a space like his current cell was equally disturbing, figured Teme, unmuting the TV once again for staged drama to break the ice. Solitude back then was a sign of danger. Isolation was the precursor to torture and rape, thus none wanted to be left alone. Privacy was off the menu, their suffering in groups was necessary. But nothing would come of harm in a land of the law, he reminded himself, as he stopped the pacing and sat back on the edge of the bed facing the toilet.

Imagining a gangster in a solitary confinement was the theme of his escapade fantasies the first few days. As in those dark Libya days, his fantasy had saved him; he had remade the many movies he had seen in the past. The heroes and villains had been reconstructed to elevate his ego.

One minute he would replay the scenes from the prison break he used to indulge over and over while he was in the Sudan. That time he was Michael Scofield, convicted for a crime he never committed, plotting his intricate escape. Soon he would tire of the notion. After a while it would be another gangster movie, like one of them Guy Ritchie action-packed movies, where the hero underwent a chain of seismic hellish vicious cycle of violence to earn his freedom, annihilating anyone and everything that stood his way. Yeah, the setting indeed inspired such a superhero to spark his imagination in concocting action-packed scenes during tight situations to save the moment from the black hole of boredom. He imagined himself as the troubled but street-smart cocky hero, who was kidnapped by a brutal criminal organization that he had been evading for years. After subduing him, betrayed by a good friend, he found himself gagged and tied to a dinghy underground basement of an abandoned car factory. He cracked a smile with how the plot was thickening, but he would soon tire of it.

Teme was besieged with a craving for a smoke, but he knew better than to endure it until the next day when they were let out to buy one from the commissary. Back to his imaginary cinema, he knew he had to make some adjustment as the action hero in the torture cell in the car factory basement was unsuitable for the lavish prison comfort he found himself at that moment. He had to be original. It was handy distraction back in them Libya days to escape from the stifling heat and the endless violence displayed on a daily basis. The mind was a crazy, mysterious thing, like his shrink used to say. But back to his new plot, perhaps something relevant. Maybe a government national security case, where he was abducted from the street by two civilian security men and held in a safe house to retrieve sensitive material he was suspected to possess. Ha-ha, that sound better, he would cheer himself up. So now they had cameras on every corner of the room to record and analyze his every move, he was suspicious. Even the collect calls he made had been recorded, the emails he sent hacked, analyzed for any hidden messages. *Hope they do not start water boarding or African or worse, Arab-style interrogation,* he cracked up with that. It was good to at least to know he felt no fear for the very first time in his life while under the custody of the police. After all that happened to him, all the abuse he endured, his nerves had been calm so far. Maybe controlled exposure or simulation of a traumatic event could be a healing process, like his shrink said. Maybe that was why he felt so confused a while ago, silence and lack of action while under the police was disorienting. There was nothing to look forward to there when isolation ended, he would be fed on time, let outside on the gym or library on time, escorted and watched by stern-faced but respectable guards. He laughed out loud, shaking his head on how fucked up his mind was, that there had not been any surprises so far, he was disappointed in some way. *Man, the mind was a crazy thing indeed*, he mused. He was fucked, he knew it inside though. Teme would soon lapse to the action hero. He tried his best to come up with a complex conspiracy theory to thicken the plot but stalled. Maybe best to stick to what he knew, the ghetto action boy running rampage break and blow things to get by. He imagined himself plotting to escape the prison. Shawshank Redemption style, dig a centimeter at a time; no, that took too long. Prison Break style maybe, tattoos and everything. His imagination was on override, finally engaged, shutting the rest of his problems away and escaping until the cousin of death claimed him.

****

After two days though, the isolation got to him. His imagination no longer drifted away at will. Halted at the start, restlessness grew. Pacing around his cell in circles, he was edgy. The silence was bothersome. The occasional human sounds coming from the other cells, the clinging and gliding of the steel doors of the cells, the shuffling of the guards on the corridor brought a sense of relief, a recognition that he was not alone.

Being assigned in the restrictive unit in department C 1, he had surrendered the right to congregate with other inmates. But under supervision, he was allowed to participate in some activities, the gym, the library, and the workshops as soon as he completed his isolation punishment.

Read books that resonate with your experience. Plenty of books out there. Finding yourself in a book would allow you to reflect upon your own character. Sometimes you can see your probable future played out in one of the characters. You can alter the choices you make, learning from others, had said to him his shrink a while back. But his concentration was in disarray, barely finishing a page at every try of just one book that was available in his cell. The TV was even worse, replay of the same show, the commercial breaks that salivated his appetite for the outside world, the endless talk shows bored him even more. He was cracking up or was he, he questioned himself after barely days inside of his 18-week stay.

****

The next few days were even tougher. Long nights, sapping weird vivid dreams from the past were being replayed like a movie, at times simultaneously. Weird as they were, some even coincided with present events. Even his fantasy failed to rescue him from the longest bore he could ever imagine. The football star he had created in his young, innocent days had been all over the world, playing everyone one the field, winning every football tournament and awards, but now he could not conjure the scenes as he once could for an entire day at times. It all stalled.

Write a diary, only for yourself. Seeing the dark moments in your life on paper has a very therapeutic value. And it is only for yourself and never to be revealed. But the writing pad on the desk was still blank. He just did not trust himself with the ink as if some unknown forces might flood revelations on paper oblivious to him.

****

He was gradually out on supervised congregation with the general population. After a breakfast in a cafeteria, he was escorted to his cell. And later he would go to the gym, always supervised, shadowed. Bigger intimidating figures benched three-digit kilos. There were fewer inmates than he had anticipated in his block; he had imagined it would be a crowded rowdy gang-raping gangster prison. Most were older violent offenders but sullen and mostly independent inmates, there were barely any noted cliques to watch out for. With a friendly nod he greeted everyone but never made friends with other inmates. He could sense their reputation in their eyes, but no one was threatening to his surprise. He felt right at home at the gym, a place to shut off space and time. He had taken to running on the treadmill until sweat was dripping off his t-shirt while panting for breath. And then bodybuilding until he was escorted back to his cell. The gym was indeed reinvigorating. But once back in his cell, the silence and the vastness of the cell unsettled him even more. It was so different to what he was used to as prison. All he wanted to do in his cell was fall asleep, but the cousin of death never arrived on time.

****

After the first two weeks lapsed, he adjusted to the system. Institutionalized, he accepted his fate. His anger receded. He duly obliged with the routines and never talked back to the guards. He received a letter from his girl at last, which he read and reread at times like his bible. The letter had her scent; he sniffed like a dog while lying on his bunk at night. But above all, he had begun to reflect on his action, putting aside his ego and its excuses. He jotted down some of his thoughts and reflection on the pad. Mostly questions he would ponder and debate on his own, before fading to sleep. '*Is my life going to be like this forever? Will I ever be a grown mature adult with responsibility? Ever? Or will I just be a damaged child for the rest of my days?*'

****

The prison psychologist had interviewed him thoroughly. Evaluation, they called it; jotting down what he never said, he called it. He just did not understand the man. Like any fucking other doctor, noting down his thoughts when he remained silent. *What the fuck! Was he a fucking mind reader?*

For a change though, he had quit smoking. Edgy he was the first 24 hours but felt much better afterwards. A challenge he set himself in the art of self-discipline, as one inmate had told him, "You can measure your character by how well you control your urges."

Lying on his bed, staring at the fluorescent light on the wall above the gliding door, Teme often replayed the questions the police shrink pressed him on his blackouts. How often do they occur? When did they first happen? If he recalled anything that he did during the blackouts afterwards? What usually provoked him to the point where he blacked out? Was it an insult or a physical assault or the build-up of inner tension? But the more the questions, the more Teme was confused. If it was a blackout, it meant he remembered nothing from his point of view. Did he regret it? Did he take responsibility for his actions? Getting caught up in a moment was part of his life, but yes, he did regret some of it. Though he had said he did regret it to the cop, mostly he was indifferent to his action. And that thought scared him afterwards. The fact that he was at times possessed by some force, some power taking over. As of accountability, he was doing time and he was not bitching about it, he figured. But the more the cop drilled him, the more he dissected his actions and everything that preceded it. Instead of finding the answer, it allowed him to think about his decisions in life. And boy, he had plenty of time for it.

****

Chapter 34

Five weeks into his prison sentence, Elise finally showed up. He had been dying to see her, counting every minute since the day he received a message of her upcoming visit.

The moment they sat in front of each other in the visiting booth, with a guard a couple of meters away, he could not contain his excitement. Yet Teme could not even look her straight in the eye. Her hair looked a mess. He knew it was because of him. Puffed up eyes, dark circles around them. He suddenly realized he was so in love with her but felt pity for her as he had ruined her as well. Why could not he let her be in peace? She was probably worried sick about him. But the steel in him could not say it to her face.

After the usual exchange of pleasantries, she broke down the news he had missed out. Her abortion and the complications afterwards, his so-called friends free and wild once again after selling him out.

It was not the news of his boys that broke him. He had come to terms with that, it was his doing, he had it coming. But watching her, hearing how tough it had been after the abortion, he understood she struggled more than him, despite him being locked up.

"I am so sorry, babe. About everything. I am a fuck up!"

She shook her head, fighting tears that were on the precipice of her mascara-highlighted lashes. "No, stop it. What happened is done."

"So you okay now?" There was a real concern in his voice that brought a smile on her face.

"Yeah!" She grimaced. "I get by. Was tough but I am back to work and you know me." She broke into a melodic giggle.

"I know you." Then a long stare ensued. A lot being said without a word exchanged. Both their eyes were clouded with tears. Both fighting it back. After a long transcending glare, he finally asked, "So we cool? You forgive me?"

"You will serve your sentence when you get out," she said playfully, pushing him away while drying her tears with the tip of

177

her nails. Her mascara was running down her face, but she still looked beautiful, he noted.

"So what was his name? D? I hear he has been in town."

"Don't do this now, Teme. Not now. Not here." She waved her hands around to remind him that he was behind bars. "I never lied to you. I met him a couple of times, but I am over him. You are the only person I have been with ever since I met you. YOU are the only one I think about. The only one I will ever let to touch me and the only one I want to be with. If you do not believe me, it is your problem." Tears begun drop down her cherry-red cheeks. He wished to reach out and dry her tears and hug her but he restrained himself. His body was recently imprisoned. But his soul and spirit had long been in shackles, it was not new to him.

"So the baby was mine." He looked up.

"Yeah, stupid." She smiled, reaching her hands to gently place them on his. Always cold were his hands. "Besides, I did some thinking as well. It was not the right time for both of us. We got time."

Silence.

"Say something." She squeezed his hands.

"I mean, I am not ready, you know that. Look at me." He shrugged in defeat. "I am a fuck up. But I don't want to burden you as well. But if I ever was ready, it would mean the world to me to father a child by you."

She glowed at the reply. She wanted to hear those exact words. "Romance behind bars," she broke down in a silly giggle again. She let his hands go, took out a tissue and dried off her mascara. Still looking at him with those warm, loving eyes, she sighed, tugging her wool sweater he liked over her fingers.

His heart melted. "Love behind bars."

"So all the two weeks, you don't reply my calls. Never open the door when I come by your place. Went over your workplace, turns out you were fired. Then to see your face on the newspaper. The police manhunt? Kicked out of your apartment? Why did you not call me or ask for help?"

He sighed, eyes locked on the ground. He barely moved as he listened to her running the events of the past few weeks prior to his arrest, like it was a scene from an action movie.

"No comment, huh?" She nudged his shoulders playfully. "Typical you. I guess you were punishing me for the rumors you heard about me. Your boys, the gang don't even look at me. I never knew they hated me that much, you know. As if I was to blame. In the end, you were punishing yourself, babe. As for your boys, where are they now? Has any one of them visited you? Wrote to you? Called you? No! It's just you sitting in a prison cell, baby. Stop punishing yourself, please," she pleaded, squeezing both his hands. "Look at me, babe."

He hesitantly looked at her. Looked down again, ashamed, her teary red eyes full of pain and affection stinging his cold heart. "What do you want me to say? I am, hmmm, I am sorry, okay? I wish I could have done things differently, but I am here now. I will make it right, I promise."

"No, no, no! Do not apologize to me, babe. You are the one you are torturing yourself the most. Be at peace with yourself first, babe. Let it go whatever it is, the ghost you carry on your shoulder, babe."

A moment of silence ensued. They were holding hands but lost in their own worlds. She was studying him, imagining how it would be like to be all alone in prison. Him fantasizing with Elise and a beautiful baby boy sitting next to a grown, mature older version of Teme, one day in the farther future.

The prison guard, the long flat-faced freak, approached them cordially to notify that visitation hours shall conclude in five minutes.

"So how are you doing anyway?" fighting her tears posed Elise, counting down every second of what remained of her precious five minutes.

"Not bad. They got great food. Got a TV in my room. There is even a gym, a garden, and everything," snickered Teme, wretched though inside as he was about to be separated from his love for a couple more weeks. Promising himself to treat her better, he held her ever-warm soft hands tighter and stared deeper into her eyes. Perhaps she could read for herself what he felt about her.

"Stop fronting, man!" She pulled her hands away. "Why are you trying to be tough? You are not talking to your boys, it's me, babe."

"I am serious. It's a bit too quiet. Too quiet at times, but man, much better than I expected. The guards treat you okay. You got a whole lot of time to think but got TV and everything."

"Yeah, sounds good. So nobody harassing you or anything?"

"No, it's not like in the movies. Here it is very quiet. When we are allowed in the yard, you meet others, but I stay cool with everybody, you know?"

"Okay, babe, stay out of trouble, okay? I need you back in one piece."

"Sure, babe."

"So, nobody made you a bitch, I guess?" She smiled again fighting of her tears.

"Hahaha me somebody's bitch, fuck out of here, girl." He was about to go on a macho rant but seeing those beautiful eyes boring through his soul, leafing through the holes and pain of his darkness, he held back. Despite not uttering anything about his past, he had a hunch she knew everything about him. Maybe that was why he was so attached to her.

"Okay, tough guy. No booty tapping in here, okay, mister?"

"Ha-ha, jack off to your image in my head, girl, hahah." And he meant it as they held on each other's stare.

The guard came back and stood by the cubicle to see her off. '*Unfucking believable!*' she thought to herself, looking at the dead fish eyes of the guard. '*No sympathy whatsoever!*'

"And one more thing, I know about that slut Trish or Trash and you too. But let just put that behind us, okay? Fresh start when you get out!"

With that she got up and gave him a hug, a peek, and then moist kiss. She wanted to kiss him more but sensed agitated feet shifting behind her. "Use the time inside to reflect and think right. Gather positive energy, okay? Let go of all the negative vibe. Forget everyone, nobody cares about your reputation, okay? By the way, I have transferred some money for you to buy at the commissary store. Take care of yourself, okay?" They kissed and parted.

"Bye, babe…" he mumbled, "I love you." She heard it too and smiled, satisfied. He wanted to tell her more, about the diary he had been keeping, dripping dark and light thoughts in his cell. Even about her. But there will be time when he got out. The electric doors slid closed, and she disappeared behind yet another steel door separating the convicted criminals from the rest of the society.

Chapter 35

Not all birds with wings can fly, but those who belong in the open sky shall one day be set free, was a saying he would always remember as Teme was set free. But his release had terms and conditions to be met if his wings were to flutter free. First being he had to stay away from his crew; gang-related affiliation they called it. The second being to abstain from consuming any drugs until his parole period was completed, with a drug testing every two weeks to be performed at a specified clinic. The third to attend every two weeks a counseling session at a rehabilitation center, where a psychologist along with a police officer would make assessment of his behavioral progress to be reported, to his immediate probation officer. The fourth, he had to either go back to school or secure a regular job; no more chilling, in other words.

Right from prison, Teme did not even contemplate celebrating his freedom. As part of his probation term, his girl had arranged his temporary accommodation adequately. Had a place ready for him to move in with a student at a flat far from the city center in Torshov. The very third day out of the slum, once again through Elise's contact, he appeared on a job interview. He had never been focused and determined in his entire life as he showed up on the interview wearing a cream khaki pants, a shirt and a sweater. Geeky but gets the job done in first impression, despite his criminal records.

****

His occupational migration had finally landed him into the bakery business. It paid well and the hectic routine kept his mind from wandering away into his soul wilderness. Nordland Bakery was the biggest bread and pastry baking and distribution chain in the whole of Norway. Situated among the cluster of hangars of the industrial zone of the north-east end of Oslo, it monopolized the supply daily bread sold across the supermarkets and convenience stores. With orders from all the neighboring districts, the bakery operated 24 hours of the 6 days of a week to meet the excessive demand. The 45 different bread loaves and a two dozen pastries baked, packed, sorted for delivery on a daily basis offered unskilled laborers like Teme the chance to master the sophisticated machines involved in the packaging division. The demanding aspect of the job made it less attractive for the natives and drew mostly foreigners of all nationals to toil in shifts. Despite the deservedly handsome salary, full-time jobs were rarely available for many. As a systematical cost-effective measure, the owners rotated randomly around 50 part-time employers in three shifts, which motivated a competitive and effective atmosphere among the part-timers yearning to earn a full-time stay.

The routine was knee grating, sole blistering, spine wrecking, hand burning, and bruising affair that ended with a fat check. There was never a break, nor a time to lay back and gossip as the endless bread, fresh from the gigantic ovens, raced down the multiple conveyor belts that sloped down to the packing robot at full speed. Teme's job was to monitor that the machines were functioning properly, adjust the right size of the track that led to the mouth of the bagger, feed the automatic bagger receptors with the precise plastic or paper bag, make sure the breads never bunch on the overhead rail, place five each of every packed bread into plastic boxes at a blistering pace in a race against machine. Once the entire bread for the afternoon or evening was packed, which took around seven hours, they had to count the packed breads and sort to distribute the thousands of orders ready for transportation. With no room for error, the tense, hectic tasks kept Teme occupied in a trance-like mechanical state, to match the flawless machines and maintain the flow at all times.

It took just a bread to derail the smooth operation. One lousy loaf, lodged at a corner, could jam the conveyor rail from rotating and chaos would prevail to fuck up their day. The fresh-baked produce, fed automatically from the oven into the rail, when bunched up, stalled the furious bakers and the entire schedule up to delivery was delayed. He enjoyed it somehow, the constant whining of the bakers,

"You guys too slow. Pack faster."

"More bread coming, need to hurry up."

"You are jamming track number 5."

"The bread can't wait in the oven, fucking hurry up!" would they scream.

Then there was the impatient eyeballing of the truckers pacing and raging outside for their goods yet to be sorted out. "Come on. Got to beat the traffic."

"Jesus, do we have to do this all the time?"

"You lazy fuckers need to do your job faster!" Some even went further, "Will have to report you guys, the delays are costing me time and money!"

The disappointment of the returning nightshift over unfinished tasks to be handed over, the frenzy of man vs. machine, even though his knees, back, and soles begged to differ afterwards. Teme was grateful for the job as it spared him from thinking. By the time he clocked out, he was exhausted. No room for friends nor the luxury of hanging out. Little free time he had, he spent it with Elise, recharged his soul and then back to the grind.

****

A couple of weeks into the job, one particular Friday he felt like it was killing him. His feet had never felt heavy. The soles blistered and sore as if he had been on that distasteful long trek across the Sahara. He should definitely buy one of those rubber sole boots most of his coworkers strutted about with. His back, his knees, his head all felt like they were barely hanging by a thinning thread. His girl was right, there was no way he would last forever in the unskilled manpower market. He was just some replaceable statistic. Job migrating till how long though? Most of his colleagues he barely spoke to had either studies or a career path lined up on the side. But he had none! Like it happened everywhere, his shifts would abruptly be halved due to the emergence of a renowned rival into the local bread market. The bread wars made him uncertain; soon he might find himself once again on the lookout for another job. The migration never stopped for a wandering wonderer. *What the fuck was he to do, hustle?* It was a dead end as well as he had found out. *Crime and grime was only glorified in the movies. In real life, it was just a broke ass dangerous hobby,* had said an old timer in the slum while watching a gangster movie. *Hustling was romanticized on movies. In real life, you spend most of the time just chilling and sharing tiny crumbs of big-time hustlers' droppings. The small-time gangsters were the ones making a whole lot of noise yet made not much to get out. Fast money tasted good only at the start, like beginner's luck to the gambler. Lady luck blows your way when you are fresh to the game,* recalled Teme.

Like you are on a spell, no evil lurks around you, you enjoying life and chilling. Chilling and spending cash you never had. New friends and bitches pay more attention, your confidence skyrocketing, your swag contagious, close shave with the popo but always getting way; man, life feels so good in the beginning. Then bam, all closes in like a mist in the morning man. You start making enemies left and right, cops pick on you and eyeball you when they roll by, the paranoia and the hatred in the game, the vicious violence and the revenge cycle. Shit, you are trapped before you know it and you have become a career criminal! You feel me, youngie, we are all ruined. Addicted to it but you got a chance to change before it is too late, had said another old timer who seemed to give wise rational advice for a repeat offender. Now strutting alone, he had become a target. Wearing his work overalls proudly, recounting the positive constructive inputs from prison, he sat on the tram heading to Torshov. Yawning and sighing repeatedly, he thought about all the crazy fights he used to pick up almost everywhere. It was inevitable that he will run into some of the cliques he had messed with. They would have their revenge, it was part of the game! It was only time he reckoned while still keeping an eye over the sliding door of the tram at every stop or any unruly glares thrown his way. He might be out of the game but vigilant he would always be.

****

Even lately, he had made himself available for duty on weekends. As every weekend was a torture session. Flashbacks and temptations of all the good and bad times overall. Regardless, good or bad action was guaranteed, thus less time to think or reflect. There were times when nothing happened, they hunted in packs, looking for a kick to spark the day or night. But as of here and now, his girl was all he got. And that scared him even more that he has become way too dependable on her. She may have noticed, maybe even appreciate it even more, but she might soon get tired of it and leave him hanging like his fate. Boredom strangled him so tight that he failed to enjoy anything on his free time. Movies or his Xbox, an auto mode on his joystick had been the name of the game, until he got the call or the visit of his girl on his free time; the weekend was on another level. Speaking of which, he had to clean up, no wonder his girl was always reluctant to visit or spend the night. Filth personified, trash and crumbs littered everywhere.

Teme gave the place a descent brush up. Bed made. Table arranged. Dust and leftovers cleaned up. Rug vacuumed. As of the shared kitchen, bathroom, and living room, his clean freak flatmate had it under control. Boredom enveloped his mood once again. That short fuse was beginning to snap inside. As a consolation, he flipped his phone and logged on Facebook. He had been following of late some inspirational figures from hard knock backgrounds posting some deep philosophical stuff that made sense and tempered his senseless impulses. He clicked on Troubled Troubadour's page. There was a flurry of posts that attracted enormous feedback, mostly constructive. He leafed through the recent posts one by one, until his eyes landed on one post that garnered the least likes and comments. *What happened to the thrill and the kick, all just seems ordinary, numbed by the fanatic fantasy. Detach yourself from the need and one shall have peace, cult in desire and you will only see its manifestations. Illusion of what is advertised, the real pic will never be as good as the Instagram profile... reality is the ugly twin bitchy sister of my fantasy. But got to live with her regardless. #selfcontrol #nodrama* – a troubled troubadour.

He read the post again and again. Some of the words were a bit too sophisticated, but he had the gist of the message. Got to control the impulses by not wanting or something like that, Teme figured. It was easy saying than doing; *no wonder all them people giving advice are the one that probably needed it*. All of them were fucked up big-time losers in life anyway, Teme gesticulated, throwing his phone towards his bed.

****

Sighing and pacing around his bedroom, he knew it was going to be a fucking long night. He went to the living room and switched on the TV. He did not last a mere ten minutes as he was left pacing around the apartment. He finally said, "Fuck it," he got out once again aimless into the night. He hopped on the tram and headed to city. Hopped off at Brugata and guided by some power inside his feet, hit the pedals towards Grønland. Same vibe around the bridge, laidback old men and women sipping their drinks on the sprawling bars. Commuters scurrying in and out the metro entrance, and spread out corner boys selling their products. Acting all fidgety every time a potential customer hesitantly approached them. New faces though, Teme noted. Now all he needed was one long ass fat joint to put him into some dreamless deep sleep. It sure was a violation of his parole. *But fuck it, life is too short and some nights too fucking long!*

He scored his joint from a newbie, cocky as hell. His colleague kept watch just in case. None of them recognized Teme, to his disappointment. Even one was a bit disrespectful, hurrying him, "You buying or what?" but Teme held his cool, investigating the product like a CSI. An ululating police van raced past the bridge to unnerve him. He scored his dose without a fuss and hurried out of the vicinity. Looking left and right, before any further lapses and mighty temptations, he got back on the tram and headed back to his enclave. It was a hustle by itself, looking over his shoulder over some people he had roughed up in the past.

****

Smoking the joint on his balcony of his apartment drew the ire of his neighbor, who did not respond to Teme's exaggerated greetings. After a moment of awkward stares, the dude had walked away with that I don't need problems concerned look on his face. High as a fucking Arab, everything raced about him in an accelerated loop. Now, then, and yet to come met at the roundabout and drove in circles like kids on a playground, dazzling him. Even the music failed to relax him. He changed the dub hip-hop mix to roots reggae to simmer down his disjointed nerves. No help there either. He switched off his pc and played the local radio instead on his phone. After a song or two, the intermediate conversations between the guest and the radio DJ put him off, *Why the fuck did they have to yap over everything, just play the god damn music!* he snapped and switched to another channel. No luck either, some plucky sketchy radio advertisement followed one after the other. Another channel run the daily reportage. He gave up to lock his phone into silence. Sitting with his hands strapped to his chest in the middle of his yellowing sofa bed, he contemplated how long he would have to live this way. For some reason, his entire life ahead looked as gloomy and dim as the moment he wallowed in as if on a strait jacket. He closed his eyes and tried to fantasize about one of the imaginary alter egos as a timely escapade. Yet reality had a strong hold on his imagination, like a tangled leash to a dog on a heat. Restless, he sighed, the high was receding dangerously fast; he had to keep it going with another hit.

Making his way to the shared balcony, he switched his phone back on, wondering if he should holla one of his old friends for a

186

catch-up session. But then he was in no mood to engage in any sort of conversation. Besides, it was violating his probation terms. He had already broken one term, why not all? He contemplated but quickly squashed the thought. It was a solo chill mode then. *Rehabilitation was an individual struggle,* had said to him a repeat offender in prison. Besides, so much for friendship. They sure celebrated when he got out like he was a hero. *Fuck them all!* Even though it was all his action that led to his demise, his friends did not waste time in giving him up. His downfall was their wake-up call to get their shit together. A jolt of reality that shook up the crew. Toure had reinstated himself back to school, so did one of the twins. The other twin had secured a full-time job. Some had faded in the background as the game remained; their crew was replaced by a new younger clique who owned their spot. His reputation meant nothing to them. The whole point of it, life goes on. He was still stuck in a limbo state, all he got was Elise. It was probably the right decision to move to another neighborhood, where the temptation was out of reach. The drama reduced but isolation was very troubling.

After he had three hits, three long good ones, he was relieved, with a numbing effect taking over like morning mist. He had got back to smoking cigarettes again. So much for self-discipline. All of a sudden though the dark morbid thought of ending it all, this so-called hapless headless chicken bout of a life conjured vividly in his mind. Despite the agitation, the sulking, and oscillating between rage and anger, suicide thoughts rarely possessed his thoughts. If such notions indeed rented the penthouse of his mind, he was definitely assured of their manifestations one day. But death was not the issue. He would welcome it. He knew what she smelled, looked, felt, and sounded like. All overwhelming but then natural, assimilating to the ground. Decimated, disintegrated right in front of one's eye and gone. Dust to dust. The bloating, the grotesque discoloring, and oh God that pungency of a rotting maggoty flesh was just a bluff. As soon it shall be just bones. He pictured all the dead bodies he had encountered along the way. Vivid flashbacks of all the still and stiff figures that oddly stared back. What had been planned as the pathway to heaven and riches had indeed become the corridor of hell. He had witnessed people bleeding to death in his hands after being shot. He had literally felt the last breath, cold breath in that searing midday heat brush his neck before all had went still in the middle of nowhere. Shallow graves to fallen ones, and life continued. It was remarkable how people just die and the memory nearly deleted the details of their features. Watching their souls depart tainted the memory of the persons while they were alive. The Sahara Desert was indeed the hot bed of hell. That was the proper acquaintance to the brutal artist in death. Migrants his age left behind by smugglers in the Libyan Desert, the thinning crowd was dropping like flies. Water bottles drain long ago, dry and cracked lips barely moving, still humid thick air, hot breath blowing some fine sand on you face, it all came back to him. That first flash of death. That was where he got to know who and what death and life were; at times there was no line between them. When cruel ending of faces one had known for a while was a daily occurrence, one just missed the real lively thrill of being among the breathing.

There were days then he wished to bring it all to end, take some along for the ride to the shallow valley of no return, but sadly, he was just ushering others bound and gagged to their untimely departures. How heartless had they made him, or was he some cold heartless Killa as they called him, he questioned. Why did not he end it then? Teme sobbed, overwhelmed. Uncontrollable, he let it out for three long minutes, howling like a wounded coyote. Maybe his living was in a way to atone for his indecision or cowardice? How would he end if it should indeed end and is not worth proceeding with? Jump of this balcony? Jump into a moving underground metro track to be grinded by the train in front of a crowd? No, that would be a performance, too much drama and speculations, he reconsidered in a haze. *If you have to go, go quietly*, he told himself. Maybe after all was forgotten, somebody might run into his bloated frozen indistinguishable body somewhere in the ocean. Or he might feed himself to a pack of wolves. He then realized he was still standing on the shared balcony and mortified, sensed some moving shadow behind him. His flatmate must have seen him crying like a bitch, he figured. *Fuck,* he ostracized himself for displaying his vulnerable side. *Man up!* he screamed at himself. He rubbed his eyes dry with his sleeves, lit the roach and killed it. He was now properly faded. Better knock a couple of beers, maybe pop the two oxycodone pills he found in his bag, and sleep it off before his dark thoughts become a reality overnight. The mind is a scary thing, he thought to himself, casually walking to his room. Maybe best call it a night.

Chapter 36

Up and down it was life, days passed and days turn into another weekend. Same routine work and home, with less lapses. Teme woke up happy the following weekend; not happy but with less burden on his shoulders and chest, unlike some days. He indeed controlled his impulses and slept it off. Morning blues had long become his company. The doctor had diagnosed that maybe the lethargy was due to the lack of vitamin D or the iron mineral in his blood. Regardless of the omega 3 and vitamin tablets, Teme had always knew it was the hangover of the exerting nightmares of the night before, waking depleted bereft of energy. "Fuck it, today feels good," he repeated to himself, rubbing his morning hard bread. He longed for Elise. Her warm body next to his was often nice to wake up to. He made a lavish English breakfast Elise had shown him how to make with the sound track of Drake blasting from his speakers.

Dressed up to impress, he packed his gym bag and embarked for some much-needed flexing. Best take advantage of his mood, he figured. He smiled towards his roommate when he ran into him in the corridor. The dude barely replied. Teme courteously helped an elderly get into the elevator and hit the road. It was spring. The pretty ladies had started to show some skin, he noted, as much as he hated the winter longing for these sunny days made it more exciting. The tram came on time to his delight. Everything seemed to be going his way, fingers crossed.

At the gym, it was cardio time; 45 minutes sweating on the treadmill left him panting and sweating. Next up he took to the bench to flex his chest. Stretch to warm up and then he was set lifting half his body weight. Suddenly, his body tensed. At the corner of his eyes he picked up unnecessary company. It was two of them, the crew from Storo. Sure had been a while, he recalled one of them. He had sent him with stiches for trespassing in their territory. Now they eyed him closely. Benching with caution, he kept one eye on them. They were vigilant, with vengeance oozing from their eyes. These days he was more vulnerable, being on his own. All that fronting, tough talking, and bullshitting indeed had some consequence. He finished the bench and moved to back press. Being conscious of the intruders fucked up his focus. It was not like they were doing their thing either, their eyes were set all upon him. Casually, he made it to the changing room, skipped the shower, gathered his bag from the locker, and snuck out. *Puff, about time to switch my gym spot,* he reckoned. Footsteps speeding on the sidewalk towards the Bislett stadium tram stop, he looked over his shoulder. He was not followed. Just for a precaution he crossed the street with the red light still on.

On the tram back on his way home, Teme sighed, frustrated about how he would ever distance himself from his former life. The ticket patrol jumped in on the third stop to finally put a smile on his face. He had the monthly card, which he proudly displayed. Watching three other kids getting nabbed and arguing their cases to the adamant control freaks, Teme felt good about himself. He now would head home and make his lunch, head to work, maybe meet his girl later on.

Chapter 37

After a hectic afternoon shift at the bread factory, he headed straight to his girl's place in Røa. He showered and dined on the lavish three-course dinner she had made for them. Switching on the TV, he was hoping to watch Ronaldo decimate his opponents like he always did. The game was live on the sport channel Elise had ordered for his benefit. Elise came and joined him on the sofa after clearing the table. Glued to his chest, slithering like a snake every time he watched football to grab his attention, he knew what was coming. Instead, she reached out for the remote and pressed the mute button.

"Listen, I need to tell you something. Something about me."

Oh no, girl! Keep your secrets and I will keep mine, Teme was screaming in his head. Shit, what was his girl now playing psychological tricks now to get him to talk? His ever-skeptic eyes scanned her mood for a hint.

She cuddled closer to him. Lifted his limp but obliging hands around her like a blanket, rolling her eyes at his lack of romance, wondering when he will ever learn to be romantic. "Seriously, you need to learn some romance some compassion. Aaaggh!" she sighed playfully.

He smiled back, shaking his head. He gave her head a brush with his goatee-bearded chin. Her head planted to his chest like a stethoscope to his heart, she began, "You know we all got some stuff we go through. Some stuff that happened to us we never could tell. And we suffer inside on our own." She felt his body tensing. Caressing the hands embracing her, she looked up. The hawk eyes were upon her, fully focused.

"I was 14 when something happened. I never told anyone, you know. But something happened that ruined me for a long time." After a momentary pause, gathering her thoughts and catching her breath, "Someone I trusted took advantage of me. It took me a long time to forget it."

That look in her eyes said it all, it glued him, that long buried hallowing pain. He knew what she was about to say and loved her more for it. He reached out to hold her hand, tighter. Comforted, she buried her head into his chest. He readjusted his seat to accommodate her. She smiled, her tears swelling up fast. She did not try to dry her eyes, she just let them flow, the pain along with the mascara. She drew one deep breath after another to compose herself.

"You remember I told you about a crisis I had in my teenage years? You know about my identity and all?"

He nodded affirmatively, she looked down, playing with his zippers, but her mind was replaying some dark scenarios from the recess of her memory in a trance-like motion. "So I felt so out of place, misplaced, and unfit anywhere, you know. My mother would not let me reach out to my father's relatives. She was right in some ways, she was just protecting me. Besides, my father left us, not the other way. But I managed to locate one relative of my father residing in Norway. Allegedly a distant cousin of my father. I was excited, I felt like I discovered my own father again, you know. My black roots being discovered and no longer a mystery on the mirror, feel me?" Elise looked up, he was attentively listening while gently caressing her temple. She continued with her narration,

"Back then I found out this guy was living in Skien. Just outside of Oslo. It was some friend of mine who helped me track him down through her African contact. You know you Africans have a wide network. Everybody knows everybody. So I called him to confirm, and we talked for hours. He sounded like a nice guy. I was thrilled to have a relative who was black, and I wanted to meet him. He told me so many things about my father on the phone that made me laugh for days. After days of corresponding, he invited me to pay him a visit. He was still living in a refugee center then. He had a sad story as well, with his asylum case being rejected, that made me sad as well. Had a part-time job as a cleaner, so I hopped on a train one day, skipping school, and headed to Skien.

"He was waiting for me at the station. I cried and embraced him. I was very emotional. When I look back, I feel so stupid. How naïve and trusting I had been. He took me to a friend's house, where we could have more privacy. His friend had made some West African food for us to eat. But something about him was different from the man I was talking on the phone. On the phone he sounded interested to meet his relative and eager to know about me and eager to tell me stories about my hometown and my family line and all. But in person he was avoiding the subject. Changing the subject all the time. And he was younger than I expected. You know, I had this image of him in my mind that he looked somehow like my father in his younger days, you know from the only picture of him I have got. But this guy was shorter, stalky, and lighter skinned. But then in the excitement I was just dazzled by the African treat. The food, the music, the colorful African ceramics and sculpture adorning the house. His stories were funny. Then he brought some drinks. I told him I was only 14 almost 15, that it was not legal for me to drink. But he insisted, telling me it was okay among Africans to drink even if you are that young. That he started drinking while he was 11 and all. And you know, I had drunk before and at that age somebody offers you a drink you worship them." She looked up to catch Teme's attentive gaze upon her. "So we drank, and he started dancing with some African music playing loud. I was just digging it, felt myself reconnecting with my lost self. I joined him in the dance, I was awful. He took my hands and started to teach me to dance. Then after a couple of drinks, I was drunk. Almost passed out. Was it something he put in the drink? I don't know. But I did not remember much afterwards. I was almost in a dream state.

"I could feel him taking my clothes off, while I lay on the sofa and could not fight him off. I felt him inside me as well. It was painful at first, then I passed out. By the time I woke up it was late in the evening. My head was damp. Apparently, he had carried me to the bathroom and washed my head. He had clumsily put my clothes back and pretended like nothing happened. I was confused. He was rushing, telling me his friend's wife will come home soon, that she is a radical Christian and disapproved off teenagers partying in her place and all. It was a dream. I could barely stand or talk. I told him to leave me alone for a minute to use the toilet. I reached down and it was wet, blood and semen. He had washed me off but not all of it. I was shocked and still did not know what to do, who to tell? Had I lost my virginity? I was so confused that I had forgotten about my roots, my father or my relatives. All I wanted to do was just go home and crawl into my bed. I put my clothes back on, washed my face, readjusted my hair, and snuck out the door. The fucker did not even see me off to the station. He was on his phone, talking loud in a strange language before he waved me off.

"I was not even 15 and could not comprehend what was going on. I went home, my mind was total blank. My mother was worried sick. She had called me like a dozen times. Called all my friends and even the police. I did not even explain, I went straight to bed. The next couple of weeks were like blur. When it sunk in, I was furious at myself. Replaying all our conversations, how he had duped me and all, I was pissed at myself. But I did not tell anyone. I tried to call him many times, you know my so-called relative, but his number was out of service. I even paid the refugee center he supposedly lived a visit, but there was no sign of him. They said he had moved to Denmark after the police attempted to deport him in the middle of the night. I went to the police station several times but could not force myself to file a rape charge. The consequences were severe. You know, it would break my mother's heart. But that encounter fucked up my teenage years, my sexuality, and all afterwards." Elise let out a sigh of relief. Let her tears drain her puffy eyes, and she felt the heavy stone lifted off her chest.

She looked up to meet Teme's face, ice cold as ever, but his eyes had some degree of warmness, sympathy towards her. His embrace had tightened as well the longer her story dragged. He kissed her lips. She held the back of his head gently and kissed him back passionately. Soon they were tearing the clothes off each other, lips conjoined, eyes closed, hands trashing to peel each other's clothes off. They finally entangled, Teme gently slid Elise to the middle of the bed and started kissing and nibbling on her body, inch by inch; her moan was the loudest he had ever heard. Then he reluctantly spread her legs and kissed her clitoris, something she always begged for but the pleasure he had denied her repeatedly, claiming unnatural too-Western behavior. Once there he devoured her.

Soon he mounted her. They rocked to each other's rhythm for five beautiful minutes. He was lost inside her. Nothing mattered. Her warmth was all that was needed in his life. He was the one penetrating her physically but through her patience, warmth, honesty, beauty, and everything, she had penetrated his unworthy being deeper than he would ever imagine, he realized. Her conscience was free. She was glad to finally tell him, and she knew she did the right thing for their relationship. Her heart was flooded with pure love and no longer guilt or grudge while he was inside her. In fact, she was holding on to this moment, praying it would never last, she felt him deeper but closer and gentler than their previous many encounters. It felt like she was making love for the very first time. She felt like having proper consensual sex. She felt like a virgin. Elise moaned and sighed, scratching his back. Then she heard him loud and clear, "I love you more than anything in the world." Her mind was about to explode, processing it all was too much, before she exploded first and he followed and collapsed on top of her. A rarity that orgasm occurred in that sequence in their case, to their delight.

Resting her head on his chest, they enjoyed the comfortable silence that followed a beautiful moment of pleasure. She was playing with the hairs on his chest and lower abdomen while he caressed her back with one hand and one arched on the pillow behind his head. His mind was racing and pacing, contemplating which story he should tell her. Instead he asked, "Do you know where this fake relative of yours resides now?" In a chilling voice that shocked and thrilled her. Realizing that he would defend her honor regardless made her feel safe. She looked up and kissed him on the lips. He kissed her back and whispered, "I meant it earlier you know when I said I love you. I do, I really love you."

She whispered back, "I know." They both laughed at that after all the times she bugged him into saying the L word, she would not reciprocate his uttering when he at last did say it proud and loud and meant it!

****

Chapter 38

Back at the shrink office after a long time, just a casual drop by, she asked him a question he had long forgotten to consider after pleasantries were exchanged.

"What was your favorite subject at school?"

It has been a while. He yawned as if the question exhausted his energy. "Now I don't think it matters..." he trailed away, beginning to dismiss the direction of her inquiry.

"No. No. No," she protested. "What subject did you really like then? You enjoyed the lecture or even you found to be less boring when doing your assignments maybe."

"Ahhh, I enjoyed Math. I enjoy the mystery of numbers, you now." His face brightened up at once. "Algebra, you know, I was very good at solving equations. Sometimes I used to do them all night. Could not get some sleep until I found the solution." Nostalgic smile.

"Oh interesting, so you like the challenge. Not many people like math, you know. Including me."

He nodded but his mind was somewhere serene, perhaps within the world of numbers, lost amid equations and formulas that once thrilled him.

She wanted to press him more on it.

"How was your grade in math then?"

"Quite good actually. Teachers used to call me genius when I felt like it. Then sloppy when I was not. You see, you have to feel it with math. When it is fun, you concentrate better. When it becomes you know..." he was lost for the term.

"An obligation you switch off," she aided him.

"Yeah, exactly."

"What other subject did you enjoy?"

"History was cool as well. Language I learn quickly as well."

"Yeah, I noticed."

"My teacher said I was the fastest student she ever had in learning a language. English and Norwegian I learned very quick, both at the same time, you know. Problem was I sucked at doing my homework. I was only active in class."

"Oh super. I knew you were smart."

"Yeah." He smiled at the compliment. That boyish smile she liked about him was back for just a few seconds before it disappeared. From 100 to zero in a record time, his face assumed a grave look.

"You know I was so terrible in math at school," she desperately wanted to keep that young amber glowing, "I dreaded every lesson. Used to cheat on tests. It just never sunk in. I never understood geometry, algebra, or even calculus in college; it was just too sophisticated. Too complex for me. Arrrgh, I lost patience with it," she cringed, rolling her eyes and playfully choking herself.

He smiled at that. "It is that part I used to enjoy. You just think in numbers. Different possibilities and probabilities until you find the right fit. But no matter how hard it is, there is always the solution."

She mentally noted the equations he solved were symbolic for his optimism in his approach and mental strength, the never giving in will. But the more complex mystery his traumatic experience threw at him, the less his belief that all problems had indeed solutions.

"So if you are good at math, algebra, and geometry, why not pursue fields you can thrive in and enjoy? You know you are still young."

"Nooo." He shifted his feet, a sign of taking flight.

"Listen, Teme, you are still young. Your natural talent never disappears just because you quit school or have a tough period in your life. Remember, the other students had a headstart on you while you went through hell and back all over the desert and the ocean. And you still excelled. So, no reason you cannot get back to what you are best in."

His head was held down, avoiding her eyes. Resigned and defeated he looked regarding academic life.

"Besides, talent is like riding a bike. Once you learn how to ride a bike, you can never unlearn it. Even after 50 years, you get on a bike you still will ride the bike with no problems. The mind is a mystery, but it always remembers what you are good at. Just think about it, okay? Take your time and see your options. And whenever you are ready, get back to school and earn your badge. Why waste your talent?"

He looked up, listening to her words, praising him; her belief in him made him feel better. But still he saw no future in him going back to school.

"Many rebels like you always struggle with the system. But once they get their life together, they excel and dominate the very field they were born to fill. Who knows, maybe you were meant to become an engineer or some IT expert in coding and stuff; I have no idea what those guys do." They both laughed at that.

"But anyway, you have time, okay? Don't convince yourself it is done. You are just in a phase. Do not slam the door behind. You can always go back and pick up where you left off. Okay?"

He nodded.

"Come on, let me hear a resounding yes, I can, and yes, I will."

That boyish smile was back from ear to ear.

"So I understand you have been assigned a new psychologist in anger management sessions, am I right?" she continued.

"Yeah, I attend the session every two weeks."

"Good. Good for you. But my door is always for you. Anytime you want to talk to me, just call and make an appointment, okay?"

"Yeah, sure."

She felt like a family member. Perhaps one of the very few people in life whom he opened up to.

"How is your girlfriend? Are you guys still together?"

"Yeah, we are still together." She was glad to see his eyes brighten up with the very mention of his girlfriend.

"I think you will be heading off to work this afternoon, right?"

"Yeah, I will be going straight to work," he replied, looking at his watch

****

Chapter 39

That weekend, accompanied by an older couple she knew at work, Elise and Teme checked in the giant cruise ship, Color Line for a two-day round trip to Kiel in Germany from Vika dock. Through her mother's connection she had been able to convince the parole office to grant Teme the permission to travel. After evaluating Teme's progress and the guarantee of an influential connection vouching for him the officer relented, under strict terms, to grant him a pass for a weekend. The cruise ship was bigger than Teme had imagined. The lobby was bigger than many of the five-star hotels he had slaved for a living. Their passports checked, they were handed their card keys. While Elise conversed with her colleagues, who did them a huge favor since unaccompanied minors under the age 21 were not allowed on board, Teme admired the floating mall. The red-carpeted main deck with bars, cafés, restaurants, and gift shops made one forget they were on a ship once you stepped inside.

On the ninth floor the couple split to their cabin as the two lovebirds entered theirs. A cozy, tiny room with a queen-size bed, a TV, fridge, and a tiny washing closet.

The ship soon embarked. One barely felt the movement though. His nerves had dissipated at last. Elise, who had been studying him, asked, "You nervous, babe?"

"No, no, I am good. Just excited," he replied, flipping through the channels on the TV.

"We can go down to the duty-free shop, do some shopping, beers and stuff, and then we will join my colleagues for late lunch or dinner at the restaurant later, okay babe?"

"Yeah, that sounds nice."

Elise joined him on the bed. Felt a bit hard for her taste. Feeling the pillowcase under her head, she was satisfied. But regardless of how rough the bed, as long as she had Teme by her side, she never minded any source of discomfort.

****

Teme sat alongside Elise and a hundred other dinners at the sprawling two-story restaurant on the sixth floor with a glamorous view of the sunset. With the cruise ship parting the sea in a silent powerful surge ahead, deeper and away from any distant city, his mind was on a distant memory of a similar trip. He sure had come a long way! The elaborate service took him by surprise. He was the only dark-skinned person in the entire row after row of tables. They were sitting in the middle like an amphitheater; he felt like everyone's eyes were planted on him, scrutinizing him, wondering what he was doing? He felt so out of place. The waiters danced around them in their rehearsed flawless manner. Orders placed in elaborate fashion, the hushed conversations, the measured tabled etiquettes, the almost synchronized fork movements, and controlled laughter; he felt like he was in a movie, like a titanic scene or something. '*Oh God, let me not have a nervous night with the knife and fork,*' he begged inside his head. Just a surreal moment trying to relate that instant with the last time he was on a ship. That crammed boat that set out for Europe felt like from another lifetime. The couple and Elise, engrossed with their inside jokes and stories, barely paid attention to him after several attempts trying to engage him into it.

"The appetizer is wonderful, isn't it?" he would just nod affirmative and keep his eyes on the plate.

"Enjoying this spectacular view and a wonderful company after a hectic year at work, cheers everyone?" The lady raised her glass, to which all drank to. The chatty lady kept asking him questions, "Which country do you come from? Where is it really, East or West Africa? How long have you been here?" He kept his answers curt and simple and avoided eye contact throughout the dinner ordeal. But the lady was relentless as she never let go of the mike and went on narrating a story about her wonderful wild African excursion. "The Serengeti lions and the Massai tribe, wow! We had so much fun in Africa. The people were poor, but they were so happy you know…" Elise occasionally searched for his hand under the table and squeezed it. He smiled whenever she inquired with those fruity eyes of her if he was okay.

After dinner and a few drinks, they all retreated to their cabins. Hand in hand they entered their cabin. In silence, they took off their clothes and collapsed on the bed.

****

After contemplating and deliberating for hours that night, cuddling and enjoying each other's warmth, Teme decided to tell Elise everything. "Listen, girl, got a lot to tell you about me. Don't interrupt me, will tell you everything, okay?" She nodded as if she had anticipated the moment. In a monotonous voice, without skipping a detail, he poured it out. Elise in silence, her tears rolling down her cheeks, uninterrupted listened. He told her everything from his childhood all the way to the Sudan and Libya.

****

In retrospect, interpolating the missing pieces with all the news coverage and the documentaries he had watched, he portrayed the last phase of the episode in a vivid manner. "It happened too fast. Everywhere you look was chaos. But an opportunity for us," Teme narrated, retracing his memory.

The armed tribal alliance with the government suddenly shifted the power along the coast. The militants at last were on the back foot, retreating and ambushing enemies on every corner. Large swaths of desert land were lost, just pockets of remotely accessible desert played out to their advantage in keeping the advancing alliance in check. The fighter jets from the neighboring Egypt were bombing the living hell out of their hideouts daily. Casualties were mounting, panic had set in. The oil revenues were hit hard, thus they heavily relied upon kidnapping, human smuggling operations. The chaos was a blessing in disguise as the Scarface and most of the battle-experienced fighters were deployed in the frontline, with depleted but heavily armed units left in charge of trafficking. Teme was soon promoted down the port to oversee the order at the departure point. He was all set, bidding his time, professional and brutal on the ground though; he was on the final stage to embark onto a peaceful adventure in Europe.

One unlikely man helped him on the final lap to ensure he made it to the boat trip. It was a conflicting moment for all the general perception he had of the people down there. It restored his faith in humanity; despite the harsh conditions, not all of them were alike. Despite the circumstances, there were always some good men. When loading the migrants on the flimsy, creaky old fishing boat, knowing the deteriorating conditions on the ground, a couple of the militants had blended in among the 185 paid customers under the guise of darkness. Once the boat anchored off, Teme and Toure had swam and jumped on the boat. The captain, known for his brutality, had looked away, giving them the final break they so much needed; he could have ordered their execution for treason right on the spot but did not. They paid back the favor in maintaining order inside the deck of the boat.

While under the deck the stench of the deck was unbearable, the diesel smoke that engulfed the packed space, the piss and the puke, the hushed prayers in different languages, the cries and grunts of pressed bodies, the cussing and scuffles they had to quell, the rocking of the boat that nearly split the wooden boat in pieces, it was inevitable as they heard on repeated occasions the creaking of the over-packed boat growing. The constant churning of the motor, which one terrified former mechanic swore was an improvised old truck motor, drew groans and prayers among the mostly male Africans that were under the deck, the Arabs and the women and children were stationed above the deck…

"It was a horrible journey. But I had a feeling along that I would make it alive. Just a gut feeling. Even when the boat capsized, I had no doubt. Many died, you know. That happened that fast." He snapped his fingers for further effect. "And holding on to the raft, we were picked up. Me and Toure, along with the remaining few by the giant coast guard boat. The struggle continued in Italy. We were living in the streets, surviving for a couple of months; the missionary church was our only savior. Then we moved on to France, the same fate living in the streets of Paris. Begging and collecting charity. It went all the way. That was how we I got here, babe. I would understand if you do not want to be with me anymore after this." He avoided her eyes in shame.

She surprisingly showed support, understanding, and forgiveness. Her heart broke. She cupped his crestfallen face with both hands and forced him to look her straight in the eyes. "It is not in you. Whatever monster you think of yourself, it is not you. I know, trust me, okay? No doubt, I have no doubt about it. I can feel your heart, babe. If you were a monster, you and me would never have happened. Don't you remember how you made an impression on me? No one, I mean none, ohh babe, come on. Look at me. You would not have stood up for me, a stranger you don't know, you would have allowed that maniac to have his way. Even though you were drunk, you defended me. What happened in the desert was beyond you. Out of your control. Not your will, with a gun to a head most people would even kill their own parents, okay baby?"

Her reaction astounded him. Her belief in him made him insecure about himself, even more as if she knew him better than he knew his own self. His love and respect for her grew out of proportion at an instant, beyond possible as he ever assumed any human could ever feel about another. The saying I love you so much it hurts, he felt it. Beautiful pain inside that eventually dissipated and spread like a warm wave inside like fever, so comforting. He reached out for her face with both hands, caressing her cheekbones and circled his fingers around her beautiful eyes like a sight impaired person would for facial recognition, to register every minute detail of the moment. Unbeknown to him, streaks of warm tears were rushing down his cheeks. She wanted to dry his tears but he looked at peace and so pure, so she let him be.

"Wow. Baby, I knew you had gone through a lot in life, but I could not imagine it was like that." She held him tighter and planted her cheeks on his chest, closer to his heart, where she could listen to his heartbeat, calm as always. A peaceful silence prevailed between them.

****

"Slow down, babe. Like that, let us sync our bodies. Move together like a wave. Take your time… I wish I could stay inside…" he went stiff and then relaxed his body, following her tip amid grunts and moans, he tightened his grip around her juicy thick ass and dug deeper inside her, this time slower and deeper at every thrust. *'God it feels so great to be inside her, like everything else ceased to matter,'* he thought, nuzzling her neck as she moaned at every deep thrust, stroking his back and then scratching him with her long nails, caressing the scars on his back aroused him even more. She felt him grow inside her, his body tensing, his pelvis tightening and pinning her to the bed. "Slow down, slow down, babe, pull out don't come yet." He was about to burst but he obliged to slow his momentum. With the tip of his penis he stoked the entry point for a second before entering back inside the gates of heaven. "Oh the warmth, nothing feels better than that!" Her soft moan and breath on the back of his ear; he had the urge to see her face. He wringed his neck to face her, she was smitten and blushed, looking so angelic. Her big passionate heart was displayed on her face, so loving and all giving, oh how he loved her! She bent forward to kiss him while his thrust went deeper by the second, but gentler. She had her eyes closed, lost in his world, she was all his. His one and only. She felt him grow inside her again, wriggling her hips she entwined her legs around him; he was penetrating her soul, she was close, *oh how good it felt!* They were one. Then her body tensed up; that was his cue to dance inside her with ferocious intensity to climax in unison. Her moaning grew louder, his mind at peace, his body in sync, he trashed inside her. Then exploded, her body froze tensed and she went still and her face distorted in blissful agony; she embraced him tightly. Tears of joy running down her left cheek, down towards her earlobe. She looked so beautiful; it was the first time he paid an up-close look at her during her orgasm. He realized how much he had not paid attention to her while he worked hard for his release. It had always been about him, sex. About the release; maybe he should let her lead next time as it was the most intense lovemaking episode he had ever experienced. Tender and everlasting. He bent lower to kiss her again; breathless she smiled and kissed him back, her hands cupping his face, studying him, reading his thoughts like she often did. "You liked it?" she whispered.

He nodded his head, "That was fucking awesome!"

"Yeah babe, that was lovemaking and not fucking; we should do it more often," she said as he slid out of her and pulled her obliging warm body towards his torso.

Face on his chest, she listened to the rhythm of his heart, steady.

"Can I ask you something? Just out of curiosity to help me understand," she eventually broke the ice.

He just nodded hesitantly, ready to defend himself.

Rolling her hair with her right index, selecting her words as she often did, "You were on the boat, right, crossing the Mediterranean ocean? And you all knew the risk right of drowning?"

He nodded affirmatively, still hawk-like watching her face, studying her.

She looked down, fiddling with her hair, aware the pace of his heart skipped a notch.

"Yeah, if you guys knew the risks, and if most of you planned this harsh journey, many people think why not learn to swim? You know it could save your life, right? Not judging you. Of course, not everybody lives by a lake, sea, or a swimming pool. I understand you can swim, I mean generally."

He thought about it for a second. In fact, he never looked at it that way. It almost made him smile that none took it seriously, blinded by the light across the ocean, most if not all ignored the risk along the way. Indeed, they spent thousands of borrowed dollars to get that far, but why not go all the way and learn to swim? But then not everybody had the luxury to take swimming lessons at a swimming pool or a hotel nearby. Always on the edge of uncertainty and danger, it was all about surviving for the day. One thing on the mind, making it to Europe. They were on the run and not on vacation. She reminded him of all those faces with blank faces slowly disappearing one by one into the deep blue sea seconds after their boat gave in to water.

She noticed that distant look in his eyes and regretted her insensitive question at once. It came out wrong, what she wanted to ask was what was going through their minds when contemplating the journey and the risk. She had to rephrase the question. Clearing her mind, she looked up with a bright smile to no avail. His stony look was a reply. Contempt! "Of course, you guys were fleeing danger and persecution wherever you went. How silly of me!"

He leaned down and kissed her instead; holding her even closer to his body, he sighed.

"Do you know it just takes like five seconds for a person to drown?" he began in that monotonous voice that captivated her earlier without looking at her. He was in a trance. "Just five seconds, you trash around for five long seconds and down you go, never to be seen again."

She gulped down a ball of spit.

"I remember while I was in Libya you hear stories of the boats that sink, the money some traffickers may have lost, you know, of those who pay the final cut upon reaching the destination lost to the sea. But we try not to think about it. I don't know why it never struck fear in us. You just don't. But now I understand why." He looked up.

She was gripped by his recount, timid she looked up, meeting his eyes, the painful memory still fresh in his face. "I watch the news. Almost 200 000 people, migrants or whatever they call us, made it across the Mediterranean last year and around 4000 died. That means only 2% of those of us who decide to take the journey die. That means 98% success. So much focus is on that number. Almost everyone makes it alive. That is why swimming is not a priority nor the risk ever going to stop the likes of us; we will keep coming, no matter how hard they make it out there. It was worth it!"

"Very insightful, wow! My baby is deep!" she was delighted, planting a kiss on his lips.

"You know it helps me to have a deeper grasp of your perspective and you eloquently painted a picture."

She smiled at him as a mother would at her proud son for his lucid analytical explanation. But this was rather enlightening coming from anyone.

He was surprised by how articulate he had been in relaying everything that happened in one go. Some he never ever told a soul before. It just poured out of him as if he was reading a script. Some details that he was not even aware he knew.

After another bout of silence, Teme was still not sure. It was all surreal. Her reaction was beyond calmness personified. Maybe after it sunk in, she would feel differently tomorrow, he wondered. Maybe it would come back to haunt him? *Maybe she would tell her mother and oh God what have I done?* he was suddenly engulfed by a sense of shame and guilt. He had to find out.

"Baby listen, after I told you all this, be honest, what do you feel? Are you frightened, shocked, disappointed, or what?"

"Stop it, sugar," she interrupted him, "I knew most of it. I sensed it, okay? Women and intuition, we see things, feel things, without words being exchanged. But I know you. Look at me." She cupped his face, forcing him to lock eyes, "You survived. Whatever happened does not define you as a person. You are a mess as everybody else. But nobody went through what you did. But as a person, I know you. Just stop beating yourself, okay babe? We are all fucked up in our own ways, but let's heal each other."

****

Chapter 40

He almost forgot he was on a big ass ship, floating on the open sea, like he was riding a whale or something. His excitement had won over his memory bank, spitting out the past. Besides, like his shrink had said, confronting his traumatic experience, almost reenacting it, normalized the experience. Maybe she was right. He had left his exhausted girl curling on their double deck cabin on the ninth floor; he was getting acquainted to every spot as if he just moved to a new neighborhood. A joy he had never felt before enveloped him. A huge relief, as if he was released from the longest prison term, out into the open. He felt like a free man.

Down on the fifth floor he was on a roll, the coins dripping, he was doubling his money. Every slot machine seemed to sing the same song, all eyes on him, a man in a uniform, probably the casino slot machine department head, kept gliding past his seat with a weary smile a couple of times. It must indeed be his day. Still, every now and then the slightest movement of the ship would cringe his abdomen muscles, yet he was yet to hit the panic button. He was in control, maybe the shrink was right, "Facing the trauma in a safe, controlled environment indeed is part of the healing process," she had said. *Nothing is ever safe though, nothing is ever sure* as the scene from Titanic seeped in his memory to skip his heartbeat up a notch. In real life though, sinking took seconds. A boat flips and it is down under at once. Never coming back. Hysterical humans, screaming prayers and curses be drifting, trashing, kicking, and grabbing at each other helplessly for seconds before gravity claimed one after the other. It was remarkable how within a matter of seconds, all would go quiet except the raging insatiable sea. The surviving heads do not even look at each other, just floating as if nothing happened. With no land on sight, darkness looming, just drift afloat… He quickly brushed off the thought, reminding himself it was the 21st century and a whole lot of white people on board for a change; if worst came, rescue was indeed guaranteed.

Chapter 41

At the probation officer hearing a week later, Teme sat fidgeting, listening to a report. He had failed the drug test. The psychologist, who looked more of a police than the plump smiling face of the lady in the uniform, kept reading the terms and conditions of his release while he occasionally cast a glare to study his reaction. All are fucking cops, he hissed inside to himself as Teme tried to keep his cool.

"As you have signed on the contract upon your release," the psychologist leafed through a pile of paper, to laboriously peel and point with the red pen the contract Teme had signed, "there were terms and conditions you needed to strictly adhere to, Teme."

Teme nodded passively, his mind racing, imagining his days back in the slum. It was over, he had fucked up again.

The policewoman interjected, "The previous tests were negative. But the last one showed traces of TGH, most probably marijuana. Be honest with us now did you smoke hashish or marijuana?"

Teme mumbled something incompressible. The psychologist was losing patience.

"You need to speak up and explain yourself or you will end up back in prison." She gave Teme a stern look through the reading glasses.

Teme remained silent, unmoved, frozen.

"Apart from this, we are so proud of your progress. You are making a hell of an effort. You received high praises at work, they say you are reliable, cooperative, and always on time. You have moved from the neighborhood and stayed out of trouble. You attend all the sessions. But be honest with us now, was it a one-off thing? Did you slip up, or was it someone you know who was smoking near you?"

After a long moment of deliberation, Teme avoided looking at the fucking criminal psychologist, instead faced the warmer policewoman. "I slipped up. I was depressed one day. And that was it. There was no one who pressured me, it was my fault."

With that he was told to stay outside as the two needed to huddle and make a decision. Pensive long five minutes passed as Teme paced around the corridor of the police station. He had a feeling this was it, they were sending him back. He had used up all his second chances in life.

They called him back in, facing the two of them, he read nothing from their faces.

"Teme, listen, we want the best for you. We know it is not easy to make changes. We do not expect you to transform yourself at once. It is a process. You have done well so far," announced the criminal psychologist with an annoying calm deep voice.

Teme nodded but felt there was a 'but' and a hammer to send him back behind bars. In his mind, he was ready for it. Convicted state of mind!

"So, we decided to overlook the drug test," added the smiling policewoman. "Since it is one slip-up, it does not define your whole transition period nor undermine your entire progress."

Teme's heart sunk. He was relieved. But he showed no sign of it outwardly.

"But I should warn you, this shall never happen again. Are we clear on that?" the spoiler psychologist quickly added.

Teme nodded again, this time with a humble smile.

Chapter 42

Teme had taken the day off, assuming the worst-case scenario, ending up behind bars again. The relief and joy he felt afterwards even confused him. But all he wanted to do was celebrate the extension of his freedom with Elise. He called the moment he left the police station. She was at home, readying herself for work in an hour or two. He took the metro to Røa to see her off to work.

While Teme was making a sandwich, Elise was doing her nails, but she kept an eye on him. Thinking how he had indeed transformed himself. How calm and at peace he had been of late, but still she was worried about him. Maybe the transformation was too swift. She smiled though, listening to him whistling a song she could not place.

"Babe, why did you stop seeing your friend Toure?" She finally could not help it.

"I thought you never liked him anyway?" he replied, his back still to her, sandwich taking all the focus.

"No, babe. I can't choose who you can be. But you two have been through thick and thin together. So you don't need to avoid him."

He brought the sandwiches on two plates and placed it on the coffee table in front of her, all improvised Teme style, one never the same as the other. He handed her over her plate and begun munching his in silence.

"No comment, huh?" She reached out her hand over his neck and drew his cheeks closer to her. He placed his sandwich back on his plate to face her. They looked at each other, smiling and giggling for no reason. He brushed his fingers over his pants and reached out for her face. Silent but he kept caressing her hair, pulling her hair like a kid does a cotton candy.

"The hanging out with the crew, you know how that ended. But Toure is still your friend. Besides, he is back to school right," she was not to let this one go he figured.

"Yeah."

"You see, maybe he is getting his shit together?"

"Maybe."

"How about you, babe? You considering it, you know school?"

"Yeah, but not now." His focus was back to his sandwich. His mouth was full within seconds. Loud open mouth chewer, he sometimes was fascinated by her watching him.

Thrilled at his answer and waiting until he swallowed the last chunk.

"You mean it?"

"Yeah, I can't keep doing this shitty job forever, you know." He locked on her studying glare.

Hiding her excitement, she cleared her throat and buried her head on his lap again. She loved it when he massaged her head and pulled her hair.

"Yeah, babe, proud of you. At least finish high school and get your diploma, you know."

"Yep, that is the plan. I might take on mechanic or electrician as a field. They pay well and work more independently, you know."

"Yeah, babe." She was so thrilled she wanted to drill him more. But held back, she knew he will figure it out by himself. She looked up again and reached out with open hands invitingly for a kiss. He grinned but did not make a move. That stubbornness she liked as she met him half way to plant a wet kiss.

Facing each other, with her legs wrapped around his hips on the sofa, in between kisses, her fantasy ran wild.

"Where do you think we will be in like five years? I mean with me as well, don't get no ideas, feel me?" Jabbing him playfully. "Not hip-hop dreams but our dream. You and me."

After a long pause, "I just want to be with you, wherever."

That was exactly what she wanted to hear. A hot blissful flash invaded her body. She kissed him again and again. Eyes locked on to each other, her hands locked behind his neck.

"In five years, I will be a qualified experienced nurse with a stable job. And you a big shot mechanic, and we might be married, living in our own house. What do you think?"

"Yeah, that sounds nice," he giggled. They kissed some more and broke off into a giggle.

"You want to marry me, don't you?"

He nodded.

"Yeah, I don't know here, but where I came from the bride's family pays some amount to the groom."

"You mean bride price?" she broke into another bout of giggles. "How much you want to get from my mom?"

"It is tradition, so I have to follow it," he jokingly said. "Besides, you got a rich grandfather anyway, he can afford it."

"What are you serious?" she giggled and studied his eyes if he somehow had meant it.

"Yeah." He looked serious. "But since it is you, you are the prize itself I have received in advance, so we are good."

"OOOhh, that is so sweet!" she nearly cried with that. Giving him another tight embrace and planting kisses on his forehead, cheeks, and his lips. "I love you too, babe, and cherish you as a gift in my life, always will."

The kisses escalated and soon they peeled off their clothes.

****

After a steamy love session while Elise rested on his chest, she contemplated introducing him properly to her family, "What do you think about meeting my mom and grandpa?"

He went stiff for a second.

"You think it is too soon? No pressure, I mean if you want to, whenever, I can introduce you to them. Sometime over lunch or whatever?" she quickly added to calm his nerves.

"Have you told them all about me?" he posed with alarm in his voice.

"Yeah, they know how crazy I am about this cute African boy." She kissed him on his chest.

"That is it? No details?"

"No, babe. What we say to each other remains between us, always."

Of course, she lied a little, some innocent stories she had leaked to her mom and her friends, especially when he pissed her off. But never the intimate details.

"Okay. No problem meeting them," he shrugged.

She was satisfied, her patience had paid off. Full circle! *Love is pain. Beautiful pain that finally gives in to bliss, blissful pain that keeps giving,* she reckoned with closed eyes.

Chapter 43

Her grandfather's house was on a hill on Voksenlia. One of the richest suburbs in the West side of Oslo. It was quiet inside the car. Elise behind the wheel, his mind was somewhere else as his eyes gorged on the greenery sparked by spring giving in to the long awaited summer. The blue sky and mild sun on the horizon, the scenery was beautiful. Pruned and well-kept lawns, spread out wooden houses with bigger gardens. Wooded parks and tilled farmed land escorted his eyes as they quietly made it up the hills. The deeper they went up, the less the density of households, and the greener and wooded the areas. The houses looked old money. The cars fancy and almost none of his kind, he noticed. Elise occasionally reached out her free hand to run her delicate fingers around her ears or touch his hands or his thighs to get his attention and study his mood.

"You okay, babe?" she asked with a smile plastered on her beautiful lips. He would reply with a nod and give her a wink before drifting back to his thoughts. She was dressed lightly, with a summer skirt and sandals. He felt like he had overdressed with a blue shirt under his coat he never wore and a cream-colored khaki that made him feel old. "Are you nervous?" she asked when they were close by. He assured her he was okay. She was in a jolly mood, singing along Beyoncé's new song on the car radio, as they wound their way up the top of the hill.

Stepping out of the driveway, Teme was taken aback by the sight. The house was like a mansion. On top of a hill, a wooden old Norwegian cabin-like house with several annexed apartments on all sides. There were half a dozen cars parked as well. Either the old man was a collector or more people had been invited. Nerves tingled along his temples. Noticing his frozen state, "Come on, I will be with you all along. It is just my aunts, cousins, and nephew and niece, and my mom." She held him closer. Walking up the marble steps the garden came to view, partitioned by fir bushes on either side, exotic flowers assaulted his vision. Trees with flowers he had never seen or heard off. Colors he had never noticed on flowers before were all around him. Following the steps, they passed the fir bushes that gave in to sparkling swimming pool with four nymph statues looking down the pool on all corners. Bamboozled by the riches in front of him, Teme almost gasped; "They are in the backyard. Let's go," his girl led the way.

Crafted stone vases lined up the marble path skirted by a green manicured grass that led to the front of the house. French windows revealed the contents of the house. It was all wood and glass, barely had he seen any metal. It all looked classic old but new as well. It was unlike any Norwegian house he had seen. Everything was elaborate and artistic, nothing ordinary.

"Wow! Your grandpa is filthy rich! You grew up here, fuck!"

Teme could no longer contain his excitement. He was now intimidated to meet the owner of the house. He could not believe he was dating the granddaughter of a man who lived in such a house.

The backyard was behind the house, giving in to the woods that ran up the hill. The delightful grill smoke was in the air. The old but fit man himself was attending to the giant grill, flipping steak and pork chops. Teme was greeted one by one. He dreaded the questions they shall rain down on him as he smiled cautiously at all of them. The mother kissed him on his forehead and brought him a plate of steak. One of the nephews pulled him a retractable chair. His girl got so animated and soon left him on his own. None badgered him with questions. The grandfather had only shook his hand firmly, and they locked stares. The only questions thrown his way but the remarkably fit man were, "You eat pork? Well done, crispy, or juicy? And give the young man a drink," ordering with authority one of his daughters before asking him, "You drink beer right, young man?" He nodded with a smile to all the generous offers.

Sipping his corona beer, Teme looked down the hill; Oslo was in full display. He could make out certain landmarks all the way to the coastline. It was like God had splashed the contents of the world from the other side of the hill toward him. The neighboring houses were farther apart but lavishly sitting on the hill as well, he noted. The family had welcomed him with a reserved but friendly manner. He was somehow sure they knew of all his run-ins with the authorities. Yet no questions bombarded him, a relief though. With Oslo city under him, his childhood seeped into his memory. It had been a while since he accessed that tender part of his life.

The only memory of his childhood that ran in loops was his grandmother humming a monotonous gospel song while she weeded their vegetable garden. In her felt colorful but old skirt and her soiled apron on top, her cornbraided gray head bobbing once in a while, she went about her business oblivious to her grandson. Crouched by a tree shade, Teme used to rest, drawing figures on the dry soil, awaiting orders on which chore to fulfill. At times she would take a break from her garden to narrate a riddle-filled myth that used to bemuse him. His inquisitive young brain would interrupt her often, patient as she was though, she would answer in her elaborate ways with some symbolic relevant examples he could comprehend, while caressing his cheeks with her hardened, gnarled fingers. His favorite tales were of the conniving trick master, the coyote. Whenever he was enthused by the mere mention of a coyote, she would remind him to keep an eye on devious people with coyote characters. He should neither befriend nor provoke them, he just should watch them from a distance. At times they could come in handy as malignant as they could be, she used to say, her eyes lost in the open skies. "Never be a sheep nor a coyote," she would rephrase her message after a moment of silence, "just be yourself, always alert and independent." Ever since he departed from her angelic shadow, he had been running into coyotes of all kinds. What bothered him the most was that nagging feeling if indeed, he had become that proverbial coyote, the devil's advocate in the end. His grandmother though, that gentle soul who barely showed the dark streak of what obviously every human including him harbored, remain a mystery. Even when admonishing him for his childhood lapses, she had a warm, caring but concerned tone that often had an impact on him. Apart from that the rest of his childhood remained a blur, insignificant bits and pieces jammed at the back of his memory.

With no phone in her village, he used to follow up on her wellbeing after strenuous phone attempts to unwilling distant relatives that seldom passed by her village. He even heard of her passing months after, right after he made it to Europe in Italy, it had been casually dropped to him as a condolence by a distant family member he ran into. It was devastating, the death of his childhood, buried behind a church cemetery along with the frail features of his grandmother. No funeral, no wake to speak of, just a passage. He never mourned either. He had completely sealed it off, to be never spoken again, even to a length of pretending she was still alive. She died before he even had the opportunity to help her. He shook off the thought of his grandmother and faced his girl's family. They were into some inner circle joke, all giggling and ogling. He scanned

215

the threshold; his girl was on the backdoor of the kitchen, leaning on the pane, watching him with a smile on her face. He winked at her.

****

Chapter 44

A couple of days later he was at his psychologist's office. He was jolly and looking forward to the meeting, despite this being his last session. He sure was going to miss talking to her. Looking at her while in a calm voice summarizing his progress and words of praise, Teme felt grateful he had been able to utilize her services. She sure had been helpful. From the days when he was so reserved and resentful towards her, it had come to a point where he was longing to see her and open up to her.

"I told my girl," he interrupted her summary.

Relief... A breakthrough. But she showed no emotion. But what a triumph! A win for science, a win for the faith in her job and to vanquish those doubts for a little while. But above all, a win for Teme. A customary smile and she allowed him to continue before saying calmly, "I am glad you did."

"Yeah," he smiled back.

He looked like he had a weight lifted off his young shoulders. He looked younger as if he had frown lines surgically removed.

"You must feel relieved, I guess."

He nodded, looking down.

"Did she take it well, your girlfriend?"

"Yeah, she has been very helpful."

"I am glad that turned out well for you, Teme." After a moment of comfortable silence, she began flipping the end of that pencil, anxious for him to take the lead and say something, fearing of spoiling his little triumph today. "What else do you want to talk about today then?"

"To be honest, I don't feel like talking at all today."

"Okay, no pressure," she was disappointed but quickly added, not giving up, "Everything going well at work?"

"Yeah," he hesitated, shaking his head inadvertently, "still not settled, you know, job hopping."

"Still, at least you are working. Take it easy on yourself. Baby steps at a time. You will get there one day."

"Yeah, the short blanket theory shit, right?"

"Excuse me?" she was baffled.

"You know that life is short blanket. Either the foot or the head is going to get cold or you have to adjust, was you who told me that?"

"Oh yeah, that is a wonderful theory, it applies well in life. But make no excuse, it will never be perfect, you know life. It is the same for all of us. Everybody is dealing with some issues, struggling, hiding it from everybody else."

"Yeah, everybody does," Teme nodded his head with the picture of his girl crying in his embrace flashing in his mind. "Everybody got issues indeed."

"So you still feel like having the session once in a while then?"

Hesitation, finally a shake of the head.

"Maybe I will take a break. And if I need to talk, I will book an appointment. Is that okay?"

"Yeah, it sounds great." She did not want to press him anymore.

"But keep talking to your girl, okay? Promise me that."

"Will do." He looked determined.

"Anytime you need to talk, don't hesitate to call me, okay?" She extended her card once again just as a reminder.

"Sure." He accepted the card and shoved it in his back pocket. Not even in his wallet, she noticed. He was restless, like a real teenager now.

"Can I ask you something?"

"Sure," he replied.

"Did you think our sessions helped you somehow?"

After a long contemplation, he plainly said,

"Yeah, in a way. It opened some windows."

She smiled like a proud mother.

Now she could sleep well. Not saved but somehow rescued on a raft from the unforgiving waves of the ever-raging inner oceans.

"To be honest, with you it fucks you up somehow, especially in the beginning. The stuff you know, the psychology. But it makes you think, question, and read and stuff. I learned a lot coming here and talking to you. But honestly, some of it is not applicable for us. You know the likes of us are not like ordinary teenagers." With that he got up and left.

She waved him off.

Watching him go, she replayed the last words he uttered to her. He had no idea how much she had learned as well talking to him, questioning, and researching on her own. It made her think as well.

We are always learning. She wanted to tell him that and thank him for it, but it was too late he had slid out the door and down the corridor. Besides, it would be unethical. *Detach, detach, and move on to the next patient*, she reminded herself. Closing the folder with Teme's name and shoving it down back the folder cabinet, she wondered if she would ever open his file nor ever talk to him again. '*But got to let them go*,' she sighed and poured herself a steamy dark coffee. Twenty minutes, then it is case number 4587.

****

On her break, right after Teme left her office, watching the international news coverage, the war on terror unleashed around the Arab world and all the way to the Sahel and Sahara was spilling all over the world. No place was safe. A car might run down pedestrians harmlessly going to work. A bus might explode full of people who were probably late to work but on time for their untimely death. Someone with a knife could go berserk in a crowd. It was frightening to be a mother these days. Often, the first thing as a mother came to her mind the wellbeing of her kids, then her immediate family, then to the extended family, before sympathizing with the victims and the rest of humanity. She avoided engaging in political debates and heated conversations with colleagues and friends.

But of late, working closely with the living, breathing rubble of the global crisis, she could not help but get involved in it. These days with all the newsreels she zoomed her attention towards the children. Their horrifying, heartbreaking reactions. The shock of repeated loss and the company of constant pain was unbearable to watch. What terrified her most though was thinking, how would those kids cope when they grow up? The battle that awaited them. At night sieges, their cruel unconsciousness playing and replaying the vivid scenes of the turbulent past in their nightmares. Then comes in the daytime in flashes. Most keep it to themselves, thinking it would go over like a rash. But boy, the subtext to the war had a prolonged effect on an entire broken generation. Ripe upon childhood, subjected beyond tender minds could muster, they would adjust. Just when they thought they were back to normal and their ability to process and comprehend grew, all they had left behind crushed back at them like an avalanche. *No escape, they trust none, all they can find is comfort in one another. Misery indeed loves company as they marinate in rage, in silence. A generation of pain,*

219

loveless, painless existence. All they could give is pain. Love is foreign. The generation incapable of loving receives nothing but pain. Addicted to pain, the subterranean war is fought in the mind. The damage is astronomical. Their pain is cyclic and one day they will unleash their rage upon a society that never understood them. The society that pitied them and worse, labeled and stereotyped them wherever they went. And they shall call that terrorism if they unleash it abroad. She shook her head. *How does one break the cycle? Psychology? Group therapy?* Oh, she felt so helpless. She turned off the TV, an expert was yapping about ideology and jihad. The war waged on the million young ones was what should be prioritized, ticking silent raging bombs spread everywhere. Kids with no core yet hardened to the core, not easily manipulated but to escape from themselves would join any cause that kept them going. If she could, she could save them one by one. But no, no one could save them. One could only guide them to find the path, untangle the knot themselves and hopefully, to find love; love for themselves. She was not being romantic or too optimistic, but only love could heal their pain not just science.

****

Later on that day Teme reached his left hand and tentatively at first and then firmly held the small of her back, drawing her body towards his side. It sent shivers, a warm sensation erupting to flood Elise's entire body. They slowed their pace like conjoined twins walk in tandem. She was overwhelmed, she wanted to kiss him but did not want to ruin the moment, and perhaps he might snap back to his withdrawn former self. Instead, she reached out with her right hand and rested it on the small of his back. He did not stiffen at all. Oh how she wished they would walk together hand in hand, forever up and down the Karl Johans Gata, window shopping shoes and jackets until the end of time to the envy of every loveless lonely soul out there. She lost track but love found her in the end with her true match! In fact, she earned it!

---The End---